Pushing Up
Daisies

Also by Jamise L. Dames

Momma's Baby, Daddy's Maybe

Pushing Up Daisies

A   N O V E L

Jamise L. Dames

ATRIA BOOKS

New York   London   Toronto   Sydney

ATRIA BOOKS

1230 Avenue of the Americas
New York, NY 10020

ISBN: 0-7434-9266-8

First Atria Books trade paperback edition May 2005

10 9 8 7 6 5 4 3 2 1

ATRIA BOOKS is a trademark of Simon & Schuster, Inc.

Manufactured in the United States of America

For information regarding special discounts for bulk purchases,
please contact Simon & Schuster Special Sales at
1-800-456-6798 or business@simonandschuster.com

IN LOVING MEMORY
of one of my greatest inspirations,
Clarence "Peanut" Miller Jr.,
who once told me that I'd one day say to him, "You told me
so." How I wish you were here so I could do just that.
But, somehow, I know that you know that you were right.
Thanks for believing and encouraging me to go after my
dreams. Thank you for being a true example
of making dreams come true.
You are never far from my thoughts or heart because you're
in both. Keep smiling down on me. Love you, still.

ACKNOWLEDGMENTS

First and foremost, I thank the Creator, the One who created and breathed life into me, my gift, and my hands that type a cazillion words a minute. Thank you for yesterday, today, and my tomorrows.

To the ones who have given love a new and improved definition and life more meaning: My beautiful daughter who introduces herself as "My name is Ms. Dames, and I'm an author." Who would've known that you'd have a career at just five years old? Keep saying it, baby, because you have the power to write your life.

For him who has designated himself my protector, my alpha twin son. You are truly magnificent and will grow up to be what women dream of and men strive to emulate: the perfect gentleman who has a lot to offer the world.

My singer, athlete, and entertainer; my omega twin son. Your drive, candor, and ambition are truly incredible. It's up to you how high you'll go.

Mr. Dames, you are something special. We've laid a foundation together and have built a solid structure. Thank you for not only feeding my creativity but for standing back and watching it bloom—applauding it.

Loving thanks to: My mother, Barbara Gill; my grandmother, Viola Box; my great-aunts: Ynobie Zackery and Charlene Jefferson; my great-grandmother, Pearlie Box, and the rest of my family.

Love to the following families: The Boxs, Greens, Pattersons, Fricks', Hollimans, Roses, Childers', Blakelys, Walkers, Blakes, Sockwells, Gulleys, Cottos & Mangols, Clays, Porters, Dansbys, Reels', Thomas', Rickersons, Whipples, Sebastians,

Randolphs, Buckners, Penixs, Artis', Dortons, Grooms, Berrys, and the Zackerys.

Kind thanks to: Sue Trinkley, Mocha D'Chateau, Divine Saddiq Dubar, Trevor Randolph, Paul Hendricks, Mrs. Randolph (Hey Ma!), Tashonda Phillips, Nickie Blakely, Jane Clay, Valerie Kilgore, Maureen Sebastian, Tracy Sebastian-Ingram, Nafeezah Shabazz, Kenny Reels, Michael Thomas, Sherryl Martin, Denise Anderson, Aunt Laura Porter, Felicia R. Box, Riccardo Box, Shelly Box, Robin Box, Sharone Box, Paradise Payne, Michael Slaughter, Tonia Crowley, Brenda (Penny) Pickett & family, Chucky & Lynne Charles, Deborah (Debbie) Davis, Carla Dean, Richard Holland, Michael Slaughter, Kyshina Chandler.

Extra special thanks to Dorothy and Leonard Wright, not only for your blessings but for raising one of the most wonderful people to have ever graced this earth with his footprints.

Here's to Leola Jean McCrorey, Doug McCory and my girls (couple guys in attendance as well) from Sister Sister Let's talk, Weaver High in Hartford, CT: Veneice McKenzie, Nadia Redway, Angie Fontenelle, Tashana Mitchell, Kimberly L. Brown, Brittany Brown D., Charity Brown, Stephanie Clark, Shantel Fraser, Nicolette Mitchell, Lakia King, Cristina Torres, Johanna Torres, Joselyn Cruz, Nelley Rosade, Kellena Nelson, Ashley Coleman, Jazmine Daniel, Shirley Minnifield, Tiara Conway, Reneé Gary, Marcia Clark, Margarie Little, Adrianne Little, Khila Wakefield, Ashley Weaver, Latiza Hales, Zoya Decarish, Kimblia Gillispie, Sidjae Hemy, and Mark A. Austin and Leord Shakes.

Warm recognition to the following authors: Brandon Massey, Brenda L. Thomas, Nikki Turner, Travis Hunter, Tracy Price-Thompson, Eric E. Pete, S. James Guitard, Yasmin Shiraz, K'wan, Marcelle Morgan Payne, V. Anthony Rivers, Noire, Carla Rowser Canty, and Earl Sewell. Gracious thanks to my AIE family: Literary manager extraordinaire, Ken Atchity; Andrea McKeown, Julie Mooney, and Margaret O'Connor. My Atria family: Brenda Copeland, you have to be the coolest editor—ever. Thanks for making it easy and comfortable. LaMarr Bruce, Jenny Voohries, and Amy Tannenbaum. My Echo Soul family: Kim Rose, publicist of publicists, you are a writer's dream. Thanks for pushing when no one else would and doing so much more than what your title entails. Nicole Childers, the behind-the-scenes person who is never behind. Thanks for taking me international. I owe you both To-Gos! Thought I forgot, hunh?

A great BIG THANKS to my readers. You've been wonderful, supportive, and very patient! I can't and couldn't do it without you. Much appreciation and love. As always, I hope you'll visit me online at www.jamiseldames.com, and/or email me when you get a chance (yes, I do answer emails!) at jamise@jamiseldames.com.

Love, laugh, and enjoy life as carefree as children!
Enjoy,
Jamise

For every woman who's had to make something
out of nothing,
was brave enough to do it, and strong enough to
see it through.

'Tis after death that we measure men.

—James Barron Hope

Pushing Up Daisies

Daisy

I *saw it coming. I knew it was coming—felt it inside. But I did the unthinkable; the thing that so many of us do and later regret. I covered my eyes and questioned, taunted myself until I made what I knew into something I wasn't so sure I knew. Then I turned against my own feelings and convinced myself that I was wrong, that I didn't have a right to feel what I felt. That's why I can't complain, that's why I can't point a finger at someone else. Yes, I was betrayed. Definitely. But I betrayed myself. Because I saw it coming, knew it was coming, and felt it coming deep down inside with all that I had. There, staring me in my face, announcing itself and poking me in my soul.*

And I ignored it.

1

Daisy Parker's blood was boiling. She balled up her boyfriend's favorite brown suede Armani jacket and threw it out the second-story window. She stuck her head out into the warm breeze, surveyed her work, and smiled wickedly. Jasper Stevens's clothes and shoes decorated her front lawn. Silk shirts in every color imaginable sprinkled the red roses that climbed the white trellis. Boxer shorts were scattered like freckles on the flagstone walkway, while an isolated pair hung from the limb of an oak tree like a gigantic moth. A beige loafer lay in the neighbor's yard across the street.

Neighbors stood outside and watched in shameless amazement.

"Mind your own business!" Daisy yanked the navy sheers closed. _Why in the hell is everybody outside so early anyway?_

She stood thinking, hands on hips. _Now for his grandmother's antique china._ As she ran down the stairs, a stabbing pain shot

3

through her right foot. She winced as blood trickled from her big toe. She shook her head in disgust and pulled out the small masonry nail.

"Ooh . . . goddamn!" She cringed, grabbing her foot. "I hate these stairs. I hate this house." Then Daisy's heart raced. "Lord, don't let him walk through that door right now, 'cause I swear I'm gonna kill him. I told him the last time that if he let the sun beat him home, it would be the last one he'd see rise." The pain from her wound, which was beginning to swell, deepened her anger. She wiped a tear from her eye and went to treat her injury.

As she limped into the first-floor bathroom, Daisy frowned at the tiny spots of blood staining the tile. *If it's not one thing, it's something worse. I wonder who it is this time—what woman has twisted his head so far up his ass that he can't see who's had his back for years.* She yanked open the medicine cabinet, and the entire contents tumbled into the sink. "Jesus!" Her heart felt as if it were jackhammering its way out of her chest.

She was not going to have another anxiety attack. No. No. No. Jasper wasn't worth it. She inhaled slowly, held her breath to the count of ten, then exhaled. The last thing she needed was to lose control. After repeating the process several times she began to relax. Seven years of yoga had taught her how to alleviate stress. As her pulse slowed, she rummaged through the fallen toiletries for the first-aid kit. After treating her wound, she found herself staring into the basin. Something wasn't right. The medicine cabinet was usually full, but the sink only contained a few items. *All of Jasper's toiletries are missing. His extra toothbrush—gone.* There was no denying the evidence. Every time Jasper had stepped out on her before, she'd found the cabinet almost bare. "Now I'm really going to throw the china out the window!"

Daisy carelessly stacked the fragile china on the table in separate piles. With each half-toss it clattered, threatening to topple to the floor. Silently she urged it to fall, dared it to break like her relationship. *Why not? Everything else Jasper claimed to love is broken.* She snatched a plate and examined it. The blue-patterned china that bore fanciful etching, navy like a perfect night sky lighted by stars, was trimmed in gold. The hazy color she once thought beautiful was now as hideous as it was gaudy and old. Ugly and disgusting. *Haunting, like the bluish lips of the dead.* She shivered. Flinging the dish on top of the stack, a vile film covered her fingertips. Smelling her hands, she realized the china smelled as bad as it looked. Its stench attacked her nostrils and made her mouth feel like cotton. Turning away, she bumped the table with her hip and watched the china shake, rattle, and fall.

She headed to the kitchen. It was nice. The cold marble floor soothed her injured foot. She took a bottle of water from the refrigerator, threw her head back, letting the water soothe her tongue and dry throat.

She needed to check on Jay, who was over at a playmate's house. She longed to hear his young, innocent voice sing the magical words that had always lifted her spirits: "Hey, Mom." Daisy's heart warmed as she thought about him. He had a knack for making her think about things bigger than her problems. He'd made it easy and desirable for her to segue into motherhood. He was Jasper's son, but became her own when she'd stepped in to raise him when he was almost two.

She dialed his friend's number, but couldn't speak to Jay. He was outside playing basketball. Daisy sighed. As upset as she was, and as proud as she was for finally taking a stand, she yearned for the comfort of someone who loved her unconditionally.

"Jay," she said out loud.

Daisy sat on the sofa waiting for Jasper to come through the front door. She was fuming. He should've had the decency to call. She picked up Jasper's photo from the end table. *You would think you'd want to spend every available minute at home, considering your job has you out of town four days a week. But no. Not you, Jasper. That would be asking too much.* She glared at the picture, then tossed it across the room. She looked at another photograph, this one of Jay and herself. Immediately a tinge of guilt coursed through her, and a sudden sadness too. What was she to do about him? She certainly wouldn't put him out.

She picked up Jay's Little League trophy that was sitting next to their photo. As she ran her finger over his engraved name, a whimper escaped her: "I'm the only mother he knows. I can't lose him." She'd taught him how to talk, potty-trained him, and nursed him when he was ill. She'd done everything that she assumed his biological mother would've if she could've. "Death stole her from you, and it'll be the only thing that'll keep me from you."

"Hell, he's *my* son," she said, setting the trophy back in its place.

A tear slid down her face. Jasper wouldn't leave Jay behind no matter how hard she fought. In her heart, Jay was her son. But biologically and legally he was Jasper's.

"I'm sorry, Jay," she whispered, thankful that he was spending the weekend at his friend's house. "I tried. One day I hope you'll realize how much. And I'll never let you go."

How can I leave the father and keep the love of the son?

Hurting her was one thing, but destroying Jay's security was another. Jasper had thrown their lives out the window just as she'd thrown out his belongings. It was always about what he wanted. She tapped her foot, willing the brass knob to turn and give her what she wanted: Jasper's head.

Where the hell was he?

Tears flowed freely now from Daisy's deep brown eyes. She paced the room, pounding her fist into her palm. As much as she loved him, she couldn't take Jasper's disrespect anymore. *Wouldn't* take it anymore. She'd pretended for too long, lived too long in her make-believe world. Her mind wandered to the time she'd smelled another woman's perfume on him, and he had convinced her it was her scent. *It wasn't perfume that I smelled. It was pussy.* She plopped down on the sofa, laughing at her naïveté. How could she have been so stupid? She'd give Jasper one more hour, she decided. If he didn't come home, she'd change the locks.

Settling back into the soft cushions, Daisy questioned herself. Why did she sit around and drown in thoughts of Jasper? Obviously, he wasn't thinking about her—or Jay. The longer she sat, the angrier she got. And not only at him, but at herself. Why did she allow him to drain her of her happiness? He didn't deserve her undivided attention. He wasn't God. But she did have to admit that she'd treated him like a god. She had made him her alpha and omega, her personal messiah who'd convinced her that he was akin to Jesus; he was her first and last, beginning and end. Her only. In his hands she'd turned to dust and allowed him to mold her, breathe *his* version of life into her. She'd thought that he was her savior, but had been seduced by the fallen one and believed his lies. Daisy cringed because she knew that *she* had given him power. She'd placed him on a pedestal from which he'd refused to come down, and she'd been punished for being the type of woman who loved completely. There wasn't anything on the green earth that she hadn't done for him, or for Jay. So why hadn't he come home last night? "Because he thinks I'm stupid," she whispered.

No one could tell Daisy what she already knew. Inside, she knew he'd cheated before, and her gut told her that he was out doing something that he had no business doing.

As her eyes drifted around the room, Daisy realized that Jasper had fashioned her to his liking, just as he had fashioned his home. She too had been bought and paid for.

One thing she wouldn't complain about was the grandfather clock. It had accompanied her through the night without missing a beat. And it had given her the wake-up call she'd finally answered, the call that had told her to put Jasper where he belonged—out with yesterday's trash.

The clock chimed now, as if reminding her. *Time to make the doughnuts.* Daisy reached for the phone and called the locksmith, then forwarded her calls to a local psychic hotline.

The clock chimed again. The locksmith was late. How many people needed locks changed on a Sunday morning? Now she was waiting on *two* men, Jasper and the locksmith. *Isn't this a trip?* It was bad enough that she was going to have to pay a surcharge for weekend work. In the phone book his ad claimed to have the speediest service in town, but please, she had seen molasses move faster. Daisy told herself to be patient. She'd waited almost seven years for Jasper to act right, so she could certainly wait another hour for the locksmith.

The doorbell rang. Her heart leapt to her throat. *Jasper? No, he has a key.* She calmed herself, tried to smooth out her wild hair, and let the locksmith in.

Three hundred dollars and five changed locks later, Daisy was even more pissed. There went the new outfit.

She walked slowly up the stairs, counting every one of the pictures that hung on the wall in stair-step succession. Seven in all, one for every year they had been a family.

"Seven whole years, and not once did you propose," she said aloud. "And you asked me to have your baby? You must've thought I was a fool, telling me to have your baby first, and then you'd marry me. Hell, I raised your child."

Daisy smashed one photo against all the others, shattering them to pieces, leaving only the photos of Jay and Jonathan, Jasper's deceased twin, untouched. She stopped and paused in front of Jonathan's picture. He seemed to watch her in disapproval. His eyes had always made her uncomfortable; they seemed more real than camera-captured. *Sorry, Jonathan, sorry you had to see this. But your brother's acting a fool—again. Please send him some good sense from wherever you are.* She turned away and glared at the scattered pictures.

She went to the guest room and stood before the closet. She knew not to open the closet door, but still felt the temptation. Just the thought of what was hidden inside irritated her. The last thing she needed now was to come face-to-face with that haunting memory, that single piece of paper that had hurt her and served as a constant reminder of her shame. Daisy reached for the knob, then drew her hand back. She walked out of the room in a daze.

Padding down the hall, she tripped over one of Jasper's ill-placed shoes and fell face-first into the carpet.

"I can't . . . I just can't take this," she sobbed.

Daisy pushed herself up, her day-old makeup leaving faint traces of color on the carpet. "Who puts white carpet in a hallway, anyway?" she muttered, sniffing under her arms. *I need to bathe.* There was no way she'd allow herself to become like Jasper: tired and stinking.

The telephone rang while Daisy was taking off her clothes in the bedroom. She picked up, but no one was there. *My cell phone.*

"Hel-lo," Daisy snapped.

"Dai—um . . . what's wrong with you?" her best friend, Gigi, asked. "You okay?"

"Yes. I mean . . . no. Jasper didn't come home again last night, and he hasn't called."

"No? Girl, you're having all kinds of trouble today. Men problems and phone issues. Did you know something was wrong with your phone? 'Cause I just tried to call twice, and some lady who claimed to be psychic kept answering—had the nerve to ask me which credit card I'd be using. I told her since she was psychic, she should tell me."

Daisy laughed. "I forwarded my calls. They're psychic, so maybe they'll tell Jasper he doesn't have a home." Daisy paused, spreading cleanser on her face. "So what's up? You feel like going to Ming Li's and out to lunch?"

"Sure. I'll meet you at her house in about an hour."

"Make it an hour and a half. Oh, and Gigi?"

"Yeah?"

"When was the last time you talked to Marcus? Did he come to your house last night?"

"We were together until midnight. Why?"

"Just asking. Listen, if he calls you, don't say anything, okay? I'll see you at Ming Li's."

Daisy leaned against Ming Li's bar, waiting for Gigi to arrive and for Ming Li to get dressed. Her eyes roamed the trendy Manhattan loft. She imagined how peaceful she'd make her surroundings once she got on her feet. But single life scared her. Daisy had never lived alone before and she wondered if she'd be able to handle it.

Pouring herself a glass of chardonnay, she noticed black lingerie on the floor. *At least somebody's getting some.* She sipped her wine, trying to remember the last time she and Jasper had had sex.

A loud knock on the door pulled her out of her thoughts. "It's about time. Seems like I've been waiting on people all day," Daisy said as she opened the door for Gigi.

Gigi stood there smiling, beautiful in her own way. Her caked makeup made her honey complexion look flawless, almost plastic. But there was nothing phony about Gigi. She posed, then modeled a catwalk spin, showing off her newly dyed hair and baggy gym attire. "Well, what do you think?"

Daisy frowned, covered her mouth, and laughed. She pulled Gigi inside and bolted the door. "Get inside before someone calls the cops on you for disturbing the peace. New York has noise ordinances, you know."

"It's not that bright," Gigi said, patting her shocking red mane. "It's vibrant, like my personality."

"Yeah, you're right. It's not bright. It's loud."

"Whatever." Gigi shrugged off Daisy's teasing and hugged her. "Are you all right?"

"I'll be fine. It's nothing new, right?" Daisy avoided Gigi's intense gaze, diverting her attention elsewhere. "Where's Ming Li? She's always holding us up."

Just then, Ming Li sauntered into the room, naked. She hopped onto a barstool, her long black mane swaying against her back. "I'm right here." She grabbed a crystal decanter, poured herself a drink, and lit a mini-cigar before turning to her friends. "Want some?" she asked, then her eyes widened in surprise. "Damn, Gigi! What in the hell happened to your hair?"

Gigi smirked, crossing her arms. "What happened to your *clothes?*"

Daisy smiled sadly, her emotions getting the best of her. She forced herself to brighten, trying to cover her pain. "You know Ming Li doesn't like clothes, Gigi. She's Eve, remember?"

"I'll have wine too," Gigi said, laughing. "That liquor's too strong for me."

"Sweeties, if you two had what I just had, you'd say this was mild in comparison to Ian." Then Ming Li noticed Daisy's face. "Whoa . . . wait a minute. What's wrong?"

Gigi shot Ming Li a knowing look.

"Jasper disappeared again?" Ming Li huffed. "Rhetorical

question. I know the answer. What are you going to do?"

The sound of a door closing reminded Daisy that they weren't alone. "We'll talk at lunch."

Ming Li shrugged. "It's your pity party."

"Who's back there?" Gigi questioned.

"Ian." Ming Li closed her eyes and pretended to swoon.

"That good, hunh? Wait a minute, who's Ian? I thought you were seeing Ricky."

"I am seeing Ricky. And Ian. And Lucian—"

"Lucian?"

"Yes." Ming Li licked her lips. "He's Greek, and hung like a Trojan horse. Lucian Antonopoulos."

Daisy gulped her wine. "You're sleeping with all three of them? Ricky, Ian, and Lucian Anta—whoever?"

"As often as I can. Sometimes two a day."

"Oh, hell, no. Are you serious? I hope you don't sleep with two at a time."

Ming Li pursed her lips.

———————

Daisy dabbed her mouth with a napkin. The outdoor restaurant was bustling, and Greenwich Village was in full swing, as crowded as usual for a hot summer weekend.

"Girl, no. You didn't throw his clothes out." Gigi threw her napkin across the wrought-iron bistro table.

Ming Li eyed Daisy and nodded. "Oh, hell, you did. Good for you. I told you years ago that that muthafucka wasn't any good."

"I warned him before. Obviously, he didn't realize that a threat can be a promise."

Gigi fanned her face. "If he was stupid enough to stay out, he deserved it."

"He's *your* cousin."

"That he is. But you know we're not close. If it weren't for you or Marcus, Jasper and I probably wouldn't speak. Still, you can't say I didn't warn you about him. I didn't push you into his bed. You jumped in."

"Well, good for him," Ming Li said. "Screw him, but

don't fuck yourself in the process. Know what I mean?"

"Yes, I do." Daisy nodded. "I also know it's time I explored my options too," she added with a sly smile.

Ming Li returned the look. "Gigi told me some guy's been hitting on you at the gym. What about him, Daisy?"

Gigi sat back. "I don't think I should be hearing this."

"I'm not the whore; Jasper is. I'm not going to mess with Chris the personal trainer."

"Oh, that Chris."

"You've met Chris?" Daisy asked.

Ming Li winked. "A *few* times."

"Damn, Ming Li. Save some for the rest of us."

"There's always Adonis." Ming Li grinned.

Just the mention of his name gave Daisy chills. She'd spent plenty of nights thinking about Adonis. He'd been the childhood crush she'd always wanted but never pursued. "Adonis? What about him?"

"He's here," Ming Li said, nudging Gigi. "Right, Gigi?"

"Shut up, Ming Li." Gigi turned to Daisy. "You understand my position, right? With Jasper being my cousin, and Adonis my stepbrother . . ."

Daisy's expression dulled. She wished like hell that she'd thrown her insecurities to the wind and pursued the man she'd wanted, instead of settling for the one who wanted her. She'd never admit it out loud, but she'd always felt that she wasn't good enough for Adonis. He had a certain air about him so that she'd found him unapproachable.

"Yes, I understand," she replied. "Family."

"Bullshit," Ming Li said. "Jasper and Adonis aren't related. They don't share the same blood. And according to Adonis, they barely know each other. They met as adults."

Daisy shook off the thoughts of Adonis. Unrelated or not, it wouldn't look right. She also had Jay to think about. "I'm putting Jasper out with a clean conscience."

"And a job," Ming Li interjected.

"Uh-oh," Gigi said. "You're serious. You're gonna do it this time."

Daisy threw her an angry look. "What do you mean, *this* time?"

"You always say you're going to put him out," Ming Li said. "If you're going to do it, do it. Think and do for yourself. What do you think he's doing . . . playing golf? Please, you want to see Adonis again because Jasper's game has gotten rusty."

"And put the degree to use. No offense, Daisy, but what is it that you do? I mean, really, I've only seen you plant flowers—for your house," Gigi added.

Daisy rolled her eyes and exhaled. "Unbelievable, Gigi. How could you not know what I do? We shared a dorm and you don't know what I studied? How is that possible?" Daisy deadpanned, "How many summers did you help me spend my paycheck when I worked the landscaping job? For the last time, ladies, I have a degree in horticulture, not flowers. I'm an expert in plant cultivation and propagation. I specialized in floriculture, as well as commercial and residential landscape design."

"Well, damn. *Sorry,*" Gigi retorted. "Point taken, but what does it mean?"

"Seeding, cutting, layering, grafting. I protect plants from diseases and pests, and I am a specialist in all things flowers. You name it, I know it."

Ming Li cleared her throat, closed her eyes, and paused. She sat up erect and stared at Daisy. "You mean to tell me that you're a *scientist* who can actually fathom cultivation, propaganda—propagation—propa-whatever, but you can't understand why Jasper didn't come home? Book smarts won't help you, you need street smarts. It doesn't take a degree to figure out that one. It's simple. The bastard has grown an extra pair of legs *and* fangs, and he pisses with his back leg up. He's metamorphosed into a dog—simple as that. He's done everything except bite you in the ass to prove it."

Daisy glared and balled her fist under the table. Her heart picked up speed, but anxiety wasn't the cause, anger was. Ming Li's naked honesty hurt, but Daisy had to take it for what it was worth—the truth. She couldn't deny it. Wouldn't. And she refused to be mad at her friend for caring enough to express what she felt. "Can't argue with that one."

"Flower degree or no flower degree, I still say you should let your education work for you." Gigi smiled. "You plant a hell of a rosebush."

Ming Li pursed her lips and laughed. "Yeah, peddle those hybrid flowers you love to create. You could get a vendor's license, you know? Go to the flower market and sell, sell, sell. Do something besides wait for Jasper, damn."

"Okay, I've got enough drama in my life without your criticism."

"No one's criticizing you. We're telling you the truth, and you should listen. And we've known him longer than you have. Besides, no one can be *that* good in bed. Don't tell me he's fucked you so hard that you're seeing things—"

"Ming Li!"

"No, Daisy, you need to hear this," Ming Li insisted.

"Daisy, you've given him too much power. You get dressed in the morning just to sit around and keep *his* house. For what? So you have to depend on him? You already had one man raise you. What makes you think you need a second daddy?"

Daisy crossed her arms defiantly. She wanted to curse at her friends, but she knew they were right. "Well, ladies, you can rest assured. Jasper obviously had a place to stay last night, so he can live there. And as far as working, I don't know. He never wanted me to, and I didn't have to. But that doesn't matter now. He's gone, and there's nothing more to be said. A girl's gotta do—"

"You've always got us," Gigi interrupted, smiling kindly. "Remember that."

———————

"What now?!" Daisy grumbled, fumbling to find the ringing cell phone, which had awakened her for the third time. *God, please? Make it stop.* She sat up and immediately regretted it. Her lids felt twenty pounds heavier and she strained to keep her burning eyes open. Her temples pounded against her skull, threatening to explode. And her ears rang. And rang. And rang some more. "Too much wine. Much . . . too much . . . wine," she whispered while digging in the sofa cushions trying to locate the dreaded digital device that wouldn't allow her to sleep. "This better be good," she answered.

"Daisy, you up?" Gigi asked breathlessly.

"No. I'm talking in my sleep. Call me back when I wake up . . . in about five hours."

"Goddamnit, Daisy. Get up! Marcus just called. Jasper's in the hospital."

Daisy sat up and pressed her fingers against her throbbing temples, hoping to slow the pounding. But the drumming didn't shift; it sped up, accelerated like her heartbeat. Moved in rapid, short successions like her anxious breaths. *Breathe. Breathe. Goddamnit, breathe!* She'd lost track of the inhale/exhale pattern and was forced to relearn it in seconds. Seemed like years. Panic made its way in with a slow crawl and a push so steady it dominated her hangover. *"What?! He's in the hospital?* What hospital?" she managed to ask.

"University . . ."

Daisy raced down the Staten Island Expressway as rain spattered on the windshield. The slick roads and potholes added to her shakiness. She couldn't make it to Jasper fast enough. "Lord, please let him be okay," she prayed as her back tires slid, losing control for seconds, when she exited the expressway onto Lily Pond Avenue. *Let me be okay too,* she continued her plea as she fought to gain control of the vehicle. She chastised herself for acting in haste, for throwing out Jasper's clothes, for assuming that he was cheating.

She turned into the parking area at top speed. Her heart—her need—wouldn't allow her to slow. She had to get to him. She pulled into a handicap spot without a second thought. She didn't need a wheelchair tag; she was the sign, a walking billboard that screamed, "Mentally and emotionally handicapped." Every bad thought that she could think infiltrated her mind. Stole her sanity. *Please,* she begged God again, *let him be okay.*

As she ran toward the ER, the cold, wet cement reminded her

that she wore no shoes. She had no purse. The only thing that she carried was worry for Jasper.

"Excuse me," she asked, pounding on the reception counter to get attention. "I'm looking for Jasper Stevens."

"Hmm, Stevens. Stevens." The lady smiled and began searching what Daisy assumed to be an intake sheet.

What the hell is she so happy about? Doesn't she realize this is an emergency room? Emergencies aren't funny.

"Is he here?"

"I'm sorry. I don't see a Jasper Stevens listed. But, then again, they just changed the sign-in sheets. New shift. Let me check in the back for you. What's your name?"

Daisy waited a small eternity for the woman to return. Three whole minutes. One hundred and eighty ticktocks on the hospital-issued clock.

"We don't have a Jasper Stevens in the back," the receptionist said, and followed with a shrug. "I'm sorry . . ."

"Alright. Thanks." Daisy clipped her words. Frustration and anger replaced panic and worry as she turned to leave. *Liar—Jasper's a liar.*

"However . . ."

Daisy did an about-face and looked at the receptionist as she blinked back tears.

"A nurse from the last shift said that we did have a Jasper here earlier. She couldn't remember his last name, though. He wasn't her patient."

Daisy dialed, then spat wildly, frantically into her cell phone, "He's not at University, Gigi. At least I don't think so. First they said that they didn't have a Jasper Stevens registered. Then they said maybe he was there earlier, but weren't sure. They changed shifts. Goddamn shifts. And wouldn't you know it, sign-in sheets too."

"Trust me, he was there, Daisy. The doctor interrupted me and Marcus's conversation. But that doesn't matter now. All you should focus on is getting your butt home and picking up his clothes—"

"What?" Daisy asked, switching lanes and frame of mind. The

previous night's alcohol, lack of sleep, and bouncing between hurt, pain, and worry had begun to take a toll. She'd forgotten which face to put on and when. Her mood became like a voice, everyone had two. There was the happy, polite one usually reserved for business, and then the real one. *My problem is that I don't know what real is anymore.*

"Are you listening? Get home! I just got off the phone with Marcus. He wants me to meet him at your house. If he's on his way there, then Jasper's on his way too."

Daisy's heart raced as she rifled through the coat closet. No raincoat. She yanked the front door open, wincing at the sound of the mirror shattering behind it. She hurried out into the rain and began gathering the sopping clothes.

"What can be saved?" she asked herself frantically. Maybe some of the silks, but the suedes had no hope. Neither did she. What would she tell Jasper?

Once she had gathered all the clothes she could carry, she hurried back inside. "I can't believe I'm doing this," she mumbled, dumping the heavy, wet load onto the floor.

Now for the rest, she thought with a sigh. She had no idea how she was going to get Jasper's boxers out of the tree. And she still had to get the shoe from across the street in the neighbors' yard. What if they'd moved it?

Daisy gave herself a pep talk. She could do it. Had to. She sprinted across the street, feeling the cold wetness of her jeans on her thighs. No shoe to be found anywhere. She got down on her hands and knees, palms sinking into the soggy grass. Finally, she spotted the shoe under the bushes. As she reached for it, the sharp branches tore her skin. Daisy winced in pain, pulling back her hand. Blood trickled down her arm as she held up her wrist to examine her injuries.

Daisy hurried back across the street, retrieving shirts, pants, and socks. After dumping them in the foyer, she went back outside and tried to rip a branch from the rosebush. She had to get Jasper's boxers next.

She moved under the tree and looked up. There they were, dangling. She counted silently and jumped, swinging the rosebush branch, praying that the boxers would catch on a thorn. No luck. She tried again. The branch snagged the boxers and broke in two.

She gave up for the moment, deciding to get the remaining clothes first. As she ran toward the house with another pile in her arms, the wind blew the front door closed. She came to an abrupt halt, her wet feet sliding on the walkway, and fell face-first in a puddle of mud.

As Daisy lifted her face from the wet, stinking ground, a car door slammed behind her. She turned to find Gigi staring down at her, a smile plastered across her umbrella-shaded face. They both giggled.

Then Daisy's smile vanished. Jasper's Escalade had pulled up behind Gigi's car.

Daisy wanted desperately to run into the house, but the front door was closed and on automatic slam-lock. She looked at Gigi, who shrugged. Not knowing what else to do, Daisy smiled as she saw Marcus getting out from the driver's side of the Escalade.

"Hey, Marcus," she said, shaking her head. "What happened? Jasper too tired to drive again? I don't know why he does it to you."

Gigi tapped Daisy's shoulder and pointed toward Jasper's SUV, which had no other visible passengers. "Marcus, where's—"

Marcus held up his hand, silencing her. He stood two feet from Daisy, his gaze traveling up and down her body before coming to rest on her partially exposed breasts.

Daisy cleared her throat, then grabbed him under the chin, forcing him to look in her eyes. "Up here, Marcus. My face is up *here!*"

"You better act like you know, Marcus," Gigi said. "Trifling bastard," she muttered.

Marcus stood still. Rain was running down his face, drenching his clothes, but he didn't seem to notice. He was breathing heavily, his eyes blank as they moved over the lawn to the tree. "What happened? I know you didn't—"

"Where's Jasper?" Daisy snapped.

"Yeah, Marcus," Gigi intervened. "Where's Jasper?"

Marcus wiped a hand over his face and cleared his throat. His eyes were misty, and Daisy suddenly wasn't sure that it was because of the rain. "Listen, Daisy. I need to talk to you. Jasper—"

"Jasper, who? You mean the bastard who doesn't come home and sends you to clean up his mess? That Jasper? What about him?" But then Daisy realized that it *was* tears in Marcus's eyes. They were now running down his face.

"Jasper's dead," he choked.

2

*D*aisy gasped, and Jasper's clothes fell from her grip. But as she stared down at the pile by her feet, she had a revelation. She looked up knowingly at Gigi, then Marcus, and a slight smile came to her face. Jasper wasn't dead, just trying to wiggle out of a tight situation.

"Oh, Marcus, stop it. Of all the lies and excuses you and Jasper could've made up. I went to the hospital, so I know he wasn't there—"

"You went to University Hospital?" he asked, his eyes focused on the ground. "*Staten Island* University Hospital?"

Daisy nodded, although she knew he wouldn't see her. She wanted him to look at her, needed to see that his eyes were lying.

"We were at the University Hospital in *New Jersey*—Newark."

"Yeah, right." Daisy grinned victoriously. She knew she'd

beaten them at their game, and she waited for Marcus's expression to confirm it. But it didn't.

Marcus just closed his eyes, and Daisy's smile faded. She wanted to speak, even scream, but nothing came out. "No," she finally managed to whisper. *"Please,* God, noooo . . ." She sank to the ground.

Gigi pulled her up and tried to hug her, but Daisy pushed away. Her heart drummed in her ears, and everything started to fade.

Marcus grabbed Daisy, shook her, and held her face in his hands. "Look at me, Daisy. Please look at me."

Daisy mustered her strength and opened her eyes. Her heart had never beaten so fast. It raced and pulsed, yet she had no energy. Anxiety was no longer a word or a description for what she had. It *was* her, they were synonymous. Her hands shook uncontrollably as she grasped for hope and grabbed nothing but air. Jasper's spirit.

"Jasper loved you, Daisy. He told me to tell you that he loves you and he's sorry . . . those were his last words."

Daisy stared at him blindly. "How did he die?"

"He was shot . . ."

Daisy held her breath, trying to suffocate the ache that blistered through her and caused her soul to twist into knots. She formed her mouth to question how and why Jasper was shot, but couldn't. Not yet. She had to accept the death first, then deal with the cause. "I've lost the biggest part of me," she whispered as a terrifying loneliness filled her. She squeezed her eyes closed, trying to forget what she'd said about Jasper, but the words haunted her. *If I don't ever see that muthafucka again, it'll be too soon . . . I'd kill him.*

An intense heat overcame her, and she began to perspire. Daisy bent over, releasing everything she'd consumed. She finally straightened again, shaking her head as she wiped her mouth with her sleeve. "Jay," she whispered.

––––––––––

"What happened? Tell me, I have to know," Daisy broke the quiet.

Marcus wrapped his arm protectively around her shoulders as she rested her head on his chest. They'd walked for blocks in silence, the early afternoon sun an orange glow in the sky. Daisy dabbed her eyes with a Kleenex. So much had happened. And so quickly. Jasper had kissed her Saturday night, disappeared Sunday, and died early Monday morning.

Marcus turned Daisy to face him. "Daisy, I know this is hard for you, because it's difficult for me. But I want you to know that you can call on me whenever you need to. Okay?"

"How, Marcus? I know he was shot, but *why* did Jasper die?"

Marcus closed his eyes, sighing heavily. "Jasper died being Jasper. You know how he loved helping people. He was always coming to someone's aid, putting others before himself." Marcus paused, his voice dropping to a whisper. "I miss him, Daisy."

"How, Marcus? Please tell me. Just give it to me straight. I have to know." Daisy blinked hard, trying to hold back the tears.

"We'd just left the club and were riding down the street, when we thought we heard a baby crying . . . screaming. It was so intense, Daisy." Marcus swallowed hard. "I didn't know what to do. It sounded like a death cry, a painful cry. Jasper was driving and pulled into a parking lot. We both got out and followed the noise. We had to see—" Marcus started crying.

Daisy rubbed his arm. "It's okay, Marcus."

Marcus wiped his eyes, collecting himself. "We had to see where it was coming from. In the back of the parking lot, we found a man beating a woman. She was screaming, yelling like I've never heard before. It was obvious that everything wasn't all right, but you know Jasper. He asked anyway." Marcus paused, shaking his head. "But the lady didn't answer—the man gave Jasper the only excuse he needed to step in—the man hit her, made her body float through the air like wind. Before I knew it, Jasper was inches from them. The lady begged Jasper not to interfere . . ." Marcus paused. "I told him that you can't help those who don't want to be helped."

"Jasper didn't listen, did he?"

"No. I told him to come on, that the lady obviously didn't want our help. But he wouldn't listen, Daisy. He grabbed the man and they began to struggle. There was a loud bang, and Jasper fell. The man had a gun. We didn't know. Jasper couldn't have known!"

"And you . . . what did you do? The police?"

"I froze, Daisy! I froze. What kind of friend . . . no, what kind of *man* did that make me?"

Daisy put her hand to her chest, forcing herself to breathe. "The police, Marcus. What about the police?"

"They came too late. The paramedics came too late. They all came too late."

Daisy sat on the sofa, rocking from side to side, trying to decipher the blur in front of her. Too many people. Too much talking. Too many "Are you okay?"'s. She closed her eyes, waiting for the Xanax to kick in, wishing it would all go away. She prayed for Jasper to walk through the door. She needed him. Jay needed him. What would they do without him?

Poor, innocent Jay. How was she to tell him that his father was dead? There were no correct words. Death couldn't be sugar-coated.

"Okay, Daisy?" Gigi patted her back, interrupting her thoughts.

Daisy stared at her.

"Okay?"

"Okay, what?"

Gigi knelt down in front of her, looking into her eyes. "Jay. Where does his friend stay, Daisy? Where did he spend the night? We'll go get him and make the funeral arrangements. We have to before my aunt does. She'll do it her way, not Jasper's."

"Jasper's mom? They didn't speak—"

Gigi sighed loudly. "No one in our family talks to her."

Daisy nodded. "I know. Anyway, I'll go get Jay. His first big tournament is this evening. I have to be there. We were supposed to . . . Jasper and I. It was so important to Jay. To all of us. Somebody can drive me."

Marcus sat down beside her and kissed her on the cheek. "I'll take care of the funeral arrangements."

"We have it under control, Marcus," Gigi said.

"No!" Marcus shouted, then scanned the room as if he were daring everyone—anyone—to go against him. "No. I'll do it."

Daisy stared at Marcus and could read the tension on his face as his eyebrows drew close together, almost touching. She'd never seen him so angry, so adamant. "Why, Marcus? Why are you so intent on doing it?"

"I have to," he spat, and avoided Daisy's eyes. She knew something was wrong, felt a warning that she didn't have time to heed. "You don't understand—I have no choice." Manly tears spilled from his eyes and he wiped them away as fast as they came.

"What's your problem, Marcus?" Gigi asked. "Why the sudden urgency?"

"Gigi," Marcus said slowly, "I can do it. I have to. I promised Jasper before he . . ."

Gigi turned to Daisy. "Is it okay? Do you mind if Marcus handles the funeral? Because Ming Li and I can—"

"I said I'll do it, Gigi," Marcus said. "Damn!"

"All right, Marcus." Gigi nodded. "But you're going to explain yourself later—the reason you're in here carrying on like a fool."

Ming Li shook her head at Marcus. "It'll be alright, Daisy. Gigi and I'll go to Jay's game with you while Marcus handles everything else. He knows what to do. Let's hope he does."

Daisy stepped out of the shower. She hadn't even wanted to bathe, but Ming Li had insisted that it would make her feel better.

She moved to the mirror, gripping the sides of the sink. She barely recognized herself. Her eyes were puffy, and her nose was red. When she tried to put her toothbrush in her mouth, her lips split from the dryness. She was dehydrated from hours of crying.

She heard a knock on the door, then Ming Li walked in. "You alright in here? Need me to help you with anything?"

"No, thanks. I'll be okay. Really. You guys can go home if you want. Don't let me burden you."

"Daisy, you're no burden, and we're not leaving. We've made arrangements. So guess what? You're going to have to put up with us for seven days." Ming Li paused, a sympathetic smile coming to her face. "And I hate to bother you with this, but Marcus can't find Jasper's parents' number. Gigi doesn't know it, and her mother's not home to give it to her."

Daisy stared at the ceiling, thinking. "I don't know the number. They were never close. Didn't call or anything." Daisy shrugged. "Give me a minute to dress. I'll check his office. And since you two insist on staying, there are extra house keys in the jewelry box on the chest."

"Okay. I'll tell Marcus, so he can start preparing himself. He says he's never met Jasper's parents, and he can't figure out how to tell them that . . . well, you know."

"Tell him not to worry. I'll call them myself."

"Okay," Ming Li said. "But if you can't, you know you don't have to. I'll do it for you."

———————

Daisy held Jasper's PalmPilot and stared at his parents' number. She inhaled deeply, held her breath, and exhaled. She tapped her fingers against her forehead, dreading the call.

"What am I supposed to say? 'Hello, this is Jasper's girlfriend. I'm just calling to inform you that your son died,'" Daisy whispered. *How do you tell someone that they've now lost* both *of their twin boys—their only sons? Jonathan and now Jasper too?* As she reached for the cordless phone, a pile of pale-gold-and-navy custom stationery fell to the floor. She smiled faintly, remembering the pleased look on Jasper's face when she'd had it designed for him three years before.

Daisy paced, cradling the phone, waiting for an answer. But when someone picked up, she hung up. Making the call was going to be harder than she thought. Daisy set the phone down on Jasper's desk and wiped her damp palms on her jeans. She grabbed the phone and dialed again.

"Hello," a woman answered.

"Hello, may I speak with Mr. or Mrs. Stevens, please?" Daisy managed.

"This is Mrs. Stevens," Jasper's mother said sadly.

"Hi, Mrs. Stevens, this is Daisy—"

"Oh, Daisy. I remember Jasper mentioning your name," Mrs. Stevens said, sniffling. "You're the one that my baby . . . I mean, Jasper, worked with, right? I guess you're calling about the funeral."

"Yes, but Jasper and I never—"

"Well . . ." Mrs. Stevens cleared her throat and blew her nose. "I'm sorry. I just haven't been able to stop crying since the hospital called and told me that my baby was gone. Lord, rest his soul . . . the service is going to be here, in Philadelphia, at Greater Baptist. Thursday, at two. You all are welcome and wanted. Please thank everyone in your office for the beautiful flowers that Jasper's wife and I received."

"Excuse me, Mrs. Stevens. Did you say Jasper's *wife?*"

"Yes. Jasper's wife, Camille—"

Daisy hung up.

She slumped over as grief turned to anger. She'd been used and misled. She had loved a man who had obviously loved someone else. She'd spent so much time loving him that she hadn't loved herself, had invested so much of herself in him that she'd neglected her own needs, beliefs, and wants. "I knew something was wrong, but I refused to see," she mumbled.

With a scream, she threw the phone at the wall and ran out of the room. She wanted to disappear, although she was already clearly invisible to those outside of her and Jasper's immediate circle. His mother didn't know her, and neither did his coworkers. *I didn't receive flowers, or even a sympathy card. People don't send things to no one. I was Jasper's no one.*

Daisy made her way to the guest room, which no one was allowed to enter. She flung the closet door open and dropped to her knees. She opened the small safe and removed the troubling papers. Her daughter's birth certificate. She rocked back and forth, cradling the document as if it were a baby—the baby she'd given up eight years before.

When she'd visited her parents in California, Daisy had spent so many afternoons watching her from a distance, hearing her call someone else Mom. Lalani would never know Daisy was her mother, but she'd always be her baby.

Daisy collapsed onto her side and curled up in a fetal position. She held her stomach as if someone had kicked her. She'd lost a part of herself because she'd loved too hard. *I hid my baby from you, you bastard. All these years I wanted to go back and get her, and I didn't because I didn't want to lose you.*

Ming Li ran into the room with Gigi and Marcus trailing right behind. "What's wrong?"

Gigi sat on the floor beside her. "What happened, Daisy?"

Daisy stared into Gigi's eyes for truth. "You didn't know—tell me you didn't."

"Know what?"

Daisy shot Marcus an evil look. "You knew, Marcus. Didn't you?"

Marcus held up his hands.

"What, Marcus? What's Daisy talking about?" Gigi looked from Marcus to Daisy. "Daisy, tell me."

Marcus lowered his head. "I wanted to tell you. I just couldn't . . ."

Daisy jumped up. "Why? Why couldn't you tell me? You were my friend too, Marcus. You mean to tell me that you sat in my home, ate my food, and had the nerve to act concerned about me—about Jay—when all along you were lying to me? You know damn well you should've told me that Jasper was married!"

"Married?" Gigi and Ming Li echoed in unison.

"Yes, married. Can you believe it?" Daisy said, never taking her eyes off Marcus. "Leave, Marcus. Just leave."

Marcus turned away, then paused in the doorway. "Daisy, I didn't mean . . . Jasper . . ."

"Out." Daisy pointed to the door.

Ming Li held Daisy as she cried. They could hear Gigi outside the door, cursing at Marcus.

"What about Jay? What did Jasper's mom say about Jay?" Ming Li asked.

"Nothing. Didn't mention him."

———————

Daisy sat on the bleachers next to Gigi and Ming Li and tried to smile genuinely every time Jay looked at her. Jay was a talented player, taller than the rest of his teammates and clearly more athletic. They were up by ten points, thanks to Jay, and the game was almost over. *Please don't let the other team catch up.* Daisy was proud and happy for him, glad that she'd decided to let him spend one more night over at his friend's house and to break the news to him after his tournament. He'd need a pleasant memory to balance the upcoming bad news. Deep down inside, she knew a ball game wouldn't lighten his pain, but how could she rob him of two loves in one day?

Grinning, Jay ran over to Daisy, holding the ball under his arm. "Hey, Mom! Hi, Ms. Gigi, Ms. Ming Li. Did you guys see me? We whipped them, blew them away. Where's Dad?"

Daisy had prepared, but she still wasn't ready. She wrapped her arm around Jay and walked him to the other side of the court. She wouldn't tell him in front of his teammates. "Hey, you." She rubbed his head, messing up his hair. "I'm so proud of you. You did a good job—fantastic. I didn't know you could play like that." Her eyes grew misty.

"Aw, Mom, don't start crying. You're gonna embarrass me."

"Going to embarrass me." Daisy wanted to kick herself for correcting him.

"Going to. Anyway, I wasn't that good. But you really think so?" He bounced the ball back and forth between his legs, showing off. "Where's Dad?"

"He couldn't make it, sweetie. If he could, he'd be here. You know that, right?" Tears escaped and ran down her cheeks.

Jay stared into Daisy's eyes. His expression was serious, not one of a child. "Where is he?" he said, his voice cracking.

Daisy hesitated. "Well, remember the talk we had about

your real mom? How she loves you even though she's not here—"

"Dad died?"

Daisy nodded, wiping her eyes.

Jay threw the basketball across the court. "Everybody leaves me! Are you gonna leave me too?"

"Never."

———

Ming Li's dress was hiked up around her waist as she tried to stretch her too short stockings over her long legs. Daisy shook her head and smiled.

"Ming Li, thanks for going. I appreciate it."

Ming Li straightened her dress. "You don't have to thank me. I know I said a lot of bad things about him, but he was my friend. We were close once."

"I know." Daisy patted her on the back. "I'm going to check on Jay. I'll meet you downstairs." She turned to walk out of the room and collided with Gigi.

"God! You scared me."

Ming Li jumped.

"Sorry. You two ready? Jay's downstairs waiting."

"Don't scare us like that!" Ming Li said with a sigh. "Knock next time, ring the bell or something. You know I'm already nervous. I don't do funerals." Ming Li opened her purse, pulled out her flask, and took a swig.

Daisy shook her head.

"What?" Ming Li put her hand on her hip.

"We're on our way to church, remember?"

"Well, when we get there, let me know, and I won't have another sip."

Daisy grabbed her purse. "You two ready? I don't want to be late." She headed for the door.

"Okay, but are you sure you want to go?" Gigi asked. "It might just make things worse."

Daisy turned around, nodding. "I have to go, Gigi. For Jay."

"And you? Do *you* want to go?"

"No, I didn't want to. Still don't, but Jay asked me to, practically begged me to. How could I say no? Besides, seeing is believing. And I need clarity. It's hard for me to believe he's dead. It's even harder for me to believe that he was married. I just want to get a look at his wife and give Jay the opportunity to pay his respects. That's all."

"I understand. I'm trying to understand. Just please don't do anything you'll regret, Daisy."

"I already have. I was with Jasper."

Daisy held Jay's hand as they entered the church. An attendant directed them to sit in the balcony. She wanted to protest, to inform the attendant that Jay was Jasper's son, but Jay insisted that he didn't want to sit among the congregation. Relief coursed through her as she smoothed his wavy hair. The last thing she wanted was to sit among Jasper's friends and family. "It's okay, baby. Don't worry about it." She kissed Jay on the forehead, leaving a faint smudge of red lip-gloss. Whispering in his ear, she assured him that he didn't have to do anything that he wasn't comfortable with.

"Thanks, Mom. I just don't know all those people. Who are they?"

Daisy shrugged. "I'm sure we'll find out . . . who a few of them are."

Daisy peered over the railing and found the lower section filled to capacity. She hadn't realized that Jasper had had so many friends. There had to be more than two hundred people.

After they'd risen for the prayer and the choir had sung "His Eye Is on the Sparrow," the minister began the eulogy. Daisy held Jay tightly and listened intently, not wanting to miss a word.

"Jasper Stevens was a good man, an honest man. He loved his mother, his father, and his wife. But most importantly, he loved his heavenly Father. Jasper walked in the way of the Lord and did what was right. He died doing what was right and what God would've wanted . . ."

All lies. Daisy tuned out the rest. She squeezed her eyes shut, forcing the tears down her cheeks. Then she looked at Jasper's casket, and everything became a blur. She'd been with him seven years, but she was sitting in the church balcony, instead of in the front pew.

Ming Li tapped her lightly on the shoulder. "Are you ready? You don't want to go say good-bye, do you?" Ming Li pointed to the people lined up waiting to pay their last respects.

"No, I don't even want to be here. But I do want to see his wife," Daisy whispered to Ming Li and Gigi, careful not to let Jay overhear.

Gigi put a hand firmly on her shoulder. "From here, okay? See her from here."

"What about Jay?"

Gigi nodded. "I'm going to pay my respects. I'll take him."

Daisy turned to Jay and wiped his tears. "Go ahead, sweetie. Say good-bye to your dad. Don't worry about the people. No one will bother you, and I'll be right here. I promise."

Jay shook his head and squeezed Daisy's hand as if he were holding on for his life. "I don't want to go without you. Please don't make me. Only if you go."

Daisy swallowed and looked away. She had to go. She couldn't rob him of his last look at his father.

"From here, it doesn't even look like Dad. He's not smiling. I don't want to see him like that."

"It's okay, baby. It really is. I'll stay right here with you." She kissed his cheek and squeezed his hand. "We'll wait until everyone leaves."

Gigi smiled faintly and waved to someone below. "I see Adonis made it. Glad someone else from the family is here. I bet it's because of my aunt that no one else showed."

"Adonis is here? Where?" Adonis was the last person Daisy had expected to see at Jasper's funeral. She wanted to see him, almost had to. But first she needed to see her unknown opponent: the woman who carried Jasper's name.

Ming Li pointed out Adonis, then turned Gigi's chin in the opposite direction. "No, Gigi. Look over there." Ming Li pointed at Marcus.

"Wait, just wait. I'm going to slap fire out of him. I can't believe he acted as if he didn't know my aunt. Look at him. I never introduced them."

Daisy rubbed her pounding temples and popped a pill to calm her nerves. She swallowed hard, forcing it down her dry throat. Jasper had pissed her off more in death than in life. Every time she had mentioned meeting his parents, he'd insisted that they weren't worth meeting. "Jasper made the introduction. He had to. This whole display is disgusting." She felt her bile start to rise.

Marcus was hugging Jasper's mother and wiping her tears. Daisy gritted her teeth. The exchange between Marcus and Mrs. Stevens seemed familiar, almost familial. She held her chest when she noticed the flower pinned to his lapel, which was like five other men's. "Pallbearer," she mouthed.

She followed Marcus with her eyes as he walked toward a woman who was adjusting her black, veiled hat. *Camille.* Daisy held her breath as Marcus bent to kiss her and reach for her hand. She eased forward an inch, as if she couldn't get close enough. She had to see the woman who'd made Jasper love her enough to marry her. She wanted to confront her, but she'd promised Jay that she'd stay with him. Wonder filled her as Marcus's body blocked her view. *What's so special about her? Is she prettier? Smarter?* She felt a tug on her dress and turned around.

Jay grabbed her and held on. "I want to go home. There are ghosts."

Daisy bent and kissed the top of his head. "No, baby, there are no ghosts."

"Yes. Look." He pointed.

Rays of light danced on the wall. Daisy's gaze followed them to where they began: Camille's wedding ring. Even from the balcony, she could see its brilliance.

"It's just the sun," she whispered to Jay. She looked down at her own naked ring finger, which told of her unimportance. *She's the wife. I was the standby.*

———————

"Daisy?" Gigi yelled.

"In the bathroom," Daisy yelled back, combing her hair.

"Ming Li and I are going to the store. Do you or Jay want anything?"

"No. We're fine."

"Okay. We'll be back in a few."

Daisy winced at the sound of the front door slamming, then listened for movement upstairs, something to indicate whether the door had wakened Jay. She sighed at the silence. "Good. He needs all the rest he can get."

She grabbed the remote from the coffee table. "Finally, I get time to myself." She plopped down on the sofa, reveling in being alone for the first time in more than a week. Just as she was about to turn on the television, the doorbell rang.

"Come in. It's not locked," Daisy called out. "What did you guys forget this time?"

The door closed and Daisy heard the lock click slowly and deliberately. Then silence.

Daisy turned to see an unfamiliar woman standing by the door.

"I'm sorry. I know I said to come in, but do you make a habit out of walking into strangers' homes?"

"You did say come in."

"Yes, but I thought you were somebody else." Daisy studied the woman. She could've been her twin, if Daisy were older. "We're not related, are we?"

The stranger shook her head.

"This is scary . . . how much we look alike. Never mind. I'm sorry, can I help you?"

"I want to know why you were sleeping with my husband."

3

Daisy crossed her arms over her chest, trying to still her racing heart. Now that she was face-to-face with Jasper's wife, her hurt increased, and her anger settled. In Camille's presence, Daisy didn't feel like the person Jasper had once convinced her she was. She felt duped, knowing that she hadn't been as special to him as he had once made her believe. She realized she had no bearing or position compared to that of the woman standing before her. Daisy swallowed hard and bit her tongue. No way was she going to let Camille see her cry.

"Are you going to tell me why you're here, Camille?" Daisy asked, refusing to break the stare.

"So, you do know who I am," Camille said tearfully. "Well, I already asked what I want to know. Why were you sleeping with Jasper?"

Daisy laughed softly. All at once, she hated Camille. She despised her presence, her name, her very being. Daisy detested her because Camille had been married to Jasper and she wasn't.

But Daisy composed herself. She eyed Camille from head to toe: her shoes, her legs . . . her stomach. *Oh, no.* Daisy was consumed with sympathy, anger, and jealousy.

"You're pregnant?" Daisy whispered, more to herself than to Camille.

Camille placed her hands over her protruding belly. "Oh, what? Jasper forgot to mention that part?"

"Camille, I understand you're upset. Hell, I'm upset too. Now if you want to discuss this like civilized adults . . ." Daisy motioned for Camille to sit down, glad that Jay hadn't awakened.

Camille sat. "I wouldn't have it any other way. Now, are you going to answer the question or not?"

Daisy sat on the opposite side of the room. "Okay, let's get something straight, Camille. I wasn't sleeping with your husband. I was sleeping with *my* man. I didn't even know you existed until right after . . ." Daisy swallowed hard. "Until Jasper died. So you can do us both a favor and turn your attitude down a notch."

"*Your* man? You're going to sit right there and lie to my face? You didn't know Jasper was married?"

"Isn't that what I told you? For all I know, you were the one who interfered in *our* relationship. Hell, Jasper and I were together for seven, almost eight years."

"We were together more than ten." Camille rubbed her stomach.

Daisy dropped her head, dabbing her eyes. "You were with him first. I didn't know."

"How could you not know?"

Daisy stood and began pacing the room. "What the hell is that supposed to mean? You think I'm some sort of home wrecker or something?"

"Think about it. Where was Jasper on Valentine's and Christmas? How many times did he stay away at work just a day or two longer? How many—"

"I could ask you the same thing. He couldn't have been with you every holiday because he was with me." And Jay, she wanted to say. She had no idea if Camille knew about him, if anyone in the Stevens family knew.

Camille laughed. "Oh, I know. I know he spent more time at his office here in New York than at corporate headquarters. I know everything."

"So why in the hell are you here? You know I've been deceived as much as you have."

"No, Daisy. That's one thing I can't verify. I'll tell you this, though. Whether you want to admit it or not, you knew. You knew, and you weren't too smart about it."

"Excuse me? You have a lot of nerve—"

Camille leaned forward, her round belly resting between her legs. "So you think I'm wrong," she interrupted. "Okay, let me clear this up for you. Why don't you work? Why don't you own anything but a car? Why wasn't your name on Jasper's bank account? I'll tell you why. He had you right where he wanted you. You were a kept woman."

Daisy plopped down in the chair, glaring at her. "Who are you to judge me . . . to analyze me? Jasper didn't want me to work. *He* wanted to take care of me. You need to ask yourself why Jasper chose me after he married you—"

Camille clapped her hands. "Very nice show, Daisy. Who am I? Well, let me see." She pressed her finger to her lips. "I'm the wife, you're the mistress. I deal with pitiful women like you all day, every day. So I can analyze you," she added with a nod. "I can. That's what I do, Daisy. While you sat at home waiting for my husband's checks to roll in, I was counseling patients. I'm a psychiatrist. And what are you?"

Okay, that's it. How can I roll her round ass out of here without harming the baby?

The doorbell rang, and both women fell silent. Daisy could hear Gigi and Ming Li arguing over who had the key. A new energy drifted through Daisy's body, a feeling of certainty, as her two best friends walked in.

"Oh, Daisy, I didn't know you had company," Ming Li said.

Gigi smiled, extending her hand toward Camille. "Hi, I'm Gigi."

"I'm Jasper's wife, Camille," Camille said, refusing Gigi's hand.

"Hmm," Gigi smirked. "I'm his first cousin, and blood is thicker than mud."

Ming Li looked from Daisy to Camille. "Wife? What are you doing here? Is there a problem, Daisy?"

Daisy shook her head.

Gigi moved within two feet of Camille. "'Cause if there is, we can handle it."

"Gigi, stop it. Camille's pregnant."

"Yes, with my *husband's* child."

Ming Li tapped her mini-cigar on the pearl-pink case as if it were a cigarette. "I guess smoke isn't healthy for you, hunh?" she asked, lighting the tip. She took a deep pull and blew it toward Camille.

Camille fanned the smoke away, ignoring Gigi and Ming Li. "As I was saying, Daisy, Jasper didn't choose you after he married me. I said we've been together ten years, not married for ten. Five years," she went on, holding up her hand and spreading her fingers. "We were married five. Hope that answers your question." Camille stood and headed toward the door.

"Mom?" Jay called, emerging from the stairs.

Camille froze.

Daisy's heart pounded. From Camille's open mouth and wide eyes she could tell that Camille had never seen Jay. "Yes, baby, I'm here. Go back to your room. I'll be up in a sec, as soon as I put the trash out."

"Okay." Jay kissed Daisy on the cheek. "Can you help me pack? I can't find my shorts."

Daisy nodded. "Sure, I'll take care of it. Finish resting. There's a game coming on later that I know you don't want to miss."

Camille stared at Jay. "Mom? You have a son?" She covered her mouth. "He looks just like—"

Daisy crossed her arms. "Weren't you leaving?" She brushed past Camille and opened the front door. "Yes, you were. It was a pleasure."

"Bye," Ming Li and Gigi sang in unison.

Camille turned. "We'll meet again."

"Now what?" Gigi asked.

"Now Daisy gets an attorney, that's what," Ming Li spoke up.

Gigi laughed. "An attorney? Why? What's Camille going to do . . . sue Daisy for screwing her husband?"

"Maybe not for that, but she can haul me into court for custody of Jay." The way Camille had stared at Jay had upset Daisy. She hoped that she had rights, since she had raised him. "Do you think they can . . . *will* take him?"

"Mmm-hmm." Ming Li nodded.

"Definitely," Gigi agreed. "If my aunt finds out about Jay. Think about it. Both of her twins passed away, first Jonathan, now Jasper. Wouldn't you want custody of your grandson too? He's the only boy she has left."

"But they don't know him—he doesn't know them! He's not a part of Jasper's estate. He's a boy, not a thing to pass down generational lines . . . up for grabs to whoever gets him first. I won't let them take him. I can't, we belong together. We're all we have. I promised I wouldn't leave him, that I'll always be here for him. Losing Jay is *not* an option."

"Okay." Gigi paused, thinking. "You have to move. Stay with me until you get on your feet."

"I can't do that, Gigi. No offense, but I don't want to be near Marcus."

"So, maybe you should just go back home for a while. Get some California sunshine."

"Hell, no. I'm not going back home. I don't want to be around my family."

"So you and Jay can stay with me," Ming Li offered.

With Jay at his friend's house playing video games, Daisy lay in bed watching videos of her and Jasper's happier days. She missed him terribly. She felt empty, and her heart ached. Daisy closed her eyes, losing herself in the sound of his voice. She relaxed, allowing her body to be held by the soft fullness of the pillows. Inhaling slowly and deeply, she licked her lips sensuously, as Jasper had many times before.

Daisy grabbed Jasper's T-shirt, which she had doused with his cologne, pressed it against her nose, and lost herself in his scent. He'd always smelled so good, felt so warm, tasted so delicious. Daisy's body tingled. She needed Jasper to fill the void.

"Close your eyes, Daisy," Jasper's voice whispered.

"They're closed."

"Turn around," he commanded sensually.

"Okay."

"You don't mind, do you?" Jasper asked, placing a blindfold over Daisy's eyes.

"Anything for you, Jasper. Whatever, however you want."

"Lie back. Can I touch you? No, let me see you touch yourself. Daisy, show me where and how you want to be touched."

An intense heat overcame Daisy's body. Her hands became his hands. She moaned and arched her back as his hand caressed her breasts. The other played in her hair, massaging her scalp. Parting her legs, she begged for him. "Please, Jasper. Please," she whispered as he traced his finger along the top of her panties, gradually working his way down the V of silk that separated his hand from her flesh. In one swift motion, Daisy lifted her legs and pulled her panties off. She groaned, throbbed, and cried. Jasper's lovemaking had always made her cry. "So good." Daisy bit her lip, his touch familiar as he gently prodded her and made his way inside.

"I'll always love you, Daisy."

"Tell me you're mine, Jasper. All mine."

"I'm yours. Only yours."

Daisy sat up and looked around. Jasper's words startled her from her ecstasy. They seemed too lifelike, almost as if he were whispering in her ear. *Only yours,* she thought as she reached for the remote. She searched frantically, switching between rewind and fast-forward. Daisy became angrier each time she heard

Jasper lie. A total of eight times he had told her that he belonged to her alone.

Daisy jumped off the bed and grabbed her robe, hiding her nakedness from Jasper's ghost. "How could you? How could you lie to me all those years? You loved me, right? Only me?"

Daisy sat on the edge of the bed and sobbed. So many lies, so many half-truths, had shattered her world. Everyone was right; she'd been deceiving herself. Jasper may have been wrong, but she'd been the fool to fall victim to his game.

What happened to me? What happened to Daisy Parker—not Jasper's Daisy, but Daisy's Daisy? How could I have been so wrong? How could loving someone so much that you give in completely be a mistake?

"You did this to me, Jasper," she said out loud. "You took everything from me and gave me nothing but pain and humiliation."

Deep inside, all those times Jasper hadn't come home when he was supposed to, she'd known something was wrong. She'd always had a suspicion when Jasper conveniently had to be away most of the holidays. Daisy chided herself for not pushing to meet his family. *What kind of man is with you for seven years and doesn't introduce you to his mother? What kind of fool was I to believe that they didn't get along, and not even ask why?*

Daisy got up, went to wash Jasper's scent off her.

———————

Daisy set the table while she waited for Ming Li and Gigi to arrive.

The doorbell rang. "Hope you two are hungry," Daisy sang, opening the door.

"Daisy Parker?" asked a smiling, friendly faced man dressed in a blue suit.

"Yes?"

He handed her an envelope. "Daisy Parker, you have just been served."

4

*D*aisy, Ming Li, and Gigi sat around the dining room table eating silently. Daisy pushed her plate away. "What am I going to do now? I'm unemployed, and I've just been legally ordered to move out."

Ming Li wiped her mouth with a napkin. "Good question. What about Jasper's attorney? He had a lawyer, right?"

Gigi took a sip of chardonnay and dabbed her mouth. "Ming Li, I know where you're going with this. Do you think . . . she can't block the eviction, can she?"

Daisy sighed impatiently. "Can you two speak English, please? What are you talking about?"

Ming Li retrieved her flask from her purse, took a sip, and set it on the table. "If you think about it, Camille is Jasper's wife—"

"Tell me something I don't know." Daisy rolled her eyes, tired of being reminded.

"Listen to Ming Li, Daisy."

"Well?"

"Hear me out before you snap. I know you're tired of being reminded about Camille and Jasper, but technically, because she is . . . *was* his wife, she has legal rights that you don't. This house, for instance. Because Jasper died, everything he owned in life she owns by his death, even his Escalade. Where is it, anyway? I thought you guys said Marcus left it here."

"I let him take it to get cleaned up. Jasper's blood was in it."

"Marcus doesn't have Jasper's SUV. I would've seen it. I bet—"

"Camille! He gave it to Camille." Daisy clenched her teeth.

"Let me finish," Ming Li said. "Camille owns everything that was his, *unless* Jasper's will states otherwise. Let's not forget about Jay," she added with a wink.

Gigi laughed. "She can't overthrow his will, Daisy. Or his heir. Even if Camille has this house, as much money as Jasper had, you know you're gonna be alright."

"I hadn't even thought of that. But . . ." Daisy held up her eviction notice. "Is this any good? Do I really have thirty days to vacate?"

Ming Li nodded. "Technically."

"Call his lawyer, Daisy. Do you need me to get the phone? I gotta hear this," Gigi said.

"Ming Li, give me a sip of whatever you have in that flask first, then I'll go find the number. I have a feeling it's stronger than this wine."

"What's in that flask, anyway? And how many sips do you take a day?" Gigi asked.

"Paradis, Hennessy cognac. And not that it's any of your business, but I take about five or six swigs a day. It relaxes me." Ming Li handed the gold flask to Daisy.

Daisy gulped it, twisted her face, and banged her fist on her chest. "Damn, that's some strong stuff. What is it, again?"

"About three hundred dollars," Gigi said, laughing.

Three calls to Jasper's attorney but not one call back. Daisy tried to understand. After all, he was a busy and important man. But after the last unreturned call, Daisy became impatient. Gigi offered to try, and Ming Li said that she'd have her lawyer contact Jasper's, but Daisy declined both offers. This was something she had to do for herself.

Daisy held the phone tightly and waited for the receptionist to put her through, tapping her foot. She felt confident that Jasper's attorney, Kenneth Burgess, would tell her that everything was fine.

"Ms. Parker, this is Ronald Hayes. I'm a junior partner at the firm. How can I help you?"

Daisy sighed. "I'm calling about Jasper Stevens's will." *As if you don't know.* "Was anything left to either his son or myself?"

Mr. Hayes cleared his throat. "I'm afraid all the beneficiaries have been contacted."

Daisy's heart pounded. "Are you sure? There has to be some sort of mistake. Maybe you sent something to a wrong address or called a wrong number. There's no way he'd have forgotten his son. Will you please check?"

"Again, I'm sorry. There's been no mistake. *All* beneficiaries have been contacted, and they've met in person for the reading and execution."

Daisy dropped the phone.

She began pacing frantically. How could Jasper enjoy her loyalty for seven years and leave her without so much as a dime? Something had to be wrong. He loved Jay too much to leave him to fend for himself. She slapped her head. She'd been his fool. His whore. The woman he'd treated like his child. *Don't work, Daisy. What kind of man would I look like if my woman had to work? My mother didn't have to work. None of my coworkers' wives have to work. You're going to shame me. I'll always take care of you. Forever, Daisy. Me and you, forever.*

Jasper's lies raced through Daisy's mind. She'd done everything for him, and he'd done nothing for her. Moved her to a city where she had no relatives. Given her a home, which he would've had whether she'd lived there with him or not. Taken away her independence so that she'd be dependent on him. He had accepted her love and returned it with lies. And then he died and caused a part of her to die with him.

"Well, what did he leave you guys?" Gigi asked.

"Homeless. Penniless. Scared."

———————

As much as Daisy wanted to blame her troubles on Jasper, honesty wouldn't permit it. Everything had happened with her permission. Jasper had never held a gun to her head and forced her to do anything. She'd willingly given him control of her life because she'd wanted him to have it—needed him to.

I'm in charge of my own life now. I can do this, handle this. I can. She battled the doubt that eased in. "Why?" Daisy whispered hoarsely.

Resting her head against the wall, she peered across the room at the heap of Jasper's belongings that she had piled in the corner. Her first thought had been to burn his things, but her conscience wouldn't allow it. She needed to cremate her memories, not his clothes. She stared at the pile. Jasper's essence was in the room. Daisy couldn't resist the temptation; she walked to the pile and picked up one of Jasper's silk shirts. Rubbing the slick fabric against her cheek, she felt goose bumps travel down the nape of her neck to the bottom of her spine. Closing her eyes, she gave in to the softness of the silk. Her mind drifted to memories of Jasper's hands caressing her. She held the shirt to her nose and inhaled.

The material didn't smell like Jasper. It smelled like Camille.

Daisy's stomach turned. She knew the thought was ridiculous; the shirt had been piled among Jasper's other things for so long that it couldn't smell like anyone. It was all in her mind. The mere thought of him was making her ill one day and aroused the next. As much as she was starting to despise Jasper's memory, she still loved him. She was suffocating, trapped between love and hate.

She stood, wringing her hands, and took slow, deliberate steps toward the pile of clothes. Pain, anger, and grief took hold of her. Even in death, Jasper was controlling her. Daisy shook her head. She wouldn't allow him to overpower her anymore.

"Okay." She nodded, giving herself permission to rid herself of Jasper's things. She retrieved a box of garbage bags from the pantry, made a beeline to the living room, and tossed them across the room toward Jasper's stuff. Then she grabbed her keys, hurried outside, and backed her Jeep onto the lawn. She opened the top and bottom hatch, then went inside to finish her business with Jasper's ghost.

In the living room, she hesitated. *Boxes would be easier, neater. But I'm being put out like trash, so why shouldn't you? May your spirit always be Glad.* Daisy smirked as she stuffed Jasper's belongings into the trash bags and piled them into the back of her SUV. She ran back inside to the guest room and grabbed the jewelry box from the dresser. She removed the promise ring that Jasper had given her. She held it, studied its intricate pattern of diamonds and rubies, then stuffed it into her pocket.

———————

Daisy trudged through the grass toward Jasper's massive marble headstone. The wind blew her hair and the leaves rustled, but Daisy didn't notice. The inscription on Jasper's gravestone held her attention: *Loving and devoted husband, father, and son.* His baby wasn't even born yet. On the way to the cemetery, she wanted to shout, curse Jasper, and spit on his grave. But now, she couldn't take her eyes off the chiseled words. She'd known she wouldn't be included in the inscription. But seeing it like this was cruel, an announcement of just how unimportant she was.

" 'Lying, conniving, deadbeat dad, and two-timing boyfriend of devoted girlfriend' is how the stone should read," she sobbed. "I won't ask why, Jasper. I know now. It's written in stone."

She knelt down, digging her nails in the earth until she had made a small hole. Reaching into her pocket, she retrieved the promise ring. "You gave me this once, remember? Promised me that one day . . . you said you loved me, that you'd always be true. 'You're the only woman in my life, Daisy. The only one for me.' Do you remember that, Jasper? Hunh? You lied to me, gave me false hope, promised a lie. Now I'm giving it back to you. Take your promise and shove it up your rotting ass."

Daisy looked around and saw that she was alone. She unbuckled her pants, pulled them down with her panties in one swift motion, and pissed on Jasper's grave.

Daisy walked into the cluttered living room, stepping over boxes and avoiding bubble wrap. She'd done everything she could to avoid packing up the guest room and dealing with her demons, but she knew she had to. With every step toward the stairs, her neck stiffened and her temples throbbed. Tension spread through her back as her muscles tightened. *I can't.* She grabbed the banister and sat on the lower step. She thought about home—her real home. She needed her mother.

She hadn't called home since their last argument, almost a year before. She'd wanted to apologize, to kiss and make up, but she had refused. She was stubborn, and so was her mother. The ordeal hadn't been Daisy's fault. Her parents hadn't agreed with her wanting Lani back and didn't allow her to have her say. When she tried to speak out, her words fell on decidedly deaf ears as they sung her mistakes to her like spirituals. "You're not Lani's mother anymore, Daisy. How could you be? You gave her up. Do you honestly think it would be wise to step in and be her mother now?" her mom had said without hesitation or remorse. "But I am a mother. Damnit, I am *her* mother," Daisy'd spat back. As angry as she'd been, she now wanted to hear her mother's voice. Daisy wrapped her arms around her middle and cuddled herself. She needed someone to say that they loved her and mean it.

Daisy held the phone, staring at the lighted numbers. Her hands were sweaty, trembling as she dialed. She swallowed hard as she waited for someone to answer.

"Hello?" It was her mother, Ms. Christine Parker.

"Hey, Mom. How are you?"

"Daisy?"

"Yeah, Mom. It's me."

"Daisy, is that you? Thank God, honey. I thought something

had happened to you. You had me worried after the last time we talked. You okay?"

Daisy blinked back the tears and tried to blink back the memories of the fight they'd had over where her daughter should live. "I'm okay, I guess."

"How's Jay? And Jasper? Is he still treating you good?"

Daisy shook her head. "Jasper's dead, Mom."

"Oh, Lord. When? How? Are you and Jay okay?"

"I'm handling it the best I can. He's been gone over a month now. Shot to death. I think his family is going to try to take Jay away."

"I'm so sorry, baby. Why didn't you call sooner? I know you must've needed me. I would've flown out there—"

"I know, Mom, but that's not why I'm calling. I'm moving. I have to clean out my closet, and I can't. I want to, have to, but I can't."

"What's in the closet, baby? Why can't you?"

Daisy wiped her eyes. "The papers. All those damn papers. I can't do it, Mom. Please help me. I need you."

"Stay put. Your father and I will be on the next flight out—"

"Just you, Mom. Just you, okay?"

"Okay, baby. Just me. Hold on. Be strong now. Call Gigi and your other girlfriend and have them come over and keep you company until I get there. I'll be there as soon as I can. And call an ambulance if you feel one of those breakdowns coming on, okay? Daisy?"

"Hmm?"

"I love you. No matter what's happened between us over the years, I love you. You're my baby girl."

"I love you too, Mom." Daisy cradled the phone to her chest and cried until she had no more tears.

Knowing that her mother was coming, Daisy felt stronger. She willed herself up on her feet. *I can do this. I can.* She repeated her mantra. Preparing herself for what lay ahead, Daisy decided to clean house.

5

*D*aisy poured steaming water into the coffee cup and dunked the tea bag until the water became the color of mud. She held the mug under her nose, allowing the rising steam to tickle her nostrils and open her nasal passages. Too much crying had made her stuffy. She inhaled the peppermint aroma, held it in, then released the minty coolness through her mouth. She smiled and did it again.

She gazed out the window at the swimming pool. The aqua-colored ripples shimmered under the moon's glow. The weeping willow swayed in the breeze. She'd forgotten about the pool in the midst of her turmoil. She promised herself that if she didn't do anything else before she left the house, she'd have one final swim, one last moment to immerse her body in twelve feet of heated water.

Slipping out of her shoes, Daisy walked along the edge of the pool. Every other step she took, she'd dip her toes in the luke-warm water until tiny circles appeared on the surface. She thought of Jay. "Almost done, baby," she said as she rolled up her jeans, sat down, and put her feet in the water. *The house is almost empty; most of the furniture is in storage, and our clothes are packed.* She closed her eyes and said a short prayer. She needed strength—they all did.

"Am I disturbing you, baby?" Ms. Christine walked toward Daisy holding two goblets of iced tea. "I figured we'd need these."

"No, Ma. Come join me," Daisy said, patting the spot next to her.

Ms. Christine handed Daisy the glasses, eased down, and stuck her feet in the pool. "Whew! Squatting gets difficult when you get older. Everything isn't as easy as it looks, I guess."

"You got that right." Daisy handed her mother a glass. "Thanks for coming, Ma. And for helping me get it all together. I know you don't like to fly alone. I appreciate it."

Ms. Christine took a sip of tea and looked at the sky. "My, it sure is beautiful out here at night. You see that star right there, Daisy? That bright one?" Ms. Christine pointed. "That's ours: mine and yours—our connection. When I was younger, around your age, your great-grandmother Ma Dear showed me that star the very night she died; the brightest star. She said it was our family connection, between the living and the dead. Kind of a stairway to those we love who are gone, and a meeting place for those of us who live far away from one another. I've watched that star for the past year or so, and I knew that you could see it too."

Daisy nodded and blinked back the tears. Ms. Christine's love had always been her weak spot.

"The point is, I'll never be too far away for you to reach me. Whether I'm home in L.A., or up there in heaven with Ma Dear, I'm always going to be here for you. Don't ever do this to me—or yourself—again. Don't try to go through something so painful without me. I'm your mother. I'm here to help you." Ms. Christine reached over and hugged Daisy. "Now go ahead and cry, baby. Get it all out. We can talk about the past—and the future—later."

———————

Daisy awoke, twisted her body in a stretch, and yawned. She was still tired, and her head was ringing. She groaned, turned over, and rolled her eyes. Who had set the alarm? Forcing herself to sit up, she turned it off. *Had to be Ma.*

"You up yet, baby?" Ms. Christine said, knocking on the bedroom door.

"Unh-uh," Daisy lied.

Ms. Christine opened the door. "What did I tell you about lying? Come on, Daisy. It's after nine. I'm going downstairs to make some coffee. I've already drawn you a bath, and I ironed two different outfits for you . . . didn't know which one you'd want to wear. You've always been picky, just like me." Ms. Christine closed the door, chuckling.

"Tea, Ma. Tea!" Daisy yelled.

Daisy could her Ms. Christine mumbling as she went down the stairs. "I swear, coffee one day and tea the next. These kids."

Daisy smiled as she walked into the kitchen and saw Ms. Christine seated at the breakfast table. "I'm glad you're here, Ma," she said, pouring herself a cup of coffee.

"I know that's not coffee in that cup, is it?"

"I'm sorry I had you make tea, Ma. I just remembered how nice it was when we used to drink coffee together."

Ms. Christine giggled. "I didn't make tea. I knew you'd change your mind."

"So, where are we going? I know you want to go somewhere."

"That's my baby. You know me, don't you? Well, I thought we'd do a little shopping, then grab a bite to eat and talk."

Daisy gulped her coffee and slammed the cup on the table. She stuck out her tongue, waving her hand over it.

"Burnt your mouth, baby?"

Daisy nodded, still fanning.

Ms. Christine snickered and went to get her some water. "Still my Daisy. Next time, sip it. You have to learn to take things slowly, otherwise you might get hurt."

Daisy filled her mouth with water and ice chips. She knew her mother was referring to her history of moving too fast with men. "Thanks. I needed that. Listen, Ma, we can shop if you want. But honestly, I don't have any money."

"I know. We'll take care of it."

"I don't want your money, Ma."

Ms. Christine raised her eyebrows. "You're not getting my money. There's another way. Trust me."

Daisy sat inside the Sea Grill restaurant in Rockefeller Center and wolfed down her jumbo lump crab cakes, avoiding the tip of her tongue, which was still stinging from the coffee. Ms. Christine was in the powder room. Daisy closed her eyes with each bite, enjoying the succulence. *Heavenly.* She hadn't tasted anything since Jasper's death, had eaten only because she had to.

"I'm back," Ms. Christine announced, plopping back down in her chair. How're the crab cakes?"

"Ma, there's just no word for them. Too good. Let's leave it at that."

"I'm glad you enjoyed them. Finished?"

Daisy nodded.

Ms. Christine pushed her plate back. "I know you need to talk to me. But first let me talk to you, okay?"

Daisy smiled. "Sure, go ahead. There's no way I'm going to forget my subject."

"Well, what are you going to do about Jay? Are you going to be his guardian—adopt him?"

Daisy looked down. "I don't know. I want to, but I don't know the legalities, or how I'm going to take care of him. But I will, somehow. Whatever I do, I have to do it quickly. Summer's almost over. Jay starts school in a month. And Jasper left everything to his wife, nothing to his son—or me, for that matter."

"Is his family that bad? You couldn't trust Jay in their care?"

"Ma, they don't know him, were never there for him. Please,

they didn't even know he existed. But I'm sure they do now. I told you Jasper's wife came over to confront me. She saw Jay, and she had to have known that he was Jasper's. Who wouldn't know? He's the spitting image of his father. Still, she put us out."

Ms. Christine sat quietly for a moment, staring into space. "I got it," she finally said, to no one in particular. "I'll take Jay home with me for the rest of the summer while you get yourself together. It'll be good for both of you. Besides, he's always enjoyed his visits—"

"Wait, Ma—" Daisy started to protest.

"Don't interrupt me, Daisy. Listen. Jay can come home with me, and you can get his paperwork together. Jasper may not have left you two any money, but he worked the majority of his life, and he made good money. Jay's eligible for Social Security."

"Damn. You're absolutely right. That never crossed my mind."

"Watch your mouth."

"Sorry. But I can't let you take Jay. He's already confused and hurt. He needs me right now."

"Yes, he does. But what are you going to do when they come to take him away? And believe me, they're going to come. You don't have the money to whisk him away and hide him. Let him come home with me, get a few weeks of stability in his life. He and Lani can play together. Let the boy learn to laugh again."

Daisy nodded and smiled on the inside. She fantasized about her children playing together and longed for the day that it wouldn't be temporary. She knew Jay's going would be best for both of them. She could use the time to get on her feet, and he could enjoy himself, finally—hopefully.

Ms. Christine reached into her purse. "Now, about what you wanted to talk about. I have a feeling I know what else is bothering you, besides Jasper. Once you cleaned out the closet I knew your memories would come back to haunt you again." Ms. Christine slid a picture across the table in front Daisy. "Lalani. You want Lani back, right?"

Daisy stared at Lani's picture and picked it up gently, as if it might break.

"She looks just like you," Ms. Christine went on, "but I guess you can see that. Answer me this: How come you haven't seen your daughter in almost seven years?"

Daisy held the picture and traced Lani's pretty smile with the tip of her nail. She couldn't believe how much her daughter had grown. She was even missing a couple of teeth. Daisy grinned at that, wondering if anyone teased her at school.

"Well?" Ms. Christine leaned back and drummed her fingers on the table.

"Well what, Ma? Well, do I want Lani back, or, well, how come I haven't seen her?" Daisy laid Lani's picture on the table.

"Don't get cute, Daisy."

Daisy's mouth was dry. She reached for her glass of water but found it empty. Ms. Christine slid her glass of water across the table. "Thanks, Ma." Daisy gulped the water. "Ooh, I needed that."

"I know. My mouth gets dry too when I'm nervous."

"I'm not nervous. Okay, so I am. It's just hard for me to explain about Lani."

"I know, Daisy, just like I know you. You do want Lani back, right?"

Daisy nodded.

"Well, I don't understand—"

"She's my child, Ma."

"Okay, I'll grant you that. You did birth her. But Lani is Brea's daughter."

"No, she's my daughter, Ma. And I'd have her, if you guys—"

"We what? Say it, Daisy."

Daisy looked around the restaurant. She didn't want to cause a scene. "If you guys hadn't made me give her up."

"Oh, really? You think we made you? Daisy, look at me. No one made you give Lani to Brea. You know that. Do you remember how you cried about school? You'd call me and say, 'Ma, how am I going to do it? I have to graduate. What am I going to do?' Do you remember all that? I do. I remember it plain as day. I was the one you'd wake up at three, sometimes four in the morning."

"Yes, I remember," Daisy mumbled.

"So how can you sit there and accuse us of making you give Lani away?"

Daisy looked into her mother's eyes. "Ma, you came up with the idea."

"No, I didn't. I don't know what you've talked yourself into believing, but you're wrong—dead wrong—and you know it. What I suggested, baby, is that you come home for the remainder of your pregnancy. But you refused. You took Brea up on her offer to live with her."

"I know, Ma. I thought that's what you wanted. You said I was an embarrassment to the family." Daisy wiped her tears with a linen napkin.

"Oh, Lord, Daisy. I may have. If I did, I apologize. I didn't mean to. I was just so upset about it back then. *My baby* was having a baby. It's just that you—all of my children—always made me so proud. I used to brag all the time about you kids. To me, you all were perfect. We'd never had a problem before that. You children never gave your dad and me any trouble. You went to school, helped out around the house, graduated, and went to college."

Daisy nodded.

"I guess I was so blessed with great children that I didn't know how to handle the unexpected. I never meant for you to think . . . I'd never ask you, or anyone else, to give up their child. With all that I had to put up with as a mother—the labor pangs, colic, teething . . . hmm . . . and, Lord, puberty," Ms. Christine said with a smile. "I'd do it all over again—twice. I've never regretted you all. I know what that love's like, between a mother and a child. I wouldn't take that away from anyone."

"But you think I don't deserve to know that kind of love with Lani."

"You have that with Jay. You may have given birth to Lani, but *Jay's* your child. Tell me why you believe you have a right to Lani if Jasper's family doesn't deserve custody of Jay. The same argument applies, Daisy. You don't know Lalani, and you haven't been there for her, either."

Daisy frowned, repositioning her leg to get into a comfortable position. With each attempt she made to get her foot within reach, she held her breath. She soaked a cotton ball with fingernail-polish remover and immediately regretted holding the acetone too close to her face. The fumes were making her nauseous. "Ick," she said as she rubbed the cotton across her toenail.

"Why don't you just go to Ming Li's shop and get a pedicure?" Ms. Christine asked.

Daisy jumped. "Ma, I didn't know you were there. What's that you used to tell us, to announce ourselves before we enter a room?"

Ms. Christine laughed. "Yes. Yes, I did. I said for you to announce yourselves; I didn't say that *I* had to." Ms. Christine sat on the floor next to Daisy. "Pass me those cotton balls and the remover. I'll take the polish off for you. I still don't understand why you don't just go get a pedicure."

"I haven't had a professional pedicure in almost eight years. Jasper used to do my feet. He'd wash them and massage them. He'd even put cuticle remover around the edges of my nail beds before he'd put them in the foot massager."

"He did?"

"Yeah, he did. He used to hold my feet as if they were the most beautiful things he'd ever laid eyes on." A dreamy smile spread across Daisy's face, and tears welled up in her eyes. "He used to file and buff my nails. He'd even polish them. He said my feet were too pretty to be overdone. He wanted them accentuated, not disguised."

"Disguised?" Ms. Christine wrinkled her nose. "How does someone disguise toes?"

"Designs and loud colors. I had tiny orange swirls painted on my toes when I met Jasper. You know, at that time I was always after something different. I think that's what attracted to me to Jasper. He *was* different. He wasn't like Calvin, or the other deadbeats I'd dated in college . . . he actually seemed to care about me . . . right from the start. You remember when that guy tried to rob me and I didn't have any money? Not a dime." Daisy laughed.

"Lord, how could I forget? I wanted to kill him, whoever he was."

"Well, that's the day I met Jasper. Gigi and I had just come out of the nail salon and had just spent our last cent on our nails. We were headed to the subway station and I was walking ahead of her because she was on her cell. I turned the corner before she did, and the next thing I knew I was pressed against a building and had a knife pointed to my face."

"*Oh, God.* You didn't tell me all of that . . . only that you were almost robbed . . ." Ms. Christine clutched her chest.

"Then I saw Jasper. At the time I didn't know that he was supposed to be meeting Gigi, I didn't even know who he was. So, it was like he appeared out of nowhere. You should've seen him, Ma. He stepped up and said, 'If you want to rob someone, rob me. Try to take my money.' Then he reached into his pocket, threw his money on the ground, and dared the man to pick it up."

"That was awfully bold of him. But what does that have to do with having swirl designs on your toes?"

"After the robber ran off, I hugged Jasper and got fingernail polish on his shirt. You know I never wait for my nails to dry. I felt so bad because I knew he'd never get the stain out. But then he accidentally stepped on my toes, and I felt like we were even. Then he insisted that I let him make it up to me, so I did. That's also the day Gigi and I met Ming Li. Anyway, he walked me back to the nail salon and removed the polish himself. Then he picked out a new color for me. I was so happy," Daisy added, her voice cracking. "I thought that was the cutest thing on earth, him picking out which color he thought was best for me. Jasper controlled me before he even knew my name. He hadn't even asked me what it was yet."

Ms. Christine took Daisy in her arms and rocked her. "It's going to be okay, baby. It's all going to surface . . . it has to. That's one of the first steps in healing."

"Ma, how could I have been so stupid? I loved him. I thought he loved me. Why does it have to be so hard? No one told me love could be so cold."

Ms. Christine held Daisy at arm's length. "Now you listen to me, Daisy. Don't you ever let anyone tell you different. Love isn't cold, baby. It's nice and warm. It's an emotional home. If it feels any other way, it's not love. You understand me?"

Daisy nodded.

"Now, I won't bad-mouth Jasper, because he's gone. But Lord knows, I'd curse him to hell if he were here. There are four things I don't play around with: my life, my children, my husband, and my money. Not necessarily in that order." Ms. Christine paused, shaking her head. "What Jasper did to you was awful. Disgusting. You know it, I know it. And wherever he's at, he knows it. You were a good woman—naive, but good. But now you've got to finish pulling yourself together. You allowed him to break you in life; don't give him the upper hand over you in death too. He's gone, Daisy. It's time for you to let his spirit go and lift your own."

Daisy rested her head on Ms. Christine's shoulder and thought about what she'd said. Like Ming Li and Gigi, her mother was right. It was time for Daisy to take care of Daisy.

"Ma?"

"Yes, baby?"

"I'm going to get Lani back. You and I didn't speak for months, and you have me back in your life. I want my baby back too."

Ms. Christine kissed her on the forehead and looked into her eyes. "I know you do, baby. But think of Lani first, not yourself. Don't rip her from the only home she's known—the home that your sister Brea has given her. Try to focus on yourself right now. You can't do anything for anyone else if you can't do it for yourself."

———

Daisy rang the bell hesitantly. Although she and Ming Li were close, and Daisy appreciated Ming Li's offer to let her stay until she found a place of her own, she wasn't comfortable living with her. She'd heard enough horror stories of friendships dissolving once people moved in together. *I can't stay here long.*

Ming Li opened the door with a smile. "You don't have to ring the bell, you know . . . oh, I forgot. I haven't given you a key yet. Come in and lock the door."

Daisy gently closed the door and bolted it. She leaned her weight against it, dropping her purse on the floor. "Whew. I don't ever want to see another box again."

Ming Li closed her red silk robe around her. "That bad, hunh? You'll be okay, trust me. You just need something hard and stiff."

"Ming Li! Is sex all you think about?"

Ming Li laughed. "I was talking about a drink."

Daisy sat down on the sofa. Ming Li sat opposite, putting her perfectly French-manicured foot on the coffee table. She shook her head. "But you do need a man."

"For what?"

"Whatever you want. They come in handy, you know?"

"I already had one . . . didn't do me any good."

Ming Li shook her head. "You had a boy. Boys play; men please. Watch this. First, tell me where your things are."

"In the Jeep. Why?"

Ming Li ran her fingers through her hair and raised her eyebrows. "Ricky, honey, can you come out here for a minute?"

Daisy gasped as six-foot-four Ricky walked into the room. His height was intimidating, but his eyes were soft and friendly. He smiled as Ming Li whispered in his ear. "Daisy, give him your car keys," Ming Li said, never taking her eyes off Ricky.

Ricky nodded and took Daisy's keys without uttering a word. He speed-walked to the bar, humming. Although he was only steps away from Daisy and Ming Li, he seemed to be in another world. He returned in less than a minute, smiling, and placed their drinks on the table, then kissed the top of Ming Li's head and disappeared into the foyer.

Daisy waited until she heard the front door close. "What—"

Ming Li placed a finger to her pouted lips, shushing Daisy, and smiled. "It's really very simple . . . what I do. It's all about P's and Q's. First you gotta put the P down." Ming Li cupped her mouth and whispered, "P-U-S-S-Y. Whip that on them and they'll bow to your *power*. Q's are what they bring to the table because no one can come to mine with only a knife and fork and expect to be served."

"Q's?"

"Qualifications. Quantity. Quality." Ming Li counted on her fingers as she spoke. "They have to be competent and worthy of my time. Give me only the best. And give me a helluva lot of it."

"Okay, so it helps to have a man around. But it doesn't mean that I need one."

"Yes, it does. You're unhappy; I'm not. I please him; he pleases me. He's happy as hell right now because I just gave him some. Why do you think he's walking around here humming and shit? As long as I can make him sing, I can make him dance to my tune."

Daisy stood. "Girl, you're crazy. I'm going to help Ricky—"

Ming Li wagged her index finger. "No, don't do that. I have him just like I want him. Give me a few weeks, just twenty-one days, and I'll teach you how to make a man do anything."

6

*D*aisy sat on her bed staring at the newspaper. She'd been searching for a job for over a week. She'd posted her résumé on monster.com and careerbuilder.com, contacted the New York State Nursery/Landscape Association of Nurserymen, the American Horticultural Society, and the American Horticultural Therapy Association. She'd applied for several nursery, buyer, and landscape-design positions, but hadn't received a call yet. Education without experience wasn't good enough. *Tomorrow, I'll try the flower shops. Somebody has to need someone with "growing" hands.*

Ming Li barged into Daisy's room, opened the closet, and slid hangers side to side, obviously searching through Daisy's clothes. "Where have you been? I've been calling you all day."

"I was out looking for a job. Why? Where else would you expect me to be?" Daisy tilted her head and watched Ming Li intently as she rifled through Daisy's clothes. She'd gotten a strong vibe that Ming Li was up to something, because there was no way Ming Li needed to borrow from Daisy's wardrobe; Ming Li had clothing that designers would envy. "Why are you in my stuff? I know you don't need anything to wear."

"No, you do. Listen, you've been here almost two weeks and we haven't had a bit of fun. You've been killing yourself looking for a job. Up at six in the morning, and back in at seven P.M. I'm proud of you; you're doing what you have to do. But, damn, can we grab a bite to eat or something? Maybe go to the movies?" Ming Li retrieved an outfit. She shook her head and mumbled, "Not sexy enough. Now *this* is nice." She pulled out a dress.

"I wish I could, Ming Li, but I can't afford it."

Ming Li shifted her weight to one side and put her hands on her hips. "No, you can't afford not to. Besides, the treat's on me. Don't blow it."

"Okay, you win. Sounds good to me. I need a break. I'm tired, broke, and desperate." Daisy looked at what Ming Li was holding. "What's wrong with what I have on? If we're only going to dinner and a movie, why are you looking for something sexy?"

Ming Li winked. "Who said it'd just be us? You may meet a man, who knows," Ming Li purred like a cat. "Just because you're tired and broke doesn't mean you have to look like it."

Daisy shut the closet firmly and crossed her arms over her chest. "Jasper was the dresser, not me. He bought most of those clothes. I don't know the difference between Payless and Prada. If I like it, I'll wear it, and I'm not wearing that. The hem's too short."

"You *do* know the difference, and it's not too short. Show your legs—they're nice. Besides, you never know who'll be looking."

Daisy eyed Ming Li. "Okay, fess up. Who's the mystery man that you keep alluding to?"

"If I gave you a wrapped gift, would you ask what's in it? No, you'd open it. Have some patience."

Deciding to go along with Ming Li's game, Daisy shook her head and took a plain yellow dress from the closet. "Okay, but I'll wear this, not that. Sexy doesn't have to be skimpy."

Ming Li smiled. "Turning a head works wonders, trust me. You'll thank me later," she said, then left the room.

Minutes later, Daisy walked into the living room and turned around slowly. "Sexy enough?"

Ming Li laughed. "Yes. It looks better on you than the hanger."

"So, are you ready to go? I can't wait to see what you've been plotting behind my back."

Ming Li sighed. "Give me a second, I'm recovering." She fanned her hand dramatically and wiped pretend sweat from her cleavage. "You have to excuse me. I just got a call from Lucian, my Trojan horse I was telling you about. He's taking me for a ride in the morning and I can't wait to see what tricks he can do."

"Uh, too much information."

"No, really. He's taking me horseback riding *and* he can do tricks while mounted."

"Okay, if you say so."

Ming Li smiled suspiciously. "Guess what? Adonis is in town. He just called. Here, this is his number and the address where he's staying."

Daisy grinned. *Yes. Yes. Yes.* She'd dressed sexy, pushed thoughts of being unemployed and a minute from homeless to the back of her mind, and mentally prepared for whatever surprise Ming Li had for her, but now she didn't want to go—not with Ming Li. "Ming Li, where's Lucian?"

"Midtown. Why?"

"You should go see him. We can go out another time."

"He'll wait for me. Always does. Besides, you need to have some fun."

"I will, don't worry. I hope you don't mind, but I think I'll put this paper to use." Daisy waved the slip of paper in the air. "We're old friends. I can visit him, right?"

"Of course, why shouldn't you? I'm sure he'll be much more fun than me. So I'll meet you back here—tonight, tomorrow, who knows." Ming Li kissed Daisy on the cheek. "Have fun, sweetie, and remember . . . *control.* Well, I guess I'll go see a man about a horse."

Daisy's pulse quickened as she approached Adonis' building. *Maybe I shouldn't have come.* Looking at the paper in her hand, which had dampened from nervous excitement, she regretted not calling first. Wiping her sweaty palms on her hips, she straightened her back and held up her head. *We're friends. It's okay.* She forced one foot in front of the other and entered the apartment building.

"Hello. I'm here for Adonis Mitchell, apartment 1901," she greeted the doorman.

"And whom shall I say is calling for Mr. Mitchell?"

"Uh . . . Parker. Ms. Parker," Daisy stammered.

As the doorman picked up the receiver and dialed, Daisy closed her eyes and prayed that Adonis wasn't home. *If he refuses my visit, I wouldn't blame him. Who drops by someone's house without calling first? Besides, it's too soon.*

"Ms. Parker, Mr. Mitchell said for you to go on up. The express elevator is the second on the right."

Daisy held her breath and rang Adonis's bell. She didn't know what to say, what her excuse would be for popping up. "Here we go," she hummed under her breath, hoping to God that Adonis wasn't still breathtaking.

"Come in, Daisy. It's open."

The apartment's cool atmosphere was welcoming as Daisy stepped into the room. The sensual, sweet scent of myrrh wafted from the vents. Daisy walked into the living room and sat down on one of the fluffy, butter-yellow sofas that sat opposite each other. Not wanting to give Adonis the wrong impression, she hugged one of the accent pillows, covering her breasts. She knew what the coldness of the room would do to her, and she didn't want her girls standing at attention.

As her eyes scanned the room, she regretted that she'd come. Sexy jazz was playing, and several candles were lit. *Damn, he must be having company.* Daisy cursed the thought of Adonis welcoming another woman.

"Hey, you." Adonis took her hand, pulled her from her seat,

and embraced her. He squeezed her against his hard body before she'd had a chance to look at his face.

"Hey, Adonis." Daisy pulled back and took in every inch of him. She froze in his gaze. Her heart backflipped, and her womanhood throbbed. She couldn't believe her eyes. His Hershey's-brown frame towered over her. His goatee, trimmed to perfection, emphasized his full, luscious lips, and his eyes, as deep as a midnight sky, engulfed her. He was still the finest man she had ever seen.

"Look at you, Daisy." He smiled. "You sure have it together. Come by the window so I can get a good look."

"I'm still the same." *Pull yourself together, girl. He's only a man.*

Adonis put his hands on Daisy's shoulders and leaned close to her face, his minty breath tickling her nostrils. "Stop that. Don't tell me you're shy." He grabbed her hand and pulled her in front of the windows.

Daisy held her breath and let it out in small, unnoticeable—she hoped—spurts. "I'm . . . not . . . shy."

She studied Adonis. She knew his every movement by heart, how his veins protruded on his forearm when he turned it a certain way. She prepared herself for his killer smile and anxiously awaited the wink that accompanied the twinkle in his eyes. She knew him because she had always wanted him.

"So how've you been, Daisy? Still beautiful as ever." He winked confidently. "I swear, you haven't changed. What's it been . . . five, six years? And you haven't aged a day, have you? Have a seat. I'll get you something to drink. It's hot out there." He disappeared into the kitchen and returned with two tall glasses. "Here you go, lovely. Freshly squeezed lemonade."

Daisy sat down, basking in the compliments. Adonis was hallelujah-praise-the-Lord fine, but he didn't know it, and that made him more attractive. He had always been more beautiful inside than out, which was no small feat.

His features could have been chiseled out of stone. He had smooth, flawless skin, the kind that teenagers prayed for. His chocolate complexion was sweet enough to cause toothaches. *Delicious.* Daisy felt her heart skip.

Lord, what am I thinking? I know better than this. He and my son are practically related.

As much as Jay still haunted her thoughts, Daisy couldn't help flirting. "Oh, Adonis, stop it. *You're* the one who's looking good. So what brought you to New York?" She sipped her drink nervously, flushing when she felt the wet coldness run down her chin. She'd been trying to play it cool and had practically drooled on herself.

Adonis grabbed a napkin from the table, reached over and dabbed her face, then her blouse. Daisy flinched.

He pulled away. "I'm sorry. I didn't mean anything—"

"No, no. Don't worry about it. It's me, not you. You didn't do anything wrong."

Daisy could still feel his hand at the top of her cleavage. She hadn't been this jittery in years.

Adonis took her hand. "Daisy, are you okay? You seem uneasy."

"No, I'm fine. I guess I'm just a little nervous. I haven't seen you in a while, you know. I guess I shouldn't have come." Daisy gestured toward the candles. "It seems you're having company."

"You're right. It's been too long. And I *am* having company— you. I knew you were coming. Ming Li and Gigi arranged everything. I took the liberty of ordering some food. I hope you don't mind. After dinner, I was hoping we could go out or something."

Something? Sure, something sounds good to me. I've wanted to do something with you forever.

"I'd love to, but maybe another time. I have to get up in the morning and look for a job. And my being here isn't exactly a good example for Jay."

Adonis stood up and gently pulled Daisy to her feet. "I promise not to keep you out too long. I know you're busy . . . I know what happened. And your being here is the best thing for Jay, and for you. Better to be with someone who's always cared for you than being alone. And it'd be good for Jay to have two people in his life who've always loved him. You haven't forgotten that he's always liked me. You also have my word as a man that I'll have you home before bags form under your eyes." He laughed as Daisy yanked her hand away and pushed him playfully.

"What else do you promise?"

Adonis smiled and winked. "Our dinner's getting cold. Aren't you coming?"

I'd follow this man anywhere. She smiled as she walked beside the man she'd always dreamed of having at her side.

7

*T*he day was ruined. Daisy had been planning to celebrate her first job, but the letter she was holding had crushed her mood. Social Security had denied Jay survivor benefits. She raked her fingers through her hair. "This can't be right. No way."

She dialed Gigi at work. "I need you to come over right away."

"Daisy, you know I don't get off until—"

"Gigi, I've never asked you for anything. Swore that I wouldn't. But now, for Jay's sake, I'm asking you to come."

"Okay, I'll make up some excuse. I'll be right over."

"I'll be waiting outside."

———

Confused, angry, and skeptical, Daisy paced the sidewalk waiting for her medication to slow her pulse. The house made her feel claustrophobic, as if the walls were swallowing her whole. Breathing didn't come easily and she needed every ounce of air she inhaled, but more important, she needed answers, and someone was going to give them to her, even if that someone was Jasper's mother. She stopped pacing when she saw Ming Li pull up with Gigi right behind her.

"You two know, don't you?"

Gigi stopped in her tracks. "Know what?"

"You know what I'm talking about. You two know. That's why Ming Li's here."

"I'm here because Gigi called me and told me something happened to Jay. What's going on?"

Damn. "I'm sorry. I just don't know what the hell is real anymore. I'm talking about this." Daisy held the envelope in the air.

Gigi grabbed it and read. "Oh, God."

Ming Li took it from Gigi, glanced at it, and covered her mouth. "Oh, shit."

———

The three women sat thinking in Ming Li's living room.

Gigi finally broke the silence. "Okay, we gotta figure this out."

"It's impossible," Daisy said.

"It's a mistake, that's what it is. A simple mistake."

"But what if it's not?" Ming Li asked.

"How could it not be?" Gigi replied.

Daisy grabbed the letter from Ming Li. "I'm looking at it. It's here." She tapped the letter. "It's right here, written in black and white."

"Computers make mistakes."

Daisy sighed. "Yeah, and people lie."

She read a portion aloud:

Ms. Parker,

We must regretfully decline your application for Surviving Child Benefits. Although you've submitted required notarized documents as evidence of paternity, our records on file at U.S. Social Security Administration indicate that the deceased, Jasper Stevens, is not the father of your son. Because our records, as well as your son's original birth certificate, which we have on file, list a different Social Security number and name for the biological father, which we are not at liberty to release, we can be of no further assistance unless ordered by a court of law or appeals committee.

"He's Jasper's son. There has to be some clerical error," Gigi insisted.

Ming Li stared straight ahead.

Daisy stood. "Fuck that. Gigi, do you know where your aunt lives?"

Ming Li jumped up. "No! Don't go over there. Please don't." Her eyes were teary, something Daisy and Gigi had never seen before. "I know. I know everything."

"What in the hell?" Gigi said, dumbfounded.

Daisy approached Ming Li. "Spit it out."

Ming Li slumped on the sofa. "I knew Desiree, Jay's mother. Jay is Jonathan's son, not Jasper's."

"Jasper's twin?" Daisy asked. "Wait. I'm not understanding this. None of it. If Jay is Jonathan's son, why didn't the family know about him?"

"I'm speechless," Gigi said.

Tears streamed down Ming Li's face. "Jonathan and I were best friends. I knew him before I met Jasper. And I know for a fact that he and Desiree were together. They were a couple. Desiree was wild. She slept around a lot—more than I do. After Jay was born, she contracted HIV and gave it to Jonathan. She died first . . . and fast. Didn't get treated soon enough."

Daisy couldn't take the half-truths, half-stories. "Ming Li, get to the point. Where does Jasper fit into all this?"

Ming Li swallowed. "Jasper knew Jonathan's secret. When they were kids, their stepfather doted on Jasper, but he hated Jonathan. Jonathan was a threat, and his stepfather beat him mercilessly. Somehow Jonathan had discovered that his stepdad had a past, that he'd been accused of fondling some little boy. He confronted him about it. Jonathan later told his mother everything, about the beatings and the molestation. She never did a thing. Didn't protect her son, or question it—"

"Oh . . . my . . . God," Gigi said. "I had no idea. How could they? It had to be the money. Their stepfather was loaded. After they married, she started acting different, treating the family like shit. That's why she's an outcast."

Ming Li nodded. "Right. And Jonathan disappeared as soon as he was old enough to make it on his own. Their mother never heard from him again, and Jasper never admitted to knowing his whereabouts. She never knew she had a grandson. Before Jonathan died, Jasper promised him he'd keep Jay away from that dysfunctional household. Jay's safety was not to be gambled with."

———————

Daisy couldn't concentrate. Orders were rushing in and flowing out in vases, elaborate arrangements, and boxes. The clock was ticking fast, but time stood still every moment she thought about Jay. Beauty filled every corner of the flower shop and burst into full blooms in the storefront window. But all Daisy pictured was the ugliness of Jasper's family that Ming Li had told her about. She prayed Jay wouldn't have to see it.

One more order and I'm out of here. She looked at her watch and pepped up as she did every day around closing time. She selected a handful of white carnations and began to arrange them in a circle. "Is this for a man or a woman?" she asked no one, then reread the order slip. She shook her head in disbelief. *Not again,* she thought. She was supposed to be creating a wedding arrangement, not a funeral spray. But she hadn't been able to help it; death had knocked on her door when Jasper had died and kept finding ways to stay—to remind her of who he really was.

Daisy locked up the flower shop, relieved. She hadn't been able to think straight for over a week, and she'd almost mixed up two orders. The house had been tense. She and Ming Li had been avoiding each other ever since the revelation. Daisy understood the principle of the matter, and she still loved Ming Li, but she now had to question whether she could trust her. Eventually, she knew, one of them had to give in. Ming Li was in the wrong, but Daisy would have to take the first step. She hated to acquiesce, but she was living under Ming Li's roof. The last thing she wanted was for Jay to return to a tense house.

She didn't want to go back to the house, so she walked around the neighborhood to kill time. After an hour or so, and one too many coffees, her bladder felt as if it were going to burst. Just then, she noticed an office building with scaffolding in the front. *Please let them have a restroom I can sneak into.* She walked through the glass doors and spotted a security guard, who was busy reading a newspaper. She hated to disturb him, but Mother Nature left her no choice.

"Hi." She danced in place the way children do when they can't hold it.

"May I help you?" he asked without looking up.

"Yes, may I use your restroom?"

"Not open to the public." He still didn't make eye contact.

"Please. No one will know. It's after hours."

The security officer looked up now and scowled at her. "No."

"Damn," Daisy said, slapping the counter. She turned to leave.

"Wait," the man called out.

Yes, thank you. "Yes?"

"Try two doors down. Their security isn't as tight."

Daisy walked out without saying a word. *New Yorkers! He knows he could've let me use the bathroom.* She speed-walked to the building two doors down to the right, but found it locked. *Was he talking about two doors down to the left, or to the right?*

Daisy turned away. If she didn't find a bathroom soon, she was going to cry. *Times like this, I wish I were a man.*

She doubled back and went two doors to the left and peeked inside the glass doors of an office building. "Whew," she breathed when she didn't see anyone inside. The marble-tiled halls and wood-grained walls made her think of lawyers.

As she entered the seemingly empty building, Daisy noticed pots of plants and flowers strewn on the floor. She hoped they weren't going to be planted together; the ones that would help each other thrive weren't next to each other. She squeezed her legs together and tried to think what should go where, but her bladder ballooned a reminder of why she'd come in here. *When I come out.* She jigged and began her mission for the bathroom.

On her way out, she started rearranging the pots. After inspecting the leaves that were turning brown on some, and moving the wilted ones into brighter light, she stopped to move one more, but felt a presence behind her.

"Excuse me. Are you supposed to be here?"

Daisy turned to find an older gentleman standing behind her. "I'm sorry. I just needed to use the facilities." She started for the exit.

"Wait. What were you doing with the plants? Weren't you just moving them?"

Daisy smiled. "Sorry about that. But if they were going to be planted in the order they were lined up, they were in the wrong place."

"Really? How do you know?"

"It's what I do."

"Landscape, hunh?"

"Not really. I work in a flower shop. But I have a degree in horticulture, and I used to work for my dad. He had his own landscape company, Great Escapes." Daisy held up her hand. " 'Growing' hands run in our family."

"You're not a native New Yorker, are you? I hear an accent." He extended his hand and offered Daisy a business card. "I'm Mr. Wiles. And you are . . . ?"

"Daisy Parker. I'm originally from California," she said, shaking his hand. "Nice to meet you. I apologize for intruding."

"No, I'd love for you to intrude again. Did you say you do landscaping? I just fired the company that does mine. They just never get it right, and I can't keep paying for dead plants. You seem to have a genuine love for greenery, a knack. I'd love to give you a shot at the job, especially since I'm a native Californian myself."

Daisy was overwhelmed. "I'd love to!"

"Great. You have my card. See you Monday at nine?"

"Mr. Wiles, I don't know if I can. I have to be at the flower shop at eight. Can I go at lunchtime? I really don't want to call in. I just started a week ago."

"I see."

"But I . . . I want the job," Daisy stammered.

He laughed. "I believe you do, and you can have it. I'm just impressed with your dedication, that's all. I don't see too much of that around here. Tell me, do you plan on working two jobs?"

"If I can."

Mr. Wiles shook his head. "Did you look at the card? I own several buildings and a couple of atriums. I'll need you full-time." He reached for the business card he had given Daisy and scribbled on the back, then handed it back to her. "That's your starting salary, with benefits. And you can hire a couple of helpers, of course."

Daisy gasped. *Salary?* There was no way she could turn him down. The measly $7.50 an hour she was getting at the flower shop couldn't support her and Jay. "You'd really hire me without seeing my work?"

"No." Mr. Wiles laughed. "I've seen you work here for free. Anyone who does that *must* love what they do. I trust you'll do even better with a paycheck. Call it instinct. Good deeds never go unrecognized, not by me. I'll see you Monday at lunchtime."

———————

Daisy was beaming with excitement as she walked out of the building. She called her mother immediately from her cell to tell her the exciting news. Both Jay and Ms. Christine sounded just as excited as she was, although Jay didn't realize what an accomplishment it was. Adult problems had never been discussed with him. Blowing him a kiss through the phone, Daisy told him that she couldn't wait for him to come home. He'd be back in a few days, and she knew that soon she'd be able to afford a place for them.

Daisy felt lighter on her feet than she had in a long time. She had to refrain from skipping down the street. Things were finally starting to look up.

———————

Leaning against the metal barrier, Daisy stood watching the currents on the Hudson River. A faint salty scent tinged the air. The Manhattan Promenade was serenely beautiful at night, tucked behind tall buildings on the West Side Highway. Blue lights glowed from the three-level deck situated at the end of the pier.

Adonis's warm hands massaged her shoulders. She felt completely at ease with him. In the cab, she had shared everything with him, given him all the details about her stroke of good luck. He'd listened intently, then agreed to help her find an apartment.

Daisy couldn't believe how much time they were spending together. She enjoyed his company, and the hours always flashed by. She knew she needed to go home but couldn't make herself do it. "I hate to leave you."

"You don't have to. You know you're welcome to spend the night."

"It's still too soon."

Adonis turned her toward him. They were standing a breath apart, and every inch of her wanted him.

"Daisy, I swear that I wouldn't try a thing. I'm just offering, that's all. I wouldn't feel comfortable letting you go back to Ming Li's when I know you don't want to."

Daisy couldn't resist the temptation. She threw her arms around Adonis's neck, resting her head on his chest as his strong arms embraced her.

"It's okay." She looked up, and they locked eyes. Daisy shivered at the intensity of his gaze. A man had never looked at her that way before, as if he were looking through her, searching her depths for answers she didn't possess.

"Are you cold?"

"No. A chill just ran through me."

"Could it be me?" He grinned, unbuttoned his shirt, and draped it around her.

"Maybe."

"I hope so," he said, smiling mischievously.

Daisy grinned, his smile infectious. Her cheeks flushed, and her eyes lit up. She had no control over her body. Or her soul, for that matter, if he asked for it.

"Why the smile, Daisy? Do I make you smile?"

Daisy nodded.

"Good. I'm glad. Somebody should. You have a beautiful smile. You should show it more often. Are you ready to go? It's almost two in the morning."

"No, not really. But I guess I should be getting home," Daisy said reluctantly.

"Not home, Daisy. I'm not letting you go there tonight. And I know you won't be comfortable at my place either. Not yet, anyway. So pick a hotel, because you need time to yourself."

Daisy hesitated, considering. "Well, if the offer still stands, I'm coming to your place. I don't want to be alone."

———

Adonis emerged from the balcony doors with two glasses and a towel. He sank down in the wicker chair across from Daisy. "Here," he said with a smile, handing her a glass. "I thought you'd like something to drink."

"Thanks." Daisy held the cold drink to her head before taking a sip.

Adonis's eyes sparkled in the moonlight. "Ming Li shared a secret of yours with me."

Daisy almost spat out her drink. "She did *what?*"

"She told me you've always wanted me. Do you?"

Heat filled Daisy's body. She was going to kill Ming Li. "I don't know if *want* is the right word . . ."

Adonis laughed and kissed her hand. "No need to be bashful. You won't know what you're capable of getting unless you go after it."

Thank you, Jesus! She leaned her head on his arm.

Adonis rubbed her shoulder, then pulled her close and hugged her. She felt as if he were squeezing away all of her pain. He released her, swept her hair out of her eyes, and kissed her gently on the cheek. It took everything she had not to grab his face and guide his mouth to hers.

"Come on, baby, let's get you settled." Adonis took her hand and led her into the apartment.

Her face lit up when she noticed the large portrait of Adonis's mother sitting on the limestone fireplace mantel. *You know what they say about a man who loves his mother.* Daisy scanned the room. Adonis had taste. In front of the fireplace were two matching high-backed chairs separated by a chess table. The game wasn't finished yet, and she wondered who his opponent was. The original art adorning the walls drew her in. Africa . . . she remembered Africa.

Back in college, they'd all taken a trip to the motherland for spring break. Adonis had joined them, even though he was in grad school. They'd longed for a piece of their identity, but Daisy had discovered more than culture on that trip; she'd discovered her lust for Adonis.

Daisy rose from the sofa and felt herself glide to the wall as the memories returned, running deep. Unsettled sand had drifted on the dry, bittersweet air, attaching itself to any exposed bare flesh. It had come to rest on her feet, becoming her sandals. Intense heat had chaperoned their nights and days, and the sun had deemed itself mother, warming and lighting the way for her children.

"Remember that one?"

Daisy jumped, her hand flying to her chest.

"I didn't mean to scare you."

"That's okay. Yes, I remember that one, and I'm taking it home—"

"No, no, no," Adonis scolded, wagging a finger. "You gave that to me, remember? Right after I saved you—"

"Saved me? Oh, Adonis, please. You didn't save me."

"Yes, I did. Remember, I was your husband for one night?"

Yes, Daisy thought, he had been her husband. And she should've kept him. But in those days, Adonis wasn't meant to be kept. He had been a football star, a wide receiver, popular on the field and widely received by the ladies.

She crossed her arms. "Yeah, you were my husband all right, only because you didn't like the attention I was getting. But why, Adonis? We didn't have anything between us, except mutual friends . . . and Gigi. I never asked you to claim me as your wife."

Adonis flashed his killer smile. "You didn't have to. I was jealous and I didn't want anyone else to have you. I've wanted you for years, even back then. But you were too wholesome, too vulnerable. Gigi would've killed me if I hurt you. You weren't the type of girl . . . excuse me, woman, that a man could have a fling with. You were never a fly-by-night."

"Thank you." Daisy was squirming on the inside, praying that Adonis couldn't tell. Her heart kissed her soul, and her spirit laughed. She was glad that the feeling had been mutual.

"And then there was him—Jasper. We'd already clashed when my father married into the family. . . ."

A quiet fell over the room. Daisy stood and stretched, then felt Adonis's arms embracing her middle. She relaxed and nestled her head against his chest. He eased her closer. Amel Larrieux's pretty voice filled the air. Adonis took Daisy's hand, whirled her around, and held her tightly. Centimeters apart, they swayed to "Make Me Whole."

Daisy could have swayed with him forever. Lust had left her. They didn't have to make love, and she didn't even care if he spoke. But she needed him to hold her. With Adonis, she felt safe and protected. His arms felt like home, a home she wanted to move into.

Not wanting to give him too much too soon, Daisy grabbed his hand and led him to the fireplace. "I love your art collection. Especially this one." She pointed to a painting of an elderly man looking toward the sky, and then she noticed a picture on the mantel. She picked it up and stared at it. *Oh, God. Calvin.*

"That's my frat brother. You remember Calvin Harris, don't you?"

Daisy nodded. *Lalani's father.* "I didn't know you knew him."

"Oh, yeah. We became good friends after college. I haven't seen him in years, though—"

Daisy turned and forced a smile. *Good.*

"—but we talk pretty often and try to hook up when I go home to visit. But we'll see him soon; he comes to New York often. One of his sisters moved to Queens. Maybe we can all have dinner together. I'm sure he'll be interested in seeing you."

Did he say "we'll see him"? He knows, doesn't he? "What would make you think that?" Daisy quizzed.

"Don't look so shocked. As beautiful as you are, who wouldn't want to see you?"

Relief splashed into Daisy's soul, easing her for the moment. She weighed her options. If she wanted to be with Adonis, she'd have to tell him about her and Calvin eventually because he was "connected" to both of them. *But if I spill now, he may not want me. After all, they're friends—frat brothers.*

"I think I should go now."

"I thought you were staying. Is it something I said?"

"No, it's me. Staying with you is tempting. But I'll eventually have to get back to reality." She rushed out the front door.

As Daisy waited for the doorman to hail a cab, she felt a tap on her shoulder. When she turned around, Adonis grabbed her and kissed her deeply. The warmth of his lips and the slight wetness of his mouth beckoned her to stay. She wanted to see what more he had to offer. Their tongues danced rhythmically, their breaths becoming one. She had never been kissed so passionately, so intensely. Daisy moaned, feeling his hardness against her abdomen. She tried to pull away but couldn't. His lips invited her to stay and she couldn't turn them down. She gave in to his deliciousness, and before she knew it, she was on the elevator with her back pressed against the wall.

The doors opened and neither uttered a word with their mouths, but their eyes spoke. She couldn't get enough of Adonis and hadn't even *had* him yet. She envisioned what it'd be like to be with him and knew she'd drink him with her soul. Suck up every drop of him and carry him inside her for as long as he would stay.

"I've wanted you for so long," Adonis whispered in her ear once they were back in the apartment.

Daisy panted. She had no words, only desires she wanted him to fulfill. She was tired of being empty and guessed—hoped—he was the one to fill her voids.

"I'm glad you came." He kissed her forehead.

"Me too."

"Can I do something for you? No, let me rephrase that. I'll be right back, there's something I want to do for you." He went to the back of the apartment.

Daisy sat down and waited. She heard the rush of running water coming from the bathroom. Her day had been filled with surprises and she was thankful. She closed her eyes to absorb the good feeling that pervaded her.

The phone rang.

"Can you get that, baby?" Adonis yelled from the back.

"Yes," Daisy answered. "I can't believe he wants me to answer his phone," she squealed under her breath, happy that he'd asked. She took it as a confirmation of his singleness.

"Hello?"

"Hi, is Adonis home?"

"I'm sorry, who are you looking for?" Daisy asked, knowing whom the woman asked for, but wishing she'd heard wrong. She hoped Adonis didn't have the audacity to expect her to take messages from his admirers.

"Oh, I apologize for being so rude. I have a husband too. I wouldn't want some woman calling my house and not introducing herself. This is Denise, Calvin Harris's sister. Is Adonis in?"

"I'm afraid you have the wrong number."

"Is this 212–387- . . ."

Daisy ignored Denise as she spoke. She knew it wasn't her place to lie, but she had to. She couldn't allow Adonis and Calvin to speak. On cue she answered, "Yes, this is the number. But no one lives here by that name."

Daisy fixed her clothes and headed to the door. "Wrong number," she yelled. "I'm sorry, but I have to go. Something urgent came up," she lied, and ran out praying that Calvin's sister wouldn't call back.

_____

Daisy pulled out of the storage facility where her belongings were stored. Her hands were dirty, covered with God only knew what from carrying all of Jay's necessities. *This is only the first of many trips.*

Jay had always been fortunate—spoiled. While Daisy had taken care of his needs, Jasper had supplied his wants. He had become Noah and spoiled Jay with *every* single thing he'd asked for, in twos. He had two PlayStations, Xboxes, GameCubes, and Game Boy SPs along with the respective games for each. He had a double collection of all things DVD: players, camcorders, burners. A wardrobe of high-priced designer clothes and equally expensive sneakers and boots. Bikes, traditional and motorized. Computers, laptops, and PCs. And a Plasma TV that hung on the wall. He had it all. All the things Daisy couldn't give him on her own and wouldn't if she could afford to. She smiled, imagining the expression on his face when he learned that they'd have to share a bedroom. She hoped it wouldn't feel too awkward, but she knew that they'd both find comfort in each other's presence. She missed Jay, and the fullness and life he brought to barren rooms. She turned down the radio and drove in silence. She needed quiet, to be surrounded by her thoughts and nothing else. *Today is a new day,* she thought, *and tomorrow will be the same. I'm a new woman now, all Jay's got. Our new life starts right here.*

_____

Daisy sat at Ming Li's kitchen table, trying to figure out how she was going to fit all of their stuff into Ming Li's space. Her stomach growled as the tangy scent of the jambalaya teased her nostrils. *What's gotten into Ming Li? She doesn't cook.*

"How's it going over there?" Ming Li asked, wiping her hands with a paper towel.

"It's going. I can't complain. I have a job. Now I just have to find us a place to live and pay the last installment on my Jeep."

"Well, I know it seems like a lot—and it is—but you can do it. As your mom would say, you've got to have faith."

"Yeah, I've got to have faith—and money. I don't know which is going to come first, but I wish it'd hurry."

"Daisy, you know I really didn't mean . . . I promised not to tell. I just never thought . . ."

"It's okay. I understand. I was going to talk to you anyway. I didn't want Jay to come home and see us walking around avoiding each other like the plague."

"So we're cool?"

Daisy smiled. "Of course."

"So, where've you been? You're gone a lot."

Daisy smiled again.

"Adonis, hunh? I should've known you had a little bad girl in you. You've been releasing stress with him. I don't blame you; he's gorgeous. But judging by that glow on your face, he's more than that to you."

"I can't tell you the half of it. The man is more than gorgeous. Adonis was, *is,* everything I've ever desired. I used to dream about how I'd give myself to him in every way imaginable. I still do."

"You need to unwrap that gift and enjoy the present. You've spent too much time worrying about tomorrows."

"I know, and you're right. But I still think about how stupid I was. As I sat here going over my to-do list, I realized that all the nice clothes, the fancy, overpriced house, the . . . the *everything,* was for nothing. I mean, excuse me for saying this, but even the sex. Really, it wasn't worth what I sacrificed. Jasper wasn't that good."

"All cash, no flash? Well, at least now you can look back on it and laugh."

"Dependence is a joke. That's why I haven't slept with Adonis. Don't get me wrong. I want him as badly as I need stability. I'm just not going to allow anyone else to toy with me. I've given too much of myself. He may just want to satisfy his curiosity."

Ming Li shook her head. "Nah. It's more than that. Gigi told me that he's always asked about you—for years. If you want him, I say go get him."

"That's exactly what I should—"

The telephone rang, interrupting Daisy. Ming Li answered, then handed it to Daisy. "It's Ms. Christine. She says it's important."

"Ma, it's not Jay is it?"

"No, baby. Jay's fine. He's all packed up and ready to go. It's Lani."

Tears surfaced immediately. Daisy couldn't bear the thought of anything happening to her daughter. Panic filled her voice. "What about her?"

"Calvin petitioned for a DNA test."

"What?" *But I never told him that I was pregnant.*

"You heard me. He wants to know if Lani is his daughter."

"Who told him? How does he know about Lani?"

"I don't know how he found out, but he did. It was something new to me, I can tell you that. I always had suspicions . . . but you never gave us a name, just the runaround. But anyway, now he wants to know his daughter."

"You've got to hide her. Send her here—"

"I've already taken care of it. He thinks she's somewhere with you. I told him I didn't know where y'all were. He's not falling for it, though. But it'll buy us some time."

"Ma, put her on the plane with Jay."

"Baby, I would. But how are you going to take care of three people when you can't take care of one?"

Daisy sighed. "Just when I thought it was all coming together . . ."

8

Fall

"**I** don't want to go to school," Jay said as Daisy stood above him, holding his uniform. He'd been trying to avoid it all week.

"Well, you're going. Do you want to be held back a grade?" She sat on the edge of the bed and gently pulled the cover off him. "What's wrong? You used to love school."

Jay grabbed the cover back and pulled it to his chin, then rolled back onto his side, away from her. "I'm not going," he mumbled.

Daisy stood there for a moment, staring at his back. It was taking everything she had not to yank him out of bed. They'd been going at it for weeks. She understood how difficult the transition had been for him, but she'd had enough. She knew that he'd been testing her, despite what the school counselor had said. Besides, she couldn't depend on the advice of a woman who didn't have children. Jay knew exactly what he was doing.

She snatched the cover from him in one swift motion. "You have five seconds to get your butt out of bed! Try me if you want to."

Jay glared at her. If looks could kill, she'd be fully decomposed. He lay there defiantly.

"Did you hear me? I'm going to finish cooking breakfast. Be downstairs in fifteen minutes. If I come back up here and find that you're not dressed . . ." Daisy slammed the door behind her.

———————

Daisy took her time buttering the toast, delaying the inevitable. As much as she wanted to put her foot down with Jay, she found it almost impossible. She'd never hit him before, and she didn't believe in doing so. There had to be some other way. But she was seconds away from snapping.

"Mmm, that smells good." Ming Li opened the refrigerator and removed the carton of orange juice.

"It's just turkey bacon, scrambled eggs, English muffins, and fruit, nothing spectacular." Daisy nodded toward the spread on the table. "Oh, and toast for Jay. He doesn't eat muffins."

"So, you're making him go to school today?"

"He has no choice, and neither do I. I'm starting on a new project today. The boss is going to be there. I can't keep taking Jay to work with me."

Ming Li sat down and began nibbling on a piece of bacon. "You shouldn't have taken him with you in the first place. He's going to run you ragged."

Daisy placed two slices of buttered toast on Jay's plate and joined Ming Li at the table. "I don't know what to do about him. On one hand I feel sorry for him—"

"And he knows it. That's why he's been doing this. He's taking advantage of you. He may be a child, but he doesn't think like one." Ming Li took a sip of her juice. "How do you think he was able to manipulate you into buying those clothes and expensive sneakers? Like you could really afford to spend a hundred and fifty dollars on shoes."

"He needed the clothes. He grew a lot over the summer. And the other kids had the sneakers."

"The other kids, my ass. That boy has everything he could possibly want. He's had more in nine years than some people have in their entire lives. 'What the other kids have' is nonsense. Anyway, the last time I dropped him off, everyone had on uniforms."

Ming Li was right. Jay had been taking her for granted. It would be a hard task to change the monster she'd helped create, but she'd get through it. And so would Jay, if he knew what was good for him.

Daisy glanced up at the clock. Jay was late. Adrenaline started coursing through her veins. She needed to calm down, she told herself as she headed up the stairs, before she accidentally hurt him. "Jay, get your butt down these stairs now!"

"I don't feel good. My head hurts."

"We can fix that." *You won't feel a thing after I knock you out.*

Daisy sat on a bench in Central Park and finished off her tuna on rye. She turned her face into the cool breeze and slowly inhaled its crisp scent. She'd always felt rooted in the park, almost one with nature. She thought it spectacular and dreamed that one day she'd be able to design her own magnificent oasis.

Looking at her watch, she realized that Adonis was running late. Any other day, she would have been annoyed, but today she needed the time alone to weigh her options. Jay had been driving her crazy. On several occasions, she'd had to remind herself that he was just a child; he couldn't possibly appreciate all that she'd done. Daisy sighed, wondering if she was doing the right thing by keeping him. She had abandoned her own child and was struggling to raise that of someone else—someone she'd never met.

"I just don't know what to do," she whispered. She'd never be able to provide him with all that he was used to, but she had a wealth of love to give. Money came and went, but love was forever.

"Hey, you." Adonis strolled toward her on the wide cement path, looking delicious as usual in a pair of dark jeans and a black turtleneck.

"Hey, yourself." Daisy stood to hug him. "I was getting a little worried."

"Sorry. I got caught up at work. You should see the amazing architecture of the building I'm restoring. I don't know how they came up with it." He smiled, then gave her shoulder a squeeze. "I'm sorry for going on about my work. So what's up?"

"Let's walk," she said, taking his arm. "I need to walk off some of this tension."

"What's wrong? Anything I can help with?"

They walked hand in hand for over an hour. His warmth and caring put her at ease, made her feel that she didn't have to hide any of her emotions or problems. He seemed to accept her as she was, flaws and all. After chatting about trivial things, she explained her problem with Jay. Adonis reassured her, said it was just a part of bereavement, that Jay was having a hard time coping with his father's death. He wasn't just being difficult; he was angry.

Adonis looked at his watch, then led Daisy by the hand to the other side of the park. "Come on, we're going to be late."

Daisy stopped. "Late for what? Where are we going?"

"It's a surprise."

"Sorry," she said, shaking her head. "I can't. I have to be there when Jay gets home from his after-school program."

Adonis smiled slyly. "I've taken care of everything. Ming Li's going to watch him."

"You asked Ming Li to babysit Jay?"

"No, she volunteered. Said she'd keep him all weekend if we wanted."

Daisy fell silent, deciding to follow Adonis wherever he was taking her. But jealousy crept in. She trusted Adonis, but she didn't want him talking to Ming Li when she wasn't around. Ming Li was not only promiscuous, but secretive.

Adonis stopped when they reached West Fifty-seventh Street. Daisy looked around. "Where are we going?"

Adonis pointed. "Right here."

"To the spa?"

"Yes, for a couple's massage. Trust me . . . you'll love it."

"Couldn't you just massage me yourself?" she teased, feeling bold.

"I can do anything you want."

———————

Daisy sat quietly between Adonis's legs on the floor of his bedroom, listening to the sultry ballads flowing from the speakers. She rolled her head slowly as he gently rubbed her shoulders and kneaded her neck, then rested it on his thigh and took in the room. As many times as she had been to his apartment, she'd never seen his bedroom, had avoided the temptation of it. Suppressing a grin, she remembered how often she had dreamed of lying in his bed. *I'm really here. Now what?*

As if he could read her mind, Adonis stood, slowly slid his hands under her arms, and pulled her to her feet. She tried to turn to face him, but he held her in place. He pressed his body into her back and swept her hair to one side, exposing her neck. She moaned, her heart pounding, as she felt his warm lips on her nape. As much as she had dreamed about being with him, as badly as she'd always wanted him, she was nervous. It had been a long time since she'd had sex, years since she'd had great sex. *Maybe we shouldn't. What if he can't live up to my expectations? What if I can't satisfy him?* She was afraid to ruin the perfect fantasy that she'd created, but her uncertainty faded with the warmth of his mouth on her earlobe.

She gave in to it, leaned her head on his chest. As Adonis's hands moved to her breasts, gently cupping and squeezing them, her nipples hardened. All of his moves were slow and deliberate. She decided that he was intentionally trying to drive her crazy, push her over the edge.

"Let me turn around," Daisy pleaded breathlessly. "Please."

"Ssh."

His hands moved from her breasts to the hem of her sweater. She lifted her arms as he pulled it off in one quick motion, then unfastened her plum lace bra. She arched her back as he planted delicious kisses from the top of her shoulders to her waist. She wanted to reach out and grab his head but couldn't.

"Turn around," he commanded in a seductively deep voice as breathy as hers.

Daisy turned, and he went down on his knees, his lips meeting her navel. Gently, he grabbed her by the waist and licked her stomach. Their eyes met as she looked down at him. *That's right, beg for it.* But if he kept up this slow, teasing pace, Daisy knew, she'd soon be the one who'd be begging.

She felt her jeans fall down to her ankles, and she stepped out of them. Her lace panties followed seconds later. And so did Adonis's succulent lips. She shivered as Adonis's mouth traveled up her body, planting erogenous kisses on the inside of her knees, inner thighs, cleavage, and then neck as he stood tall. She couldn't take it anymore. Daisy stood on her tiptoes and hungrily kissed his full lips, her hand tracing his jawline, her eyes inviting him to do whatever he wanted. Whatever he asked, she'd give it.

Selfishly, she stepped back and watched Adonis undress. She didn't help—and didn't want to. What she wanted was to take in every delectable inch of his nakedness. She stared first at his face, then his chest, then his rippled abdomen, but her gaze traveled no farther. She was afraid to look down. She wanted the rest to be a surprise—a pleasant one.

Pushing him onto the bed, she climbed on top of him. She'd never been so eager, or hot, before. Her legs were throbbing in time with her heartbeat. She had to have him. As she reached out to grab him and lead him inside her, Adonis stopped her and flipped her over. He grabbed her by the hips and pulled her up on all fours. Daisy squeezed her eyes shut as she felt his face between her legs, his razor stubble tickling her thighs. His warm breath increased her heat as his skilled tongue danced between her lower lips. Daisy grabbed the headboard, trying to keep her balance as his tongue traveled from her slit to her rear. "Oh, God," she moaned, then held her breath and braced herself as Adonis's tongue moved into unexplored territory.

Daisy inched up as she felt his hardness between her split. She wiggled as he moved the tip up and down, teasing her. Quickly, she turned over. "I want to see you. I want to see your face."

Adonis moved her hair from her eyes and pulled her legs over his shoulders. Again, he tasted her. He looked into her eyes, licked his lips, and positioned himself. His hardness spread her, and her pulse quickened as he gently worked himself inside.

———————

Daisy awoke thirsty. The delicious sex from the night before had left her dehydrated. She carefully removed Adonis's arm from her waist and sat up on the edge of the mattress, smiling to herself. It had been some time since she'd spooned. She eased out of the bed and flinched, the ache between her legs a reminder of the wonderful, long night she'd had. Adonis had been magnificent. His desire to please had caused her to throw all inhibitions to the wind. After her first climax, she'd become as carefree as him. She'd done things she'd only heard about, things she'd always said she'd never do. *If pleasure is pain, pain is pleasure.*

"Hey, you," Adonis said, walking into the kitchen.

"Hey," Daisy echoed, avoiding his eyes. She felt a little embarrassed about having let herself go. Although she had enjoyed their night, she didn't want him to think that she'd always been so loose.

He kissed her on the cheek. "You okay?"

"What makes you ask that?" Daisy laughed.

"Just wondering."

"I'm fine. Oh, and about last night . . . I don't want you to think that I'm always—"

Adonis waved her off and grinned. "Don't worry, baby. I could tell. Anyway, we're adults." His eyes narrowed seductively. "But you sure learn fast," he added, patting her butt.

"Stop it."

"So, what's up? Wanna do something today?"

Daisy sighed. "I need to get back to the house. I promised Jay we'd do something today."

"Let's all do something together. It'll be good for him. I can be like a big brother. He needs a man in his life. We can catch a couple of games, drink a few beers. You know . . . man stuff." Daisy's eyes widened, and Adonis laughed. "I'm teasing. But I can pick him up weekly and take him out. You know, do things with him that a man should do."

Daisy punched him on the arm playfully. "I'll think about it."

———————

Daisy walked into the bedroom and found Jay huddled in the corner with his basketball blanket wrapped around him. His eyes were wide and unreadable.

"What's wrong, baby?" she said as she moved closer.

He grabbed her knees and held on tightly, almost making her lose her balance. "Ms. Ming Li's dead!"

Daisy's heart began pounding. What was he talking about? She'd just seen Ming Li. "No, baby. You must've had a nightmare. She left as soon as I came in."

Jay shook his head and started crying. "No, Mom, I'm telling you, she's dead! I heard her screaming all night, and she was still screaming this morning."

Daisy started to interrupt him, then something told her to let him have his say.

"Someone was hurting her. I ran downstairs and called her name, but she didn't hear me, she was screaming *so* loud. I opened her door and saw a man on top of her. The covers were moving up and down."

Daisy rolled her eyes, sighing. She couldn't believe that Ming Li would volunteer to babysit, then have a man in the house. "No, baby. Ming Li's fine. That man wasn't hurting her."

Jay's expression changed from fear to curiosity. Then he snapped his fingers in understanding. "Ohhh . . . okay. They were doing what I was watching on Cinemax last night—"

"What? What were you watching?" Daisy put her hands on her hips.

"I saw this man and woman on TV doing 'the nasty.'" Jay paused, looked at Daisy fearfully. "I'm not in trouble, am I? Ms. Ming Li said I could stay up and watch whatever I wanted, as long as I didn't disturb her."

Daisy felt as though someone had knocked the wind out of her. *What the hell is wrong with that bitch? We're leaving.* "Go take a shower and get dressed, Jay," she said in an I-dare-you-not-to-listen tone. "Now!"

Daisy rifled through her oversize, overfilled purse and re-trieved her wallet. She selected the credit cards that were still good and could be used for cash advances, then counted the money that she'd been saving to move.

She shook her head at the one thousand and some odd dollars that she held. It wouldn't be enough, but she'd have to make do somehow.

Grabbing an old newspaper from the corner desk, she flipped to the real estate section and pulled a pen from her purse. Apart-ments rented quickly in New York. Sometimes it took weeks, even months, to find something suitable. She'd give it a shot.

After circling and calling several that were within her budget, Daisy rested her forehead in her hand, exhausted from the ef-fort. Finally, exhaling deeply, she decided to go through the ads once more. If she didn't find something this time, she'd have to go out and buy a current newspaper. There was one ad she hadn't called, one that she'd avoided: a crime-infested section of Hell's Kitchen. She swallowed hard and thought about Jay. She assumed he'd never seen a neighborhood like that one. But it had its good points, and it was being renovated. *Everyone needs a little culture. Better for him to learn about struggling than to end up emotionally screwed up, thinking that someone is killing the nymphomaniac.*

Daisy and Gigi turned onto Forty-third Street for the fourth time and finally found a space to park. The block was a mix-ture of newer buildings and horrible, aging ones. Daisy knew she probably couldn't afford the better ones, but prayed not to get a raggedy one.

"Well, maybe it won't be so bad," she said to Gigi.

Disgust was written all over Gigi's expression. "You sure you want to do this? It could be awful. I told you that you guys could stay with me."

Daisy opened her car door. "Come on. And thanks anyway. But

you know I don't want to be around Marcus. Anyway, who knows? Maybe it'll be nice."

"Yeah, right. I don't know why you can't just hear him out. You'd forgive him if you knew his side of the story."

Daisy shot Gigi a don't-try-it look.

"Whatever, then," Gigi muttered, following reluctantly. "Well, I *can* loan you some money, you know."

Daisy waved her off, stopping in front of the five-story walk-up. The steps were a little cracked and could have used a new cement job, but the entrance was clean and graffiti-free. She looked at Gigi and nodded. "If the inside looks like the outside, we might be okay."

———

Daisy walked around the tiny studio apartment, which didn't require much more than turning around. The place was a lot smaller than what they were used to, but larger than the bedroom they shared at Ming Li's.

She took in the dingy paint and scuffed floors. "All it needs is a good cleaning," she whispered to Gigi.

"The hallway stinks. Sort of reminds me of mopped-up piss—lingering."

Daisy turned to the building super, Mrs. Janowski, who was leaning against the door in a multicolored muumuu, holding a broom in her large, age-spotted hands. Daisy focused on her eyes and tried not to stare at her purplish-blue-tinged gray hair, or the huge mole on her cheek.

"I thought the ad said this was a one-bedroom."

Mrs. Janowski coughed and wheezed, then smiled genuinely. "Turn to the right, just off the kitchen."

Gigi laughed. "I thought that was a breakfast area."

"Me, too."

"No, it's a one-bedroom." She pulled a pocket door from the wall and slid it closed. "Much bigger than a studio, trust me." She pinched her thumb and index finger together. "This big, I tell you. If you want it, let me know. I'll have someone come in to paint and clean it. The stove and refrigerator will be replaced." She shrugged, then went on, "Probably secondhand and small, but clean."

Daisy looked at Gigi, who shook her head.

Daisy turned to Mrs. Janowski. "Is it okay if I clean it and buy my own paint to save money? I don't have much, and my son and I really need a place. My credit's okay, and I have a pretty good job. Salary."

The super waved her hand. "Don't worry about it. I understand. I don't do credit checks, and I don't do rental agreements. This is one of my son's buildings. He lives on Long Island in a big fancy-schmancy house. Can you believe the schmuck leaves me here? He'd let his own mother live like this, while his wife lives like a queen. So I do what I want. You want it, you got it."

"Thanks."

"Sure. Just give me two months' rent up front. And forget the deposit. But you hafta buy your own paint."

Daisy sat on the sofa in the living area, smiling smugly at her accomplishment. So what if it wasn't their home in Staten Island . . . it would do. The eggshell-colored satin paint gave the apartment a clean, warm feeling. She hated that Jay would have to sleep in the room off the kitchen, but she refused to put him close to the front door and the street.

Daisy had managed to give the place a homey feel, but it didn't feel safe at night. By day, it was quiet, but in the evenings it was loud and rambunctious, and filled with loiterers. She'd complained to Mrs. Janowski, only to be told that all the tenants had the same complaint. Daisy even called the police on several occasions to report the noise, to no avail. Apparently, a bunch of street people had decided to squat in front of their building. Mrs. Janowski assured her that they wouldn't stay long; they tended to move from block to block. Whenever the police ran them off from one location, they'd find another place to congregate.

Still, Daisy tried to take solace within her own four walls. As long as she and Jay went out for what they needed during the day, they didn't have to go out at night. She just wished her apartment didn't face the front. More than that, she wished that she could catch up to Ming Li. She hadn't spoken to her since Jay had told her what had happened that night Daisy wasn't there. According to Gigi, Ming Li was out of town with Lucian. Eventually, I'll catch up to her, Daisy thought.

A knock on the front door snapped Daisy out of her thoughts and off the sofa that doubled as her bed. It had to be Mrs. Janowski. Anyone else would have needed to be buzzed in. "I'm coming, Mrs. J.," she hollered, then smiled. Mrs. Janowski had become as much of a presence in the apartment as the new paint. She was obviously old and lonely, needed someone to talk to as much as Daisy did.

But when she opened the door, Daisy got a surprise: Marcus.

"What do you want?" she asked.

"I need to talk to you. Can I come in?"

Reluctantly, she opened the door.

"I came to explain."

She had better things to do besides listen to a grown man plead his case, but she decided to hear him out. "I'm listening."

"Daisy, I don't know where to begin. I know sorry isn't enough."

"No, it isn't," Daisy said drily, sitting down on the sofa. "So why don't you just tell me the truth, Marcus? The truth shouldn't require a lot of thought, so how about you start explaining?"

He grabbed her hand. "Daisy, I never meant to hurt you. Never. I just got caught in the middle. I mean, what was I supposed to do? You were my friend, and so was Jasper—"

Daisy snatched her hand away. "Yes, I was your friend, Marcus. I thought that meant something."

"Daisy, it did—it does. Believe me. I didn't know about Jasper being married until recently, about a year before—"

"A year? You knew for three hundred and sixty-five days and couldn't take just one minute out of one day to tell me?"

"Daisy, put yourself in my shoes for a minute. Last year we were out in Jersey and this lady comes up and kisses Jasper on the cheek. I thought it was you—"

"I know, Marcus," she interrupted. "I saw Camille already. I know we look alike. Don't act like you don't know."

Marcus nodded. "Fair enough. But as I was saying, I thought she was you. I grabbed her and hugged her, and she pushed me back. It shocked me. I almost called her by your name, but Jasper interrupted me and introduced her as his wife. I was burnt, Daisy. Truly pissed."

"So why didn't you tell me then?"

"What was I supposed to say? 'Daisy, the man you've been with for years is married to another woman who looks like your twin?' Everybody knew Jasper was your world. I didn't want to be the one to shatter it for you."

Daisy stood. "So you mean to tell me that you were willing to just sacrifice our relationship, that Jasper's friendship meant more to you—"

"No, what I'm saying is that no matter what I told you, you wouldn't have believed me."

Daisy wiped a tear from her eye. "That's asinine."

"It's true."

"But the house . . . you showed her where we lived."

"No. When Jasper passed, all his affairs had to be settled—you know, his estate: properties, bills, and so forth. When Jasper's lawyer gave Camille the paperwork, she discovered the property listed under Jasper's assets."

"The Escalade?"

"She had it towed from my apartment. I didn't even know it was gone until she called to inform me that she had a wrecker pick it up."

"I don't know, Marcus," Daisy said, running her fingers through her hair. "This is all too smooth for me. It just doesn't ring true."

"So what am I to do, Daisy? If I don't tell you the truth, I'm wrong. If I do tell you, I'm still wrong."

Daisy's eyes dropped to the floor. Marcus was right. She bit her lip, trying to fight back the tears, but it was a losing battle. Marcus scooted closer to her and tried to kiss her on the forehead, but she flinched and pushed him away.

"Well, I guess I should go. I love you, Daisy. You've been like a little sister to me, and I honor that. I'm sorry I hurt you, but I can tell that you're not ready to forgive me. I'll give you some time. I'm here, always remember that." Marcus turned to get up.

Daisy stood up. "It's not a problem. I'm over Jasper. I've moved on, and I'm with someone else. As a matter of fact, he and Jay are at the movies right now. Jasper wasn't man enough to make sure his son was taken care of. And now I've finally found someone who wants me as much as I want him."

"Want who?" Marcus interrupted.

"It's none of your business. But if you must know—and I can't believe no one has told you—Adonis."

"It's not going to happen, Daisy."

"Excuse me? What did you just say? I know you didn't just sit here in my apartment and try to tell me—"

"What about Jasper? I thought you loved him *so much*. The man's body isn't even cold yet, and you're plotting your life with Adonis?"

"Let's get something straight here, Marcus. I can do whatever and whomever I want. Furthermore, get your facts straight. I wasn't plotting out anything with anybody. *But,* if I were, that's my business. Yes, Jasper's gone, and, no, he hasn't been dead long. But even if he were here, he still wouldn't be doing right by me. Did you forget that, Marcus? Did you forget how your friend played me, how he left us with no money and no home? We won't even talk about all the shit that Jay's going to have to contend with when he gets older."

"You and Adonis . . ." Marcus shook his head. "It's not going to happen. How many times are you going to play the fool? Adonis is engaged, Daisy. Engaged."

9

*U*nable to reach Adonis by phone, Daisy went to his apartment building. She seethed, wanting to ring his neck just as she'd rung his line. The click of her heels against the clay-colored stone floor echoed frustration. *He knows I've already been played like a fiddle once. Who the hell is he? The accompaniment?* Pacing fluidly between the entry and the ornately carved limestone bench in the center of the lobby, she rubbed her hands on her jeans and nodded at the doorman for the umpteenth time. *How dare Adonis take Jay out for the day and pretend to be someone he wasn't?* Yes, he was a man, and a gorgeous one at that, Daisy admitted. But he was somebody else's.

Starting to feel as though the walls were closing in on her, she stepped out into the street for some air. Gratefully, she inhaled the cool breeze, which was quickly becoming a wild, gusty wind.

Looking into the sky, she noticed the clouds rushing together. *Perfect,* she thought. *A storm.* Just what she needed: more tension. If it thundered, she'd be up all night comforting Jay.

She removed a candy bar from her pocket, opened it, and bit into it. Three more bites and it was finished. She'd been craving chocolate for the past five days, and she was retaining water. As inconspicuously as she could, she reached down and unfastened her pants, careful to make sure her shirt covered them. Her stomach ached, and a dreadful heat warmed her lower abdomen. Adonis had truly picked the wrong time to piss her off. Pushed too hard, a bloated, PMS-ing woman could be deadly.

"Hey, you," she heard Adonis's voice calling from behind.

She turned, sneering, "How dare you?" She hurried up to them and took Jay by the hand. "The next time you want to play nice guy, become an actor. Your show's already old."

Adonis held his hands up in surrender. "What are you talking about?" he asked, looking genuinely surprised.

"We don't need sympathy," Daisy said, just as the rain began pouring down violently. She shielded Jay with her jacket, then went on, "You don't have to be kind to us. He's not an experiment. This isn't the Boy Scouts, and you won't get a badge for being a Good Samaritan. So from now on, if you want to do a good deed, do one for your fiancée." Daisy turned to walk away.

"Who?"

"Your fiancée—the woman you're going to marry."

"Christy?"

Daisy turned back to him, eyes blazing. His were bulging. Obviously, she had caught him by surprise. He stood stock-still, as if his feet were glued to the ground. "Oh, you forgot your fiancée already? Just stay the hell away from us!"

Propped on a few throw pillows, Daisy relaxed on the sofa with a warm comforter around her. Staring absently at the wall as the television watched her, she waited for the double dose of Midol to kick in. She wasn't one for pain and didn't care what the recommended dosage was. She needed immediate relief, not only from cramps, but from the strain.

She heard Jay padding around in his so-called bedroom. *It's about time.* She needed to shower, and she assumed that he was now very clean; he'd been in the bathtub for over an hour. The wind whistled, and the window rattled. Daisy felt a slight breeze slip through the cracks. Wrapping the comforter tightly around her, she got up to make hot chocolate. Then a loud bump coming from Jay's area startled her.

"Jay? You all right?" She walked toward his room and saw something fly past before she could reach the doorway.

"I hate," he said, throwing another ball, "being here!" He started crying like a baby.

Daisy wasn't ready for a tantrum, and she didn't know how to console him if he was ranting about Jasper. "What's the matter, baby?" She reached out to hold him.

He pulled away. "Why does *every*body keep leaving me? Why'd you tell Adonis not to talk to us anymore? I bet you said the same thing to Dad, and that's why he died. You probably killed him!"

Daisy held her breath. *Not today.* The pain reliever hadn't kicked in yet, and she was just as irritable as Jay was. "Listen. Not right now, okay? I'll explain later. It's an adult thing. Now, pick up this stuff and we'll have some hot chocolate and watch a movie."

She turned away, hoping the strategy she'd seen on TV would work. The show's host had said that if the parent ignored the child's tantrums, the child would eventually realize that his actions were pointless.

Not Jay. He cupped his ears and hollered as loud as he could. "It's your fault!" he cried, pointing. "Yours!"

Daisy stood quietly and counted to ten, trying to calm her nerves. *If you don't pick up this mess and clean this room, I'm going to bounce your ass like that basketball you just threw* was what she thought, but she said, "I said clean up your room, Jay. Now!"

"I'm not picking up a *damn* thing." He ran into the living area.

"Jay, if you don't do as I say *and* apologize, I'm going to warm your ass."

Jay ran out of the apartment and into the rain, with Daisy trailing right behind him.

She jogged out into the heavy downpour, clutching her robe around her. The drops pelted her skin and seeped into her eyes. She could only see a few feet in front of her. Turning corner after corner, ignoring catcall after catcall from the loiterers, she pushed on. Rocks, and what she assumed to be crack vials, crunched under her feet as she continued searching in the dark. She had to find Jay.

Stopping to catch her breath, she leaned against a doorway, clutching her chest. Anxiety attacked her, rushed through her like the violent shower that blurred her sight. She couldn't afford to let it get the best of her. Wouldn't. She shook her head, rebuking the panic like the demon that it was. "Not now, damnit!" she ordered. She looked around and realized that she had no idea where she was. Gathering her composure, she headed back into the storm toward the nearest street sign, hoping she'd spot Jay.

———————

Daisy sat on the radiator and vigorously rubbed her hands on her arms, warming herself as she looked out the window. She'd run in the rain for over forty-five minutes, searching for Jay, before she'd given up. She racked her brain. *Where did he disappear to so quickly?* It was as if he'd vanished the moment he stepped out the door.

She knew she should have phoned the police, but instead she'd called Gigi, who had taken it upon herself to bring the whole crew. Under normal circumstances, Daisy would have protested, but she needed them—even Marcus and Ming Li. *I'll talk to Ming Li later,* Daisy promised herself.

"Does he know anyone in the neighborhood?" Gigi asked.

Daisy shook her head.

"Well, he's not upstairs. Your landlady said she hasn't seen him since yesterday."

"I don't know where he's at, where he could be. It was like one minute he was in front of me, and the next . . ." Daisy shrugged.

Gigi patted her gently on the back. "Marcus will find him . . . let's hope."

"I'm going to stand on the stoop and try to spot them," Ming Li said.

"Ming Li, you don't have to go outside."

Ming Li held up a cigar.

"Don't worry about it," Daisy said, beginning to cry as she sat down on the sofa. "Just smoke in here. Give me a sip of your liquor. I know you have some on you."

Gigi sat next to Daisy and hugged her. "It'll be all right."

Ming Li pulled a bag from her knapsack. "Actually, I have a whole bottle. I was just coming out of the liquor store when Gigi called."

Daisy wiped her eyes. "Give me one of those cigars too. I need something to do with my hands." She held them up to show they were trembling.

Ming Li gave Daisy a glass and a Monte Cristo, then put a palm on her forehead. "Damn, you're burning up."

Gigi got up and started toward the back. "I'll get you some medicine," she said, then turned back to Ming Li. "Ming Li, go in the closet and get Daisy some dry clothes."

Daisy sat and cried. She couldn't lose Jay. What if something had happened to him? But then, she thought, he could be okay. He had disappeared quickly; maybe he had someplace to go. She gulped down the cognac and pulled nervously on the cigar. She didn't feel the burn in her throat or taste the smoke. Numbness engulfed her.

The front door opened and Marcus walked in. He was as wet as she'd been when she'd first come in. "I don't know where he's at. I searched for blocks, went into every store, walked through an alley." He shook his head. "Nowhere."

Daisy jumped from her seat and stubbed the cigar out in a plant. She began to pace frantically, to the window and back. Panic raced through her, digging up a memory. She'd felt the same way the night that Jasper hadn't come home.

"Go change, Daisy," Ming Li instructed, while Gigi gave her a small dosage cup to drink.

"I guess I should." Daisy walked toward the bathroom. "I have to get back out there and find Jay."

"I'll go back out," Marcus said, then left.

Daisy sat on the closed commode with her head in her hands and listened through the doorway. Gigi and Ming Li were discussing what should be done. Apparently, they'd both decided that Daisy and Jay had no business living in that environment. *Gigi means well, but Ming Li's got her nerve. Who'd made her the authority on children all of a sudden?*

Daisy flung open the door, charging into the living area. She glared. "How dare you sit in my house and say that we shouldn't live here! It may not be upscale—hell, it may not even be comfortable—but it's ours. Jay's had a better life here. At least he doesn't have to hear you fucking all night. And, no, he's not allowed to watch people fucking on television, either."

"What?" Ming Li said, glaring back at her.

"Y'all stop. It's not the time for that," Gigi interjected.

"I said, Ming Li, that he's safe here. He's not huddled up in a corner, thinking that someone died because he heard moaning and screaming all night."

"Well, excuse me for thinking I could screw in my own house—"

"It's not about whether you can screw in your home or not. It's that you volunteered to babysit him, and then not only had him around one of your countless men, but couldn't control your hormones. I can't say who can or can't visit you in your house. But I can say, and any other responsible adult would agree, that a child shouldn't be subjected to hearing adults fuck. What part of that is healthy?"

Gigi waved her hand in defeat. "Well, y'all just get it all out . . . get it over with."

Ming Li's face flushed red with anger. "Responsible? I know you're not lecturing me on responsibility. Maybe you need to find another word, because you're talking about something that you know nothing of. You sat on your ass for years and let someone dictate your life. You didn't have a job, never paid a bill, and didn't bring anything to the table but your appetite. But *you're* responsible? Please! Jasper owned you from your panties to your pedicures. On top of that he used you—"

"Used me for what? Since you claim that I didn't have anything, what could he possibly have used me for?"

"To raise his—no, I take that back—to raise *someone else's* son."

Gigi quickly moved between them. "Okay now, that's enough." She turned to Ming Li. "You were wrong, and you're sorry. I know because you told me so. So you may as well just say it." Gigi turned to Daisy. "A lot has happened, and you're upset. Understandable. And I agree she shouldn't have done it. But, and I emphasize *but,* we can't tell her what to do in her own house."

Just then, Marcus walked in. The women fell silent. Daisy looked behind him, hoping that Jay would follow. She swallowed hard. "You couldn't find—"

Her phone rang.

"Hello?" she said breathlessly. "Jay?"

"Hello, I'm calling from St. Vincent's Hospital. Are you Jay's mother?"

———

Gigi, Ming Li, and Marcus sat silently in the hospital waiting room, watching Daisy pace the carpet. She'd paused every time someone had come to the door, stopped just about every doctor or nurse she'd seen. No one knew anything—or was pretending not to. Even the receptionist played dumb. *This is crazy,* she thought.

A police officer came in. "I'm looking for Mrs. Stevens."

Daisy nodded. "It's me you want. But my name is Ms. Parker."

"Okay. Could you follow me?"

What the hell does he want? Why isn't a doctor or a nurse here instead? "I'll be right back," she said to the others.

As she walked down the tiled corridor, her heartbeat matched the hollow footsteps. *God, please let Jay be all right.*

"In here, ma'am." The officer pointed to a door and walked in.

Daisy stepped inside the bland office, which was decorated in dull browns and dusty pinks. Hanging on the walls were reproduction prints and a floral painting, the usual hospital decor. She looked at the oversize wooden desk, which had too many knickknacks and obligatory family photos, and her eyes froze on the nameplate on the desk. She didn't recognize the name, but the job title scared her: *Social Services.* She held her breath. *What do they want?*

"We'll fill you in on everything in a minute," the officer said without looking at her.

"Okay," Daisy managed, feeling as though she were about to be punished. She sensed that he was avoiding her eyes for a reason.

A woman in a navy blue suit walked in, wearing a pleasant smile. Daisy guessed that the grin was as manufactured as her clothes, something she put on and took off at will. "Hello," the woman said, extending her hand. "You must be Jay's mother. I'm Mrs. Tompkins, the Social Services administrator."

Reluctantly, Daisy shook her hand. "Nice to meet you. When am I going to see Jay? Is he alright? What happened?"

Mrs. Tompkins opened the folder that she'd had under her arm. "Well, we need to ask you a few questions. But first, let me assure you that Jay's alright. The police found him in the street without any shoes or jacket. He was badly bruised, with a split lip—"

"No shoes? What happened to him?" Daisy asked. *Jay had on shoes when he left.*

"He was robbed. Are you Jay's biological mother?"

Shit. "No, I'm not. I've raised him since before he was two— me and his biological father."

"He's dead now, right? What about his biological mother?"

Daisy nodded, realizing that Mrs. Tompkins must have questioned Jay thoroughly. "Yes, his father is dead. He passed recently. His biological mother is also dead. Jay is in my care."

"By order of the court, I assume. What about any other living relatives?"

"Mrs. Tompkins, do I need an attorney? Because I have no idea what's going on here. Jay is well taken care of."

Mrs. Tompkins smirked. "I believe that he is. But when the police bring in a runaway, it's my job to intervene. For the well-being of the child, you understand."

Daisy stood with her feet firmly planted. "Yes, I understand. But you should be spending your time talking to someone else, perhaps a child that *needs* you to intervene. Jay and I got into it, and he ran out. We've been searching for hours. Now I just want to see him, make sure he's alright, and take him home. Unless you have a problem with that, or a court order to stop me, that's exactly what I'm going to do."

Mrs. Tompkins looked at the officer. "Ms. Parker, please cooperate—"

"I have cooperated. But quite frankly, I'm offended. As you said, he had a couple of minor scratches and was without shoes—all of which are not my doing—"

"We know that, Ms. Parker," the officer intervened. "He was robbed."

Daisy looked from the officer to Mrs. Tompkins. "Where is he? I need to see him—now."

"And you will, in a second."

"You mean to tell me that you're going to make me wait to see my son?" Daisy huffed. "You know I didn't harm him, yet you're treating me as if I did." Daisy reached into her pocket and got her phone. "Okay, now I call my attorney."

"But you did threaten to hurt him. According to Jay, you told him you'd warm his ass."

———————

Mixed emotions flowed through Daisy as she turned off Jay's light and slid the bedroom door closed. She was upset with him, but she was happy that he was safely back home. She walked into the living area and joined Gigi and Marcus, sorry that Ming Li wasn't there. Daisy may have been mad at her the week before, but after their argument she'd decided to let the past remain in the past. They'd both had their say. It was time to move forward.

"He okay?" Gigi asked.

"He'll be fine. He's a big boy," Marcus answered.

"Yes. I just gave him some children's Advil and an antibiotic. The cuts shouldn't get infected."

Marcus stood and hugged Daisy. "I'm sorry."

"It's not your fault."

"No, about earlier. If I hadn't said anything, then this wouldn't have—"

"Then I would've been mad at you for not telling me," Daisy said with a smile. "Don't you think we've had enough of that?"

"Yes, y'all have. Now what are we going to do? You guys can't live here anymore. Not after tonight."

"You're right. I still don't know who took Jay's shoes. But I've put just about all of my money into this place. It wasn't much, just enough to make us comfortable." Daisy looked around. "Well, sort of."

Marcus extended his hand. "You don't hate me anymore, do you?"

"No."

"Well, now you don't have a reason not to stay with Gigi. I know you don't want to, but do it for Jay."

"Only until I get on my feet—again."

10

*D*aisy sat beside Gigi in Ming Li's shop, Ming Li's Nails of New York, patiently waiting for her nails to dry. She smiled as she absorbed her surroundings. Gold-framed art adorned the celery-green walls, music wafted through the air, and the televisions broadcasted videos.

Daisy blew on her nails. "Gigi, can you do me a favor? Would you look in my purse and hand me a fifty?"

Gigi looked over at her in surprise. "For what? Don't tell me Ming Li's gonna start charging us now."

Daisy covered Gigi's mouth. "Girl, stop worrying. It's for a bet."

"The fight? Don't tell me you lost your money betting on—"

"*Please.* I don't have money to lose. I won. I don't bet unless it's a sure thing. I do have a son to take care of, remember? This is Ming Li's change."

"I know your nails aren't dry yet. Don't mess them up," Ming Li ordered.

"Do I look like Gigi to you? You know I'm careful with my nails," Daisy joked.

"Yeah, right. Tell me another one."

"I know you two heifers aren't talking about me!" Gigi yelled from across the room.

Ming Li rolled her eyes dramatically at Gigi and turned to Daisy. "So, what do you think, now that the renovation's finished?"

"It's nice. Real nice." Daisy's eyes lit up. She'd forgotten about the investment.

"I'll write you a check later."

"A check for what?" Gigi asked, walking up from behind.

"I paid for the renovation."

"You paid for it? How? Why? Don't tell me that Ming Li needed money."

"She didn't need the money. It was an investment. She offered Jasper the opportunity, and he hesitated, so I jumped on it. And I'm glad I did because it'll definitely come in handy now. She used the renovation money to buy a foreclosure in Los Angeles. She's branching out, going national."

"And where—"

"I got the money from Jasper . . . sort of. Let's just say that I wrote myself a check."

Ming Li waved at them from across the almost empty salon. "I'm closing up, ladies. Not to be rude, but I have a date."

Daisy and Gigi looked at each other and laughed.

"I thought you didn't date."

"And wouldn't be seen with one of your toys in public."

Ming Li smiled.

———————

Daisy and Gigi both sat quietly on Gigi's deck, absorbed in their thoughts, drinking cappuccinos with a splash of Frangelico. The colorful autumn leaves rustled and scattered across the small lawn. It was cold, but serene.

Daisy got up and leaned on the wooden banister, trying to get comfortable. She decided that once she had the money, she'd get Gigi's deck restored and not leave it neglected, the way she'd left so many other things. Closing her eyes, she massaged her temples and reassured herself for the millionth time that her life would take a turn for the better. She smiled, and warmth spread through her as she recalled what her father had told her when she had been a teenager with a broken heart. *If it keeps raining, be assured that it means the sun is coming. Rain is just the opening act.* "My sun *is* coming," Daisy mouthed, then winced. Wood splinters poked her as she twisted, turned, and scooted, trying to find the right position. She could have joined Gigi at the patio table, but she wanted to enjoy a quiet moment alone. She looked over at Gigi and wondered what her secret was. She seemed so happy and content with her life. Daisy assumed that people used to think the same about her. She knew now that she'd never been as happy as she'd once believed, and that she had no idea how to define it. Her life had consisted of men, money, and material possessions. Daisy pushed off the banister and wiped her hands, promising herself that she would find out what happiness was and experience it firsthand. She went back to join Gigi.

"Hey, nice of you to join me again," Gigi said, pulling a chair out for her.

Daisy sat. "I had some thinking to do. Sorry if I was rude."

"We're family. No such thing as rude. I was doing some thinking myself," Gigi said, then looked down.

"What's wrong?" Daisy couldn't remember the last time she'd seen Gigi so sullen.

"It's Marcus . . . I'm not sure how I feel about him anymore."

Daisy's jaw dropped. She'd thought that Gigi and Marcus were the perfect loving couple. They'd seemed so meant-to-be. "What do you mean? I thought you two were made for each other."

"He's too needy. He has to be under me twenty-four/seven. Sometimes I feel like I can't breathe. And now that Jasper's gone, it's worse."

Daisy nodded. "Yeah, I can imagine. They were so close. He doesn't have any other friends?"

"If he does, I don't know anything about them. I've never heard him mention anyone."

Daisy picked up her cup. "But is that a bad thing, him wanting to be around you all the time? Because a long time ago, I would've given limbs to have Jasper want me so badly. I received the opposite."

Gigi held her head in her hands. "I know it sounds crazy, but it's not. When I go left, he goes left. If I go to the bathroom, he knocks on the door, wanting to come in."

Daisy crinkled her nose. "Ill."

"Exactly. But on top of that, he's jealous. I mean raging with jealousy. It's ridiculous. When I'm freshening my lipstick to go to the store, he wants to know who I'm going to meet. Wants to know who I'm trying to look good for when I buy new makeup. And truth be told, I don't even like to wear makeup."

"Then why do you wear it?"

"Him! When we first started dating, we went to a wedding or the theater—somewhere that required me to get dolled up. He'd never seen me in makeup before, and he loved it. He literally kissed my feet all day. So I decided if it made him feel that good, that attracted to me, I'd wear it every day."

"Wow. I guess we've both made sacrifices to please men. But you know what I've learned? We have to make ourselves happy."

Gigi nodded. "Yes, we do."

Daisy got up and walked into the house.

"Can you do me a favor and bring a blanket when you come back, please?"

Daisy smiled. "I'll do you a favor, but it won't be the one you asked for, it'll be one that you need."

"What?"

"I'm going to throw your makeup away. As of today, we wear no more masks."

Gigi ran into the house and followed Daisy. They both laughed as they took turns making jump shots, throwing away the cosmetics. Giggling like schoolgirls, they fell over each other, slipping on loose face powder. They ignored the telephone when it rang. After all of Gigi's cosmetics were in the trash, they hugged. The phone rang again.

"It sure feels good, letting things go," Gigi said as she went to answer it.

"Yes, it does," Daisy said, wiping the traces of color out of the sink. "I need a broom and a mop."

Gigi returned with the same sullen look on her face that she'd had before. "Bad news."

"What is it this time?"

"Let's go sit down."

"Tell me now. Whatever it is, I can handle it."

"That was my mom, calling to warn us that my aunt's looking for you. Social Services tracked her down, and apparently she's going to file for custody of Jay."

Daisy sank to the floor and covered her face with her hands. "Oh, God, I'm going to lose both my babies."

"Both of what babies?" Gigi asked, looking confused. "You mean one baby, right?"

Daisy shook her head. "Two. A long time ago, I did a terrible thing. A really horrible thing." She locked eyes with Gigi. "Do you remember when I took a year off from college junior year to help out my sister Brea during her pregnancy?"

Gigi nodded. "When you went to Hawaii."

"Yes, Hawaii. That's where her husband, Phillip, was stationed at the time. Well, that was a lie. I didn't want to lie to you, but I had to. The truth is . . ." Tears started running down Daisy's cheeks.

Gigi patted her back. "It's okay, Daisy."

"The truth is, I went away because *I* was pregnant, not Brea. I went to Hawaii because I didn't want to shame my parents."

"What? Are you serious?"

Daisy nodded.

Gigi stood and wrapped her arms around Daisy. "I didn't know. But what happened to the baby?"

"Brea has my baby."

"Lani?"

"Yes, Lalani is my daughter. That's her real name. I gave her a Hawaiian name."

"How come you never told me, Daisy? As long as we've been friends . . . I always thought she was Brea's. I've seen her a couple of times, when I went home to visit. How old is she now?"

Daisy's face was blank. "She's eight. I never told you because, legally, she's not mine. Never was."

"What do you mean, never was? You had her, right?"

Daisy nodded. "Yes, I had her, but all the paperwork was under my sister's name. Nowhere on the doctor's medical records, or the hospital's, does it state that Daisy Parker had a child. Every document says that a baby girl was born to Brea Parker-Adams."

"Are you sure?"

"Positive. I filled out every form and signed Brea's name."

"Why?"

"I believed that my parents—no, *everyone*—thought that it'd be good for me. I was too young to have a baby. I wasn't married. I was just about to finish college. You name it. I had every excuse but no reasons."

Gigi sighed. "Damn, Daisy." She leaned on the windowsill. "Wow. So that's why you wouldn't have Jasper's baby, hunh? Because of Lani?"

"I couldn't. How could I give birth to his child when I didn't have my own? I mean, his child would've been mine too. You know what I mean."

Gigi cleared her throat. "I understand."

11

*D*aisy turned onto her street and saw a moving truck parked in front of the house. Men dressed in dingy blue coveralls were locking the back of the truck. *Movers,* she realized, cringing. Marcus's car was parked behind it.

Ming Li sped by on a hot-pink Ducati motorcycle, blowing her horn. "Oh, Lord," Daisy said out loud. *One day that girl's going to hurt herself, or someone else.* Daisy laughed as the moving men almost broke their necks lusting after Ming Li in her tight, fuchsia leather motorcycle suit.

Daisy eased the SUV into a parking spot, trying not to hit one of Ming Li's admirers. She sighed and got out. Marcus was the last person she wanted to see. She'd overheard him and Gigi arguing the night before, and she didn't want to get involved.

As she slammed the door shut, she overheard the movers talking to Marcus. "Damn, man! What I wouldn't give to be you. It's like the international house of whew-wee, pumpkin pie around here. You know what I really wanted to say, don't ya, boy? I swear, you got 'em all, hunh?" The man laughed.

Daisy rolled her eyes.

"Yeah, yeah. That's what I'm talking about," the mover with the big mouth said, then looked at Daisy and yelled, "You a vicious one, ain't ya, gal? Well, hurt me, bay-bee."

Daisy flipped the man the bird, walked into the house, slammed the door, and locked it. *Marcus can stay outside with the rest of those hoodlums,* she thought as she heard catcalls from outside.

Gigi and Ming Li were inside. Daisy's eyes roamed the almost empty living room. It looked as though everything that Gigi owned was gone—packed away in a truck. Daisy leaned against the wall and slid down until her butt hit the hardwood floor. *Even the rugs are gone.* She crossed her ankles, pulled her knees to her chest, and rested her chin on them, remembering how she'd once had to pack away her whole life into boxes too. She felt bad for Gigi, who'd spent years decorating the house. They'd both shopped together for weeks, choosing the right layouts and color schemes for their homes, and it had taken them months to locate just the right accessories. *Funny, it only takes the better part of a day to remove it all.*

"I see you made it," Gigi said. "Where's Jay?"

"He went to the after-school program, and he's going to practice after that."

"Sounds like he's in for a long day."

"Yes, he'll be exhausted. Are you okay?"

Gigi smiled. "Girl, I haven't been happier."

"What I don't understand is why he's taking so much."

"I told him to remove all his things, even the gifts he'd bought me over the years."

Ming Li laughed. "Damn, then it seems he furnished most of the house!"

Gigi shook her head. "No, that was the only size truck he could get at the last minute. It's too big."

Daisy touched Gigi's cheek. "How'd you get that bruise? Did he hit you?"

Gigi gave her a look of disbelief. "Trust me, nobody hits me. Not while I have a kitchen full of knives and a gun—"

"A gun?"

"Licensed, of course. Ming Li and I both have one. We used to go to the range while you were at home playing June Cleaver."

"Well, for your information, even June Cleaver knows how to shoot. Remember when Jasper and I first met, how we used to go to the Poconos? Well, we also went to the range. I'd forgotten all about that. It's funny what you remember at times."

"Oh, yeah," Gigi snapped. "You were in Junior ROTC in high school, right?"

Ming Li laughed. "We'd better be careful, or someone might mistake us for tomboys. We bet on fights, shoot guns, I ride motorcycles—"

"Don't forget about pool. We haven't shot a good game of pool in a long time," Gigi interjected.

"Well," Daisy spoke up, "how about later this week?"

"What's the ante?"

Gigi shrugged. "Whatever."

"You know I don't have any money to gamble," Daisy huffed.

"True," Ming Li agreed. "So if you win, you get the money. If you lose, you have to clean one of our houses."

"Bet," Daisy agreed, remembering that she was a better shot than both Ming Li and Gigi. "Oh, Gigi. You never said what happened to your face."

"After you went to work this morning, Marcus was becoming too belligerent for me, so I politely did what any self-respecting woman would do."

"You called the cops?"

Ming Li laughed. "No, backup. First she called me at work, but I didn't make it in time. Then she called her trusty stepbrother."

"Brother," Gigi corrected. "You know we've never considered one another to be step-anything."

"Well, it's a good thing Adonis made it here first, because I had my piece at the shop—and a full clip," Ming Li said, nodding.

Daisy shook her head. "See? You're too dangerous for me."

"She's kidding," Gigi said.

Ming Li shrugged. "Alright. If you say so."

Gigi waved off the comment. "Anyway, Adonis came over and was cool about it. His normal laid-back self, until Marcus kept calling me a bitch and said 'fuck you' to him one too many times. You know they've never cared for each other, not since Marcus and Jasper became best friends."

"They fought?" Daisy asked.

"No, but I thought they were going to. Like a fool, I jumped between them. And got knocked out of the way when Adonis yoked Marcus up by the collar and threw his ass outside."

"And then he closed the door behind him as if nothing happened," Ming Li giggled. "I don't know how the hell he did it, because Marcus is bigger."

"He seems to be," Gigi said. "Marcus is fatter, Adonis is stronger—muscular."

"Well, whatever," Ming Li went on. "All I know is that I moved out of the way as fast as I could. I don't break up fights, I bet on them." She tapped Daisy on the shoulder. "Guess what?"

"What?"

"Come see," Gigi said, taking Daisy by the hand. She led her to the room that Daisy slept in and pushed open the door. Beautiful daisies filled the room.

"Ooh . . . they're beautiful! Who did this?"

Gigi giggled. "Wait, there's more." She pulled an envelope from her pocket. "Here."

Daisy took the envelope and pulled the accompanying card out of it. She smiled at the familiar verse embossed on the front from 1 Corinthians: "And now these three remain: Faith, Hope, and Love." *I need all of these.* As she opened the card and read, her smile faded. It was from Adonis. She shook her head in disbelief, dropped it on the floor, and walked away.

"Daisy, sometimes I don't understand you."

"Well, Gigi, I don't expect you to. How can you understand me, or what I'm going through, if you haven't been in my position before? Marcus didn't cheat on you."

"Daisy, Adonis is only trying to be nice. He's sorry for not telling you about Christy."

"Yes, Ming Li, Adonis *is* sorry. Sorry that I found out. If I hadn't, he wouldn't have told me. And you don't know everything that happened, how I felt, or how much I gave. So please don't assume."

"Oh, what happened? He fucked you? See, that's the problem. You should've fucked him—"

Gigi elbowed Ming Li.

"I'm not talking about fuck as in 'fuck him over.' Nothing like that, Gigi. He's cool with me, and he's your brother. All men don't necessarily have to be treated like dogs, just ninety-nine percent of them. My point is that you, Daisy, should've been the one to initiate the sex—did it for yourself, then you wouldn't feel so bad."

Daisy plopped down on the sofa. "Look at you two. What is this, Judge Daisy Day? You expect me to just forgive him because he said he was sorry and sent me flowers?"

"No, but you haven't heard his side. How do you know Marcus wasn't lying?"

"You know, Gigi's right. Marcus didn't want to see you with anyone but Jasper, definitely not with someone Jasper didn't like. Face it, Daisy. This man wants you despite your problems. And quite frankly, you've got too many issues—"

"Everybody has issues."

"Not like yours," Ming Li pointed out. "I know you've been hurt and angry, and you've grieved. But you've got to stop thinking that everybody's out to get you."

"She's right, Daisy. You're mad."

Daisy rolled her eyes. "Wouldn't you be mad?"

"Yes, I can't say that I wouldn't be. But I wouldn't have just walked away. I'd have to know if what Marcus said was fiction or fact. With the wall you've built around you, Adonis was screwed from the beginning."

"I don't want his flowers."

"Honey, you'd better take what you can get. Don't let your pride get in the way. You're just scared. He didn't have to do a thing for you. Be grateful that he thinks enough of you to apologize for something that may not even be true. He never said he was engaged, he said he was sorry that you were hurting. Did you read the card? He cares about you and Jay," Ming Li pointed out.

"Read it. It's beautiful." Gigi held the card out.

"No, I don't want to read it." Daisy stared straight ahead. She needed time. She needed to heal and forgive herself first, for all that she'd allowed herself to become victim to, before she could forgive anyone else. She ran her fingers through her hair, sighing. *I shouldn't have gotten involved with him. It was too soon.*

"No?"

"It's nice. I believe he's sorry—he already said enough with flowers. But the only one I need to forgive right now is me." Daisy sat up.

"Forgive yourself for what?"

"Nothing!" Ming Li interjected. "Daisy, don't feel sorry for yourself. And get over Jasper. He's dead and gone. Okay, he was wrong. He cheated. He lied. He did a lot of things he shouldn't have. But, damn, stop it! It wasn't your fault that you loved him as much as you did."

"Okay, I get your point. But I'm not talking about Jasper. Gigi, you know what we talked about—Hawaii, remember? Let me just deal with this the best way I can." Daisy grabbed her keys from the end table.

Gigi grabbed her and held on. "Look, I'm sorry you're going through this. You've had a hell of a time these past few months. And you're right . . . I don't understand, because I've never been where you're at. Nobody should be where you are. But I know you'll be fine. You're strong, you're smart, you're beautiful, and you're worth loving. Remember that. That heart of yours would be a gift to anyone."

"And don't forget to demand a gift for yourself," Ming Li added.

Daisy's cell phone rang just as she was stepping into the bath. She looked at the caller ID, then powered off the phone. *Let her leave a message.* Mrs. Tompkins, the hospital social worker, was calling again. Daisy had no idea why she kept bothering her, especially at nine in the morning. For days, she'd been leaving message after message, all vague, asking Daisy to return her call. She'd even phoned Gigi's house a couple of times. God only knew how she'd gotten Gigi's unlisted number. *I'll return her call later,* Daisy decided as she sank into the warm, captivating bubbles. She closed her eyes, and the whole hectic week disappeared for a second. She'd worked overtime on a few new projects, and Mr. Wiles, being the man that he was, had told her to take the day off. She supposed he could see how tired she was. But she was thankful because he'd been commending her all along, and he'd called her "the best flower person" he'd ever hired. A cool wind swept into the room, interrupting her peace.

"Telephone, Daisy," Gigi said.

Not Mrs. Tompkins again. "Tell her I'll call her back."

Gigi smiled. "Talk about women's intuition. It sure is that heifer on the phone. I'll get rid of her. Relax. You look tired."

"I am. Can you wake me at three so I can pick up Jay? I'm tired enough to sleep through the alarm."

Gigi laughed. "I did this morning. I was supposed to be at work at eight and didn't wake up until seven thirty. Good thing I had sick days left."

———————

Daisy crawled onto the bed like a cat and dropped her weight onto the floral sheets. The fluffy pillow folded around her face, kissing her cheeks, and the fan cooled her feet. She closed her eyes and started to drift off, but then Gigi walked into the room and nudged her.

"Telephone."

"Who is it? Don't tell me it's that woman again," Daisy muttered into the pillow.

"Lani."

Daisy bolted up with wide eyes, fully alert as if she'd had one espresso too many. She held her breath as she put the phone to her ear. Her heart cha-cha'd rhythmically as if beating for the first time. It danced its way up to her throat, begging her to pour out her affections. But she didn't know what to say. "Well, this is a surprise," she finally managed.

"Hi, Aunt Daisy," Lani said in the softest, sweetest voice that Daisy had ever heard.

"Hi, sweetie. How are you?" She beamed and her eyes began to pool.

"Good. Umm . . . umm . . . are you coming home for Thanksgiving? Grandma said you might, but I wanted to be sure."

Daisy smiled. "Well, I was planning to. Why? Do you want to see me?"

"Yes!" Lani sang. "Jay too. I just got a new Xbox game, and I've been practicing. I know I can beat him now. When he was here last time, he won. Oh, and now I can ride my bike without training wheels too, and my mommy said that maybe Santa will bring me a bigger one for Christmas."

Mommy? The sound of Lani calling Brea that cut Daisy to the core. "That's wonderful, sweetie. What do you want me to buy you for Christmas?"

"My mommy says it's impolite to ask for things," Lani said, then whispered, "but I really want a puppy and a Barbie House. Don't tell Mommy, okay?"

"I won't . . . not this time."

"Can I speak to Jay?"

Daisy held her breath, wondering if that was Lani's real reason for calling. "I'm sorry, sweetie, Jay's at school. Aren't you supposed to be at school too?"

"In a few minutes, but I don't think I'm going. My mommy's stomach is sick again, and Daddy's gone already. But they promised me that after Mommy has the baby, her stomach won't get sick no more."

"Your mother is *pregnant?* I didn't know that."

"Mmm-hm. I'm having a little sister. She showed me a picture. I don't know how pretty she's going to be, though. Her face looked funny."

Daisy fell out laughing. Lani must've seen an ultrasound picture. "She'll be gorgeous, just like you."

"Aunt Daisy, I gotta go. Mommy's coming, and I'm supposed to be doing my phonics stuff. I'll see you at Thanksgiving, and don't forget to bring Jay."

Daisy cradled the phone and cried.

Getting out of bed, Daisy removed the folded papers from her safe and carefully straightened them. She looked at Lani's birth certificate and wept. She'd carried Lani almost ten months, because Lani wasn't ready to come out. Daisy remembered being anxious and uncomfortable during her overdue pregnancy. She'd wanted desperately for Lani to be born so that Daisy could breathe and be one person again instead of two. Now, she'd give anything to relive those moments, to have her daughter so close to her that they'd be as one.

She felt her muscles relax, knowing that she'd get the chance to be near her during the Thanksgiving holiday. Gently, she traced Lani's name on the birth certificate. She wished that she could've been there for Lani the same way that Ms. Christine had always been there for her. But she couldn't change the past, only look forward to the future. "I love you, little girl. Even though I gave you away, I love you."

"Hel-lo!" Daisy yelled, trying to get Ming Li's attention. "We're over here."

Ming Li's pungent smoke reached them before she did. "So, are we playing straight, eight-ball, or nine-ball?" Ming Li pulled on her cigar and tapped Daisy. "Scoot over and let me sit down. My feet hurt."

Daisy looked at Ming Li's feet. "Nobody told you to wear four-inch heels to shoot pool. And besides, I don't want to smell that stinky cigar."

Gigi laughed as she racked the balls, removed a pair of dice from her pocket, and chalked her pool stick. "Tell her, Daisy. Ming Li thinks that's attractive. I keep trying to tell her. She won't listen."

Ming Li picked up the dice and rolled a pair of sixes. She smiled, nodded, and blew smoke in Gigi's direction. "I never said it was attractive. And now that I think about it, I never asked you, either. Daisy, do you remember me asking Gigi her opinion about my smoking?"

Daisy smiled and shook her head.

"I didn't think so."

"Smart-ass." Gigi rolled an eleven. "I'm just trying to help you out. You know the surgeon general says—"

"Ssh." Ming Li held a finger to her lips. "I didn't ask him, either."

"Alright, ladies," Daisy said as she stood up and rolled a five. "Are we ready? It's almost noon, and I have to pick up Jay at five thirty."

"You'll make it in time. Have you spoken with Adonis?"

Gigi sighed loudly. "Let's just play."

"So you wouldn't even hear him out, huh? How do you know he's even engaged?" Ming Li pushed.

"I don't have time for Adonis's games. I have Jay, and he's all I need. Just hurry up and take your shot, if you know how."

"Ha, ha. Very funny. Just watch and take notes, Daisy. If you're nice, I may just let you clean up my house today. It's not too bad—about an hour's work."

Ming Li cleared the table on her first try, and then her second. *Damn.* Daisy wasn't in a cleaning mood.

———————

Ming Li and Gigi walked from room to room while Daisy sat on the sofa waiting. Every time they commented on Daisy's work, she rolled her eyes. It wasn't as if she'd had a choice about cleaning up the house. She'd lost the bet.

Daisy checked her watch. "Alright, I'm leaving. It's after four, and I don't want to be late picking up Jay."

———————

Daisy drummed her fingers on the steering wheel. She'd been waiting for Jay for over twenty minutes. Doing a 180-degree turn, she searched the grounds. She bit her lip impatiently, beginning to worry. But then it occurred to her that he'd been late once before. *He's probably on the court.* Checking her watch again, she saw that twenty minutes had turned into thirty-five.

She hopped out of her Jeep and walked toward the school entrance. A little redheaded girl who looked to be about Jay's age was coming out the door. She looked familiar.

"Excuse me," Daisy said. "Do you know Jay Stevens?"

"Mmm-hm. He's in my class."

"Have you seen him?"

"He left already. I think his mom picked him up."

Daisy's heart flipped. She ran as fast as she could to the office.

"Excuse me," she said to the receptionist who was on the phone.

The receptionist held up a finger. "Just a second," she said, then continued a personal conversation that was filled with laughter and I-told-you-sos.

"Excuse me," Daisy repeated, louder this time.

"I said, just a second—"

Daisy reached over the counter and disconnected the call. "Now, can you please tell me where Jay Stevens, my son, is? A little girl from his class just told me that his mom picked him up, which is impossible!"

The receptionist was on her feet in an instant. "Just a second. You need to talk to Principal Reynolds."

"Sure thing." Daisy followed the receptionist to the principal's office.

"Can I help you?" a woman around Daisy's age asked.

"Where's my son, Jay Stevens?"

"I'm sorry. Social Services came and got him. We couldn't stop them. They had a court order."

"You mean to tell me that you couldn't even call me?"

"We tried. The phone number we have listed for you had been disconnected, and they'd already taken your son away, so we couldn't ask him. It's not our policy to get into these matters. Our interest is the child's well-being—"

"And that's exactly why you should've phoned me," Daisy said, then hurried out of the office.

She broke down in the car, banging the steering wheel like a drum. It was all her fault. She should've returned Mrs. Tompkins's call, had promised herself that she would. But obviously, she'd let her time run out.

But why had they taken Jay? True, she'd threatened to spank him, but she'd never laid a hand on him. As a matter of fact, he'd never gotten a spanking in his life. She thought of Jasper's family. *Has to be them.* She pulled out her phone.

She dialed Mrs. Tompkins, who informed her that the case had been assigned to someone else, and that she should call back in a couple of days.

"Well, where have they taken him? I need to see him."

Mrs. Tompkins cleared her throat. "They won't allow you to see him, and I don't know to which facility he's been taken. But I do know," she went on, lowering her voice to a whisper, "that you should get an attorney. Possibly a Mr. Kenneth Burgess—I overheard his name a few times. Call me and let me know how it goes."

The line went dead.

Daisy stood stuck-on-stupid for a moment, listening to dead air. Mrs. Tompkins had given her a hint. Why else would she whisper the name of Jasper's attorney? He didn't practice family law. Daisy dried her misting eyes with the back of her hand. She wanted to scream, break down, cry as she'd never cried before. But there was no time for tears. It was time to fight.

———————

Daisy held the phone to her ear as Ms. Christine lectured. She'd called to borrow money so she could obtain a lawyer, but instead she'd been getting advice she hadn't asked for.

"I know you mean well, Ma. But really, I don't have much time. Will you and Dad loan me the money until I sell my Jeep?"

"Of course we will, but on one condition."

"What's that?"

"You have to promise me that you'll let Lani stay where she's at, that you won't disrupt her life—"

"What do you mean, *disrupt?*"

"You know, tell her that you're her real mother."

Daisy was exasperated. "Look, Ma, if I don't tell her, she'll find out in court anyway, thanks to Calvin."

"I'm not talking about Calvin. I'm concerned about what *you'll* do."

"Alright," Daisy said, sighing heavily. "I'll think about it."

"Well," Ms. Christine said, mimicking the sigh, "so will I. When you make your decision, I'll make mine."

12

*D*aisy looked at the two remaining suits lying across the bed. For the life of her, she couldn't decide which to wear. The blue one made her look like someone who meant business, but the yellow one made her appear too soft. She finally decided on the blue and hung the other one back in the closet.

She yawned. She needed a cup of coffee. An over-the-counter stimulant. An electric current to zap her awake. She'd been up all night, thinking about her options. She had no idea how she was going to get Jay back. All she knew was that she had to get her hands on two things: money and Jasper's lawyer.

"Hey, you ready?" Gigi asked from the doorway.

"Yes, I am."

"Okay. Ming Li said she'd be there in fifteen minutes. She persuaded the attorney to meet with her for an emergency consultation."

Daisy grabbed her purse. "Did she imply that she had a lot of money? Did she make him think he could make a lot of money if he handled her?"

"I don't know what she said, but whatever it was worked. Apparently, he canceled a meeting with one of his clients for her."

"She hooked him." Daisy nodded.

"Yes, she always gets the men."

"Well, then I guess I have to reel him in."

Gigi stood at the receptionist's desk, first belting the woman with a barrage of questions, then making an appointment to cover for Daisy, who sneaked past.

"Hello, Kenneth," Daisy said, barging into his office with a smile on her face.

The attorney jolted to his feet. "I'm sorry, Daisy, but I'm meeting with a client." He gestured toward Ming Li.

Ming Li stood too. "No, I'm finished here. Thanks." She turned her back to Kenneth, gave Daisy a wink, and walked out.

Daisy locked the door behind her. Crossing her arms, she leaned against the heavy, mahogany door and drank in the room. Expensive barrister bookcases. Custom wet bar. Suede furniture. A wall of windows. Small indications spoke volumes of his success or, at the very least, the money he'd been making off his clients.

"What can I help you with?" he asked, looking flustered.

Daisy removed a roll of twenties and threw it on his desk. *"Now* will you see me? It's not much, but it's all I can afford."

"Daisy, I don't understand—"

"Damn if you don't, Kenneth! You wouldn't even accept my calls after Jasper died. But I distinctly remember us eating at the same table before. You, Jasper, and I had dinner together how many times?" She waved her hand, indicating that she didn't really want him to answer. "You can sit now. I'm not here to threaten you. I want an answer, that's all."

Kenneth sat down, fumbling with his tie. "Would you like a drink?"

"Social Services took Jay," she said, ignoring the question.

Kenneth's face was blank.

"Kenneth, don't play lawyer with me. I know you know something, and I want to know what it is. Why did they take him? Furthermore, I want to know why Jasper left his son penniless. I know that you know that too, so don't pretend that you don't. You two were friends—not just business associates," Daisy spat, ready to chew and spit him out like a stale piece of gum.

"Honestly, Daisy, I don't know why they took Jay away. I can find out, of course. It's not my field, but I'll see what I can do. And about the money, I mentioned it to him when we were going over his will. He told me not to worry about it. That's all I can say. You know I'm not at liberty to discuss his personal matters—"

"But he's dead! The deceased don't have *personal* anything."

"Yes, he is. But I still must honor his wishes." He picked up the roll of money and tucked it into his pocket. "Give me until after the holidays," he added, then wrote on the back of his business card and handed it to Daisy. "Here's my home number. If anything else happens between now and then—"

"Kenneth, I can't wait a couple of weeks. I won't!"

"That's the best I can do," he snapped.

Daisy slammed her hands on his desk and bore into him with her eyes. She hadn't come to play games. Her glare seemed to cut him in half, split Kenneth in two like the Red Sea.

His expression softened. "No, you're absolutely right." He clicked on his intercom. "Nancy, can you find me the number of the contact I have over at Family Services?" He turned back to Daisy. "I'll see if I can arrange for you to see him. Call me at home in a couple of hours. It may take a little while. It's a lot of phone tag."

———

Daisy sat on her suitcase while Gigi snapped it shut. Daisy had been devastated for the past few days.

"So, they still won't let you see Jay?"

"No. Kenneth tried and tried. I didn't believe him, until he let me listen to the message."

"Well, maybe it's good that you're going home for the holidays. You'll get to see Lani," Gigi reminded her.

A faint smile came to Daisy's face. "Yes, and I'm looking forward to it, although I know my visit's going to cause turmoil."

"You're not going with the intention of starting something, are you?"

"No, but I know how my sister and mother can be when they get together. And I know my mother's told Brea that I want Lani. Truthfully, I just want to see her, maybe brush her hair. I just want to be close to her. I'm tired of fighting. It's all I've been doing since Jasper died."

"I know."

"The funny thing is, I wouldn't have had to if I'd had a job, independence, money. I wouldn't have had to struggle so much. I would've been able to provide a stable life and a comfortable home for Jay, and I would've had the money to hire an attorney immediately. I never realized what freedom independence provides."

Gigi patted her on the back. "Have a good time, and go see your daughter."

Daisy helped Ms. Christine set the dinner table, admiring the delicate bone and floral china, which had been passed down through the generations. Inhaling the fruity scent of the place, she felt warm. Her parents' house had always smelled like apples. She smiled. It was good to be home.

Her father walked into the dining room. Daisy kissed him on the cheek. "Hi, Pop." She ran her fingers over his graying hair.

"Wisdom. That's all wisdom, baby," he chuckled, and kissed her on the forehead. "It's good to have you back." He turned his attention to Ms. Christine. "Chris, have you talked to Brea and Phillip? He's supposed to bring the beer. You know the fight's on later."

"No, but they'd better hurry. They're bringing pumpkin pie."

Daisy wrinkled her nose. "Pumpkin pie? We don't eat pumpkin pie."

Her parents laughed.

"We do today," Ms. Christine said. "Lani made it. She watched a Thanksgiving special on TV, and now she's convinced that we have to have one."

"Lani made it?"

"Oh, yeah. Lani's a little chef already. We can't keep her out of the kitchen."

"Wow," Daisy breathed, realizing that she hardly knew anything about her daughter.

Mr. Parker stuffed tobacco in his old pipe.

"Oh, Dad . . . do you have to smoke in here?"

"We're having smoked turkey, right? If the turkey can smoke, why can't I?"

"It's okay," Ms. Christine said. "I don't mind, really. He'll just do it over there." She pointed out the window toward the neighbor's backyard.

Everyone laughed.

"Dai-sy," Mr. Parker sang in his baritone voice. "Guess who's coming to dinner."

The room grew silent.

"I don't know. Who?"

Ms. Christine shook her head.

"Seems like it's not a secret around here. Guess I'm the only one who doesn't know."

Ms. Christine whistled and looked in the other direction.

"I don't know," Daisy said with a shrug. "I don't know. I hope you don't expect me to sit here and call out names. Tell me, Ma."

The doorbell rang. Mr. Parker looked at his watch.

"Right on time. Always did like a fella who's punctual."

Fella? "Ma, who's Dad talking about?"

"I don't know. Why don't you go answer it?"

Daisy opened the door to find Adonis standing there with flowers in one hand and a bottle of wine in the other. She stood motionless as he handed her the flowers.

"These are for you," he murmured. He stole a kiss, then stepped inside the house. She shadowed him as he made a beeline to the dining room, as if he knew the layout of her parents' house.

"And this is for you," he said, handing the bottle to Ms. Christine.

Ms. Christine kissed him on the cheek. "Before you leave, baby, make sure you get the pecan pie I made for your mother."

Adonis grinned. "Sure, Ma."

Daisy stood in the doorway and watched in amazement. *Ma? He's calling my mother Ma? When did they all become so friendly?*

"How ya doin', boy?" Mr. Parker asked.

"Fine. And yourself?"

"Not too bad."

"Oh, I didn't forget you either," Adonis added. He reached into his coat pocket and slipped Mr. Parker a small purple-and-gold bag.

Mr. Parker held it up proudly. "Crown Royal, hunh? Oh, yeah . . . you're trying to get on my good side. You know it's my favorite. Are you staying for the game? Who's your team?"

"Let them talk," Ms. Christine said to Daisy. "Go in the kitchen and check on the food. And hand me those flowers so I can put them in some water." Ms. Christine turned to the men again. "And you two go on outside and talk."

Daisy cut her eyes at Ms. Christine. "I'll be back to talk to you in a few, Ma."

Ms. Christine laughed. "I just bet you will."

———————

Daisy sat on the porch and heard Adonis out. Marcus had unknowingly lied. Adonis had broken off his engagement months before he and Daisy had gotten involved.

"So you're positive you're not seeing Christy?"

Adonis laughed. "You say that as if you know her. But, yes, I'm positive I'm not seeing her. As a matter of fact, she's involved in a serious relationship with someone else. I think they're getting married. We're still friends, though. We didn't break up on a bad note; we just didn't love each other anymore. I work in New York, and she works in Seattle. It never would've worked, anyway. But I don't want to talk about her. I want to talk about you. So are you still mad at me?"

"No, I'm mad at myself." Daisy looked at him and got lost in his deep eyes.

Adonis flashed his killer smile. "Can we kiss and make up?"

Daisy didn't answer. She just grabbed him and kissed him passionately, hungrily, as if he were her last meal. She'd never needed him so badly. It seemed as if he had a way of stepping in just when she felt as if her world were crumbling. "We can continue this later."

"Yes, we can. I have a room on the beach. It's cold out, but we can have our own hot summer indoors." He kissed her again.

"Daisy?" a familiar voice called out from the sidewalk.

Daisy looked over Adonis's shoulder, and her breath caught in her throat as she recognized the caramel-colored complexion, the wavy, light-brown hair, and the football-player build. "Oh, shit," she mumbled.

Adonis turned around. "Calvin? Calvin Harris?"

Daisy stood with her mouth open. She wished she could disappear, evaporate in the wind, when she saw Adonis walk toward Calvin.

Adonis looked at Daisy curiously, then he gave Calvin a brotherly hug and a fraternity handshake. "What's up, man? Nice to see you. What brings you here?"

"I dropped by hoping I could see my daughter."

"Oh, I didn't realize you had a daughter. I didn't know you used to mess with Brea—"

"I didn't. I have a daughter with Daisy. She didn't tell you?"

Daisy ran into the house, slammed the door, and locked it.

13

*D*aisy woke up, instantly stiffening as she took in her surroundings. She didn't know where she was. She didn't recognize the bedroom furniture, or the decor. She waited in vain for
it to register. *Great.* She sat up and squeezed her head as the
blood rushed, her temples banging without end.

"Not too fast, Daisy. Don't sit up so fast," Ms. Christine said,
sitting down on the edge of the bed.

"Hi, Ma." Daisy smiled, then gritted her teeth. "Yuck. My
mouth is tart."

Ms. Christine laughed. "You tellin' me?" She kissed Daisy on
the cheek. "How do you feel?"

"Confused. I don't know where I am."

"You're still here, baby. You're in Brea's old room. I redeco-
rated it. That's probably why you don't recognize it."

Daisy snapped her fingers, but her recollection was foggy. She didn't remember lying down, but took some comfort in knowing that her mind hadn't completely failed her.

"So, how long have I been here?"

"Not that long. A couple of days."

Daisy leapt out of bed. "A couple of days! What about Jay? My job?"

Ms. Christine patted the spot beside her. "Sit down, Daisy. Please. You're scaring me."

"I feel like I've been in a coma or something," Daisy said, doing as her mother asked. "I woke up and I didn't—two whole days?"

"Almost three, really."

Daisy started to stand up again, but Ms. Christine held on to her and started smoothing her hair. "Ssh . . . let me finish before you speak. You were under so much pressure. I would've broken down too. We can only endure so much, you know?"

Daisy nodded, calming in the safety of her mother's arms. "I know. It just bothers me because my memory's faint."

"You really don't remember everything, do you?"

"No. The last thing I remember is running into the house."

Ms. Christine shook her head and covered her mouth with her hand. "It was ugly, Daisy. Your father and I tried to keep you in the house, but you insisted. So, what was I to do except follow you to make sure that you were okay?" Ms. Christine shrugged. "You're a grown woman—a Parker. You can be headstrong."

"I know."

"Well, you ran right up to Calvin and stood your ground. You weren't loud or obnoxious, either. You weren't putting on a show. Your demeanor was cool—cold, in fact. You kind of reminded me of thunder rumbling in the distance, letting you know the storm's coming. And you called that boy some names I didn't think you knew." Ms. Christine laughed. "You get that from your father's side."

"What did he say?"

"Nobody said anything. I think we were all too stunned. You were always a meek child, and you grew into a nonconfrontational woman . . . at least I thought so."

Daisy laughed. "Anything with teeth will bite, Ma, if pushed."

"You got that right," her mother chuckled. "Because baby, you were ready to bite that night. And I have to admit, as ugly as that whole situation was, I was proud of you. It made me realize that just because you're my youngest child doesn't mean you're a baby. And I know I've babied you. But not anymore. I'm going to let go of my little girl now and let you be the woman you are. You're an adult, and you can make the decision about keeping Lani on your own. I've done all that I can do as a mother."

"Oh, Ma. You did a great job."

Ms. Christine smiled. "I know, and you will too. Because I *knew* that night that you were a mother. You told Calvin that if he ever breathed another word about custody, you'd slit him from his temples to his toes. Your daddy and I laughed about that for days. We shouldn't have, I know, but Lord have mercy!"

Daisy held her head. "I must've made a fool out of myself. And Adonis—"

"Don't worry about Adonis. He had his say too. He was quiet throughout most of it, and I don't blame him for that. How else was he supposed to get any answers? Anyway, you were on your way back into the house when Calvin made the mistake of saying that you weren't a mother. Adonis politely but severely corrected him and told him that you were a damn good mother."

"Really?"

"Yes, he did."

Daisy started to feel better as she looked at Ms. Christine's smiling face. "But you make it sound so comical. If it was so funny . . . I don't understand how I had a nervous breakdown."

"Well, it wasn't funny at the time. Everyone who was out there that night was hurt in some form or fashion. Especially you. I knew you were angry with Calvin, and that you were embarrassed that Adonis found out about Lani the way he did, but when you threatened to kill Calvin, I realized you were broken."

"Kill Calvin? I threatened to kill him?"

A faint smile came to Ms. Christine's face. "Yes, in an old-fashioned way. I hadn't heard that threat in a long, long time. You told him that if he uttered one more word, he'd be pushing up daisies."

"Fertilizer, six feet under. Why? What did he say to make me threaten him?"

"Nothing. Brea pulled up with Lani, and then she sped off when she saw what was happening. That's when you lost it."

Daisy nodded. "I remember that part. That's when Adonis and Calvin walked off together."

Someone knocked on the bedroom door.

Gigi stuck her head in the room. "Am I interrupting?"

Daisy felt horrible but smiled. "I didn't know you were here."

Ms. Christine stood up and kissed the top of Daisy's head. "I'll be downstairs fixing something to eat."

"Last-minute trip. I was at my mother's for Thanksgiving. I wasn't planning to go, but she insisted. I arrived just in time for dinner. But enough about me. Are you feeling better?" Gigi sat down.

"Yes. Just a little worried about my job, and Jay."

Gigi dismissed her with a wave. "Girl, you know Ms. Christine took care of everything. She talked to Mr. Wiles, and she found a way to get you a prescription. I don't know how she got so re-sourceful, but she is."

"She's a woman." Daisy laughed. "We're all resourceful when we need to be. Multitasking is our job."

"Yes, I guess you're right. Oh, by the way . . . Ming Li's had dozens of flowers delivered to you. I moved them downstairs be-cause it was starting to look like a funeral parlor in here. I didn't like how it felt."

"Flowers? Ming Li?"

"Weird, hunh? I don't know what's gotten into her. I called her and told her that you were ill, and she started crying."

"Ming Li doesn't cry."

"I know. That's what was strange. The only time I've known her to cry is when she told us about Jonathan."

"What do you think it is?"

"I don't know." Gigi shrugged. "But it must be something se-rious. I haven't been able to catch up with her since. She hasn't been in the shop, she doesn't answer her phone or her door, and she's not returning calls."

14

*U*p to her elbows in dirt, Daisy searched for roots, groaning when her fingers touched the tangles buried deep within the soil. Untangling the mess would be as intricate a task as sorting and fixing her problems. Faint memories of Thanksgiving surfaced and began tormenting her again. With Jay gone, and after only a glimpse of Lani, Daisy missed not only her kids, but also the dreams of the future she might have had with Adonis.

The entire degrading scene surfaced and played over and over in her mind. Adonis's angry glare, when he'd found out about Lani, had penetrated her. She'd had no answer when he'd asked her why she'd hidden her own child from him. All she'd managed to say was "Sorry."

Daisy's eyes misted as certain memories seemed to come back with full force: things Ms. Christine had neglected to tell her. Calvin's words "Oh, you had her too?" had made her feel loose,

137

even whorish. Wearily, she wiped the sweat from her forehead, trying to erase the pain that she'd caused at the same time. She dug deeper into the soil, wishing she had stayed in the safety of her parents' home. If she had, she wouldn't have had to watch her dream man walk away in her nightmare.

Daisy's pulse tripled. *Not now.* She yanked her hands out of the dirt and stood up, holding a clump of roots. *Damn it.* She paced. She needed to move. Everything was closing in on her: the walls, the plants, the heat.

"I need air," she muttered, and hurried out of the building.

Once outside, she gasped as if she were choking and tried to slow her breathing. The cold air helped. Still, she couldn't manage the anxiety. Everything seemed to be going too fast, and she couldn't catch up. After returning to work, she'd gone into overdrive, working as many as fourteen hours a day. She'd been working too hard, worrying too much—doing too many toos.

She retrieved the small prescription bottle from her pocket, bit one of the tiny birth-control-sized pills in two, and swallowed half. No way could she function at work on a whole Xanax. She squatted and waited for the medicine to kick in.

"How's it going, Daisy?"

She looked up to see Mr. Wiles's cheery face.

"Fine," Daisy lied.

"Do you have a moment to spare? I'd like to talk to you about something. How 'bout we grab a cup of coffee?"

"Sure," she said, although she wanted to say no. *I don't have a moment, or a minute, not even a second. But I do have anxiety to spare.* "Just let me grab my purse."

Daisy walked alongside Mr. Wiles, hoping he hadn't noticed her restlessness. She had missed a considerable number of days at work, and she'd forgotten to ask Ms. Christine what excuse she'd used to cover for her. *Now I have to worry about calming down* and *my mother's lie. How am I supposed to do that?*

Mr. Wiles sat across from her at the Corner Café and drank a large black coffee, while Daisy sipped a decaffeinated cream-

and-sugar. She didn't notice the clinking of cups. The whirring sound of the cappuccino machine. Mr. Wiles's eyes on her. Her medication had taken effect and begun to lullaby her.

Mr. Wiles cleared his throat.

"I'm sorry. Did you say something, Mr. Wiles?"

Mr. Wiles smiled. "No, but I'm a little curious about something." He set his cup down and wiped his mouth with a napkin. "Can I ask you a personal question?"

Daisy nodded vaguely.

"Before I ask, I want you to know that I haven't been prying, or even inquiring. But your hours have been brought to my attention a *few* times."

"My hours?"

"Yes, the outrageous hours that you work." He laughed. "I'm not complaining, believe me. What employer doesn't want a dedicated employee? I'm just wondering why you work so much."

Daisy shrugged. She hadn't thought it would be that obvious. "I need the money."

"But you're on salary. There's no overtime."

"I know."

"Daisy, is there something wrong? You can tell me. Don't think of me as just a boss; consider me a friend."

Daisy wanted to confide in Mr. Wiles. She wanted to tell him about her harsh reality, but she couldn't. No matter how much he wanted to be her friend, the bottom line was that he was her boss. The last thing she wanted him to know was that he had an unstable employee with more problems than answers.

"I'm okay, Mr. Wiles. Really."

"Remember, Daisy, I'm a father too. I know when something is wrong."

"I just need to find an apartment, that's all. It's not the easiest thing to do around here."

Mr. Wiles slapped his hand on the table and laughed heartily. "That's it? Why didn't you just say so?"

What the hell's so funny?

"I have the perfect place for you. A nice little place off River-side Drive—"

Daisy cut him off with a shake of her head. "I wouldn't be able to afford the down payment, let alone the rent."

"I didn't say it was *on* Riverside. Anyway, it belongs to my son Jacob. He's going on a yearlong sabbatical, and he needs to sublet it to someone. I'll talk to him for you."

Daisy grinned. "That'd be great."

"Good," Mr. Wiles said, standing up. "Then it's all taken care of. One more thing . . . there's this training—an apprenticeship program that I think would be good for you. When I get more details, I'll give them to you." He downed the last of his coffee. "Well, I have a few meetings left. Why don't you take the rest of the day off? And I'm sorry about your brother Rufus. My condolences."

———————

As Daisy walked into the house, she heard the dull hum of the vacuum cleaner in the distance. She smiled as she looked around. The furniture and paintings had been rearranged, a new rug had been laid, and candles were burning. She sat down on the salmon, slip-covered damask sofa and fingered the matching pillows. *Ma definitely leaves her mark,* she thought with laughing eyes. She was happy that Ms. Christine was visiting.

"Hey, baby. What are you doing home so soon?"

"Mr. Wiles let me off early because I've been working too much. Oh . . . and he said the funniest thing today."

"What did he say?"

"He said he was sorry to hear about my brother Rufus."

Ms. Christine laughed.

"Ma, Rufus was our dog, not my brother."

"I never said he was your brother. I told him that we'd lost our baby boy. Rufus was the younger of our two dogs."

"Rufus died almost fifteen years ago, Ma."

"And I also never said when. Look, Daisy, I did what I had to do. You still have a job, right?"

Daisy shook her head and laughed. "Right. It's not exactly how I would've handled it, but I was in no position to do it. Thanks again."

"You're welcome, baby. Oh, that Mr. Burgess called—"

Daisy sat up straighter. "Kenneth? What did he say?"

"He needs more time. I don't know about him, Daisy. I don't trust him. He was Jasper's attorney, and I have a strong feeling that he knows more than he's saying."

"Of course he does. He told me there are things that he can't tell me."

"You should get a good family attorney, that's what you should do."

"I can't afford one. Not now. Unless I can sell my Jeep quickly."

"You can. I already have a buyer."

"Who?"

"Me."

"Ma, you and Dad already have three cars."

"That old red one isn't a car, it's a 1976 get-out-and-push. And besides, I need a car when I'm here, and you need the money. So give me the title, and I'll write you a check."

"I don't know . . ."

"Well, look at it this way. I won't give you the money that you need. I worked too hard for my money to give it away. But I will pay you for the Jeep, and you can buy it back from me later."

"How much choice do I have, anyway?"

"Not much."

The telephone rang, and Ms. Christine moved to answer it.

Daisy sat at the kitchen table, her attention drifting from her mother's conversation to thoughts of Jay. She knew that selling the Jeep was the only way she'd be able to obtain the services of a good lawyer. She sighed, feeling as if she were coming down from a mental and physical high. Exhaustion crept in, and her eyelids became heavy. Her body and mind wanted to relax, but she couldn't. There was still too much to do.

"You ready?" Ms. Christine asked.

"For what?"

Ms. Christine put on her jacket and grabbed her purse from the back of a chair. "That was Edmund."

"Who?"

"Oh, I'm sorry. Mr. Wiles. His said I should call him Edmund. He's such a gentleman."

"What did he say?"

"He said that we can go to his son's place now. I didn't know that he was going to rent you his place while he's away. It's so wonderful that he's going on sabbatical. He's a professor, you know. What a wonderful . . ."

Ms. Christine was still talking as they made their way to the car. As much as Daisy loved her mother, she was starting to get on her nerves. One could only tolerate so much chat. *I know I should be thankful that she's here to help, but damn, I swear she's going to burst my eardrums.*

———————

Daisy drove a little faster than usual. She didn't want to keep Jacob waiting, and she wasn't about to give Ms. Christine a chance to start talking nonstop again. She was already on edge, and she didn't want to risk snapping at her mother and putting another wedge between them. She turned on the radio and surfed through the channels, then thought better of it and turned it off. She remembered that Ms. Christine was also a singer, or thought that she was.

Then it came to her. She knew how to keep Ms. Christine quiet: give her the opportunity to eavesdrop. Adjusting her earpiece, Daisy flipped her cell phone open and dialed Ming Li. She hadn't heard from her in a while and, like Gigi, was getting worried. It wasn't like Ming Li to disappear.

"Hello?" Daisy said into the phone after she didn't hear a ring. "Hello?" She heard someone breathing on the other end of the line.

"Mom?" Jay whispered.

"Jay? Is that you, baby?" Relief, sadness, and happiness spread through her at once. She pulled over immediately, wanting to give Jay her undivided attention. Just the sound of his voice brought her comfort. She paid no attention to Ms. Christine, who'd grabbed the door handle to steady herself. Daisy didn't hear the blaring horns of the cars behind her. She'd almost caused an accident and wasn't even aware of it. "Is it really you?"

"Yes."

Daisy opened her door and got out, practically skipping as she talked. "Oh, baby. How are you? Where are you?"

"I'm okay. I'm at some strange people's house. I don't know them."

"What? Whose house? You mean your dad's parents?"

"No, some other people. The lady that came and got me from school brought me here. Me and two other kids. When are you coming to get me? You told me that you weren't going to leave me, ever."

"As soon as I can, baby. I'm doing everything possible to get you back. I'm so sorry that you've had to go through this. But I want you to know that I didn't leave you, Jay. I'd never leave you. Okay? I love you."

"I love you too, Mom. I gotta go. I'm not supposed to be on the phone."

"Okay, baby. But do you know where you are—the address?"

The line clicked off.

Daisy leaned against the front of the Jeep and tried to summon her strength. Jay's voice dominated her thoughts. "He's in foster care." She banged her fist and swallowed hard. "My poor baby."

"Are you okay?" Ms. Christine asked, her window rolled down.

"No. That Social Services bitch put Jay in fuckin' foster care like he's homeless or something," Daisy spat, too upset to watch her language in front of her mother.

Ms. Christine hopped out of the passenger side. "She did *what?* Oh, hell no! Not *my* grandson—no, she didn't. Come on, baby. We have a lot of work to do. We can cry later. I guess they don't know who they're dealing with. We're Parkers. We may bend, but we don't break."

"What can we do?"

"First, we get this apartment. That's the most important thing, having a place for Jay to stay. Then we get the lawyer, and you gather your check stubs and paperwork. We'll handle it. I don't give a damn how much it costs. When there's no bridge, you build one."

———————

Daisy and Ms. Christine slipped into the apartment building as someone walked out. Daisy had wanted to ring the bell, but Ms. Christine had insisted that they go in on their own and check out the whole building without interference from Jacob.

"It's better to see for yourself," she'd said. "That way, you can take your time and not miss anything. You don't want anyone rushing you."

After they'd inspected all ten floors, Daisy stood in front of Jacob's apartment. She pulled a note from the door. He'd had to leave for a few minutes, and he'd instructed them to go on in.

"It must be pretty safe around here," she said to her mother as they stepped inside.

"And he must trust us. I wouldn't just let some stranger walk into my house when I wasn't home."

Daisy walked through the large apartment. She'd decided to work her way from the back to the front. She could tell that Jacob Wiles was a bachelor by his sparse furniture, almost empty kitchen cupboards, and the overall lack of detail that a feminine touch would have provided.

Daisy smirked at her own thoughts. She was supposed to be checking out the place, not the man. Still, she couldn't help it. She picked up a picture from a distressed dresser, wondering if it was of Jacob. Something about this man she hadn't yet met was intriguing. She couldn't quite put her finger on it, but she knew that it had something to do with his career, and his smile—if it was him in the photo. She'd always been attracted to educated men and found herself extremely interested in meeting him all of a sudden. *I wonder what makes him tick.*

His office was in disarray, and his large bedroom seemed small because it was cluttered with books and papers. She picked up a book and nodded. *Seventeenth-century literature; he could be boring.*

She returned to the living room. Overall, the apartment was nice. Not exactly what Jay had grown accustomed to, but wonderful in comparison to their last place. The building was quiet, the neighborhood safe, and there were two bedrooms.

Daisy relaxed. She was thankful and knew that Jay would be appreciative too. *I've lucked up again.* Given her mediocre credit history, length of employment, and small salary, she would've had a hard time renting a suitable place elsewhere.

"So, what do you think?" Ms. Christine asked.

"I like it."

"I'm glad," a deep voice said from the doorway.

Daisy turned and smiled. Jacob *was* the man in the picture, only more attractive in person. He didn't look like his father, and she wondered what his ethnicity was. His complexion was a light, coppery brown. Her glance easily roamed his body. Slowly and carefully she memorized him like the alphabet. *Whew, he's beautiful!* Again she looked into his trusting, gentle hazel eyes. Marveled at his curly black hair, which was cut just above his shoulders, giving him a boyish look. She wondered if he made women's toes curl like his locks, then smiled. *Not bad at all. But a definite no-no.*

"Oh, I'm sorry. I didn't hear you come in. I'm Daisy Parker. It's nice to meet you."

Jacob grinned and shook her hand. She melted. "It's nice to meet you too, Ms. Daisy Parker. It is *Ms.,* isn't it?" He held her hand a moment too long.

"Yes, it is." She didn't pull away.

Jacob turned his attention to Ms. Christine. "Oh, hello."

"Hello." Ms. Christine nodded. "You have a nice place here. Seems my daughter likes it too." She shot Daisy an I-see-you-checking-him-out look.

"So, Ms. Daisy Parker, are you interested?"

Daisy laughed flirtatiously and wondered if he was asking about himself or his place. "Yes, as interested as I can possibly be. I want it."

"It's yours."

"That easy?"

"Why, should it be difficult? I have a need, and so do you. We can blame it on economics—supply and demand."

Daisy licked her lips. "Yes, economics."

"I'm sorry, do you two want me to leave?" Ms. Christine chuckled.

"No, please stay," Jacob said.

"So how much is the rent, Jacob?"

"Just the monthly maintenance fee." He grabbed a pen and paper, jotted something down, and handed it to Daisy.

"You're just like your father," she said. "He writes down all of his figures." She handed the paper to Ms. Christine. "I'll take it."

"And dinner too?" Jacob asked.

"With or without dessert?"

Ms. Christine stood. "Okay, that's enough. I *am* sitting in this room—"

"Ma, we're talking about food."

"Mmm-hmm. I know. I'm old, but I'm not deaf. I can hear what you're really saying. It was nice to meet you, Jacob." Ms. Christine headed toward the front door, then turned to Daisy and whispered, "Don't be foolish. What looks good to you may not be good for you. Too much to risk, and maybe nothing to gain. Remember, he's going away for a year."

———————

Daisy hummed as she covered her body in shimmering pear-scented lotion. It had been a while since she'd been in the company of a man, and she intended not only to look her best, but smell edible. Despite Ms. Christine's protests, she had agreed to meet Jacob for dinner. She needed to be wined, dined, and entertained as much as she wanted to be in his presence.

Since that first meeting, she had thought of him constantly. She hadn't felt so full of desire since Adonis. Licking her lips, she stood in front of the mirror and shimmied into a hips-ass-and-breasts red dress, as Ming Li liked to call formfitting clothes. She tousled her hair and put on translucent red lip-gloss. She puckered and blew herself a kiss.

"Ma, I'm leaving!" she hollered, running down the stairs.

Ms. Christine emerged from the kitchen. "Okay. But I still don't think you should go."

"Why?"

"You know why. Plus, there are other reasons."

Daisy kissed Ms. Christine on the cheek. "I'll see you later."

"Adonis called."

Daisy turned. "What?"

"He said he was going to—"

"Never mind, Ma. I'm not ready to deal with that now. I'll see you soon."

"Okay, but don't blame me when—"

"Love you!" Daisy called back as she walked out.

———————

Daisy glanced at her watch. It was only 7:35, and she wasn't supposed to meet Jacob until eight. She'd decided to arrive before him because she hated the feeling of being watched when she walked into a room. As she walked down Bleecker Street, the whipping wind stung her skin and blew her dress against her legs. She drew her charcoal-gray wool wrap tighter around her. It was hard to be cold and cute at the same time.

"Finally," she said, as she entered Agozar's, a cozy, trendy Cuban restaurant.

She sat on one of the colorful, padded barstools facing the entrance, ordered a Pasión de Agozar, and took in the atmosphere. The warm, gold-toned walls seemed to dance in the illumination of the flickering candles. Red and moss-green fabrics seemed to announce the upcoming holiday season. Cuban beats coupled with African drums made the standing crowd move with a slight bounce. The seated onlookers were tapping their feet.

Daisy closed her eyes and swayed to the music. She understood little Spanish but knew enough to tell that it was a song about love, and maybe loss. It had an "I'm sorry" quality to it. Feeling a presence looming over her, she opened her eyes. And froze.

Adonis was standing next to her, sandwiched between her

barstool and the one beside her. His leg was touching her thigh, his eyes sucking her in.

"Would you like another?" he asked, pointing to her drink.

Daisy dropped her gaze guiltily. "I'm okay. Thanks anyway." She checked her watch again: 7:50. *Damn. Jacob could show up any minute.*

"You look exceptionally nice. You meeting someone?"

Daisy pretended to be immersed in the hypnotic flow of the music. He could ask her anything else, but not that.

"Well?" he persisted.

"No. Yes. No. Listen, I have to go to the bathroom. I'll be back." She gaited toward the ladies' room to call Jacob.

In the bathroom, she hesitated. What excuse could she come up with? She dialed his cell number and prayed that he wasn't close to the restaurant. She breathed a sigh of relief when his voice mail came on.

"Hi, Jacob, it's Daisy. I'm at Agozar's, and I can't stay. Something unexpected's come up. I'm so sorry. I'll explain later, and I hope you'll allow me to make it up to you."

She walked out of the bathroom and checked her watch again: 7:55. She slowed her pace and paused to see if Jacob had arrived. *Good.* He was nowhere in sight. She searched for Adonis. If his back was turned, she could make a clean getaway and avoid his questions. She spotted him sitting at the bar, facing the bartender. She held her breath, snaked easily—guiltily— through the crowd, and slipped out the door. Once outside, she tried to blend in with the people walking down the street.

Then a hand touched her shoulder.

Oh, God. She turned, praying it wasn't Jacob or Adonis. No such luck.

"You were just going to leave me?" Adonis asked, his eyes piercing hers.

Her phone rang. Daisy ignored it, fearing that it would be Jacob. "Well?"

"Well, what?"

"Aren't you going to answer?"

She didn't know if he was referring to himself or her cell

phone, which still hadn't stopped ringing. Whoever it was must have wanted to talk to her pretty badly.

"Can we walk and talk? I'm freezing."

"My car's right around the corner. We can talk there."

"No, that's okay. My car's down the street. Why don't we meet another time—"

Adonis grabbed her by the arm and pulled her toward him. She could smell his scent, which had always weakened her. "No. I'll walk you to your car. We'll talk there."

Daisy walked meekly beside him. She felt overpowered but not frightened. His tone hadn't been threatening, only strong. He'd spoken to her as if she belonged to him, as if he still cared.

Her phone rang again. Again she ignored it.

"Why aren't you answering your phone?" Adonis asked as they approached her Jeep.

Daisy knew that she'd have to answer eventually.

"Where are your keys?" Adonis asked.

"Why?"

"Because I'm driving."

"Why do you want to drive?"

"Why not?" he replied, his bass deepening.

"Fine." Daisy reached into her purse, handed him the keys, and got into the car as he held open her door.

The phone rang again.

Adonis hopped into the driver's seat. "Daisy, just answer the damn phone! I already know you were meeting a man at the restaurant."

Daisy had never seen Adonis angry before. Silly as it was, she found his jealousy kind of cute. Reluctantly, she removed the ringing phone from her purse. She tried to look at the caller ID to see who it was.

Adonis grabbed it out of her hand, flipped it open, and handed it back to her.

She had no choice but to say hello. She sighed a breath of relief when she heard Gigi on the other end.

"What's so urgent, Gigi?" Daisy asked. "Why have you been ringing my phone off the hook?"

"I just called."

"Oh," Daisy replied, careful not to let Adonis know it hadn't been Gigi calling the whole time. "What's up?"

"Where are you?"

"I'm in the car with Adonis. Why?"

"If you two aren't busy, could you go to Ming Li's for me? She's on some sort of retreat, and someone fell in the shop. They're threatening to sue her. She needs her insurance policy faxed to her immediately. There's something wrong with my car, and I can't do it."

"Sure," Daisy said, hoping that she could create some sort of diversion at Ming Li's to throw Adonis off. "But I don't have a key anymore."

"There's a spare one in the back of the house, under the red potted plant. The papers are in her closet chest, in the third drawer."

Daisy turned to Adonis. "Emergency at Ming Li's. I have to go there, pronto."

He nodded and made a U-turn, as if he knew where he was going. She wanted to ask him how he knew where Ming Li lived, but then thought better of it. If she talked, it would open up an opportunity for a conversation that she didn't want to have.

Adonis swung a right, then a left. As he pulled up in front of Ming Li's, Daisy looked over at him, eyebrows raised. "Seems you know your way here like you know the back of your hand. I wonder why." She hopped out and started toward the back of the house.

Adonis opened his door and got out. "What the hell's that supposed to mean? You're the one with the secrets." He slammed the door shut and followed her.

Daisy took the key from under the plant and walked around him. "Like I'm the only one. I'm sure you looked up Christy while you were in L.A."

"Let's not even talk about L.A." He followed her into the house.

Daisy flicked on the lights. "Wait here," she said, then pointed to the bar. "Pour yourself a drink."

Daisy opened Ming Li's huge walk-in closet and turned on the light. There were two chests of drawers. She chose the one on the left and opened the drawer. She removed a thick stack of envelopes and sat down on the floor with them. As she searched through the envelopes for one with the name of an insurance firm on it, she noticed a pale-gold-and-navy one jutting out from the bottom of the stack. The colors instantly grabbed her attention— the same colors she'd used on the custom stationery that she'd designed for Jasper three years before.

Curiosity got the best of her. She pulled it out of the stack and glanced at the handwriting on the front. Her hand flew to her mouth. It was Jasper's, and it was addressed to Ming Li.

She held it up to the light and studied the postmark. *Almost two years ago. Why would Jasper write to Ming Li? All of their business was done through me.* Daisy opened it and read it out loud.

> Ming Li,
> You've been on my mind all day. I wish you'd stop playing these games, because you're driving me crazy. Every time I see you I just want to touch you, lick you, and taste you. Again. I want to give you what you can never seem to get enough of. You know you want me as badly as I want you. How could we not want each other, after all we've done for each other, with each other, and to each other? Damn, I miss you. But I've solved our problem, at least temporarily.
>
> I've arranged for us to be together. I've enclosed a roundtrip plane ticket for you to meet me in Philly. It's only a one-hour flight. I'd hate for you to have to drive, and then end up being too tired to do what only you know how to do.
>
> I love you,
> Jasper.
>
> PS. I'll see you at the airport. And don't worry about Daisy. She'll never know.

Daisy hung her head and cried. "You nasty bitch!" she bellowed, throwing the letter on the floor.

"You okay?"

Daisy turned to see Adonis standing in the doorway, holding two drinks in his hands. She shook her head.

"I heard it all. I was bringing you a drink."

Daisy got up from the floor and stepped out of the closet. Without uttering a word, she took off her red dress and shoes and handed them to Adonis. In her bra and panties, she speed-walked to the laundry room, with Adonis right on her heels. She grabbed a full gallon of bleach and headed to the living room. She twisted off the cap, sniffed the powerful liquid, then doused Ming Li's velvet sofas, ottoman, and her rugs.

When Adonis called her name, she glared at him. He quickly stepped out of her path.

She returned to the bedroom, opened Ming Li's drawers, and bleached the contents. Satisfied, she turned her attention to the bed. Then she went to the closet to finish off the rest of Ming Li's clothes.

15

*D*aisy sat in Adonis's living room, her glare glued to the wall. Her staggered thoughts inebriated her senses, catapulted her into oblivion, rapt in wonder. Her genesis and the revelation became clearer with every stroke of the clock's second hand. Repetitive. *My truth, the lie. My truth, their lie. My truth was a lie.* She vise-gripped the cup of chamomile, ignoring the pricking in her fingers, the numbness traveling through her hands. Inhaling deeply, she welcomed the anger that had ravished her the night before, robbed her of sleep. She'd tossed and turned, but couldn't avoid the nightmares. Dreams of Ming Li and Jasper making love had tormented her. The thought of them tangled and wound together like a pretzel made her stomach churn. Two people she'd loved and trusted had hurt her beyond repair. *How many daggers must I pull out of my back?*

With all that she'd discovered about Jasper, another betrayal wouldn't have surprised her much. But that Ming Li could have done such a thing, despite her insatiability, had caught Daisy completely off guard. She knew that Ming Li didn't care whether the men she slept with were attached, but she'd never expected her to cross the line with Jasper. *All that time I thought she hated him, and she was making love to him.*

The tea started to crawl its way back up her throat. Jasper had gone down on Ming Li. He'd tasted her friend, and Daisy had kissed him. Suddenly, the imaginary essence of Ming Li was in her mouth. She could taste her as sure as she was sitting there. Daisy gagged and ran for the bathroom, colliding with Adonis along the way.

"Are you okay?" he asked, rubbing her back when she finally got up from the bathroom floor and moved to the sink.

Daisy nodded, but she wished she could erase the nightmare that had been realized in her mouth. She looked at Adonis. He'd been great the night before; quiet, but supportive. He hadn't pried or rubbed anything in. Best of all, he had never questioned what she had done.

"Why don't you lie down," he suggested, wetting a towel under the faucet.

"I'm not sick—physically." Daisy threw back a shot of Scope as if it were liquor and gargled.

"I know," he said, wiping. "But it may help."

"Why are you being so nice? I don't deserve it, not after what I put you through."

"You just don't get it, do you?"

"Get what? I guess I don't get it, since I'm questioning it."

Adonis looked Daisy over from head to toe, then focused on her eyes. "I care about you. I love—"

Daisy held up her hand. "Don't say it. Don't say that you love me. Just about everyone who's said that . . . everyone who I *thought* loved me, has shown me otherwise. They wrapped a bow around bullshit and I accepted it as a gift. So, guess what? I don't believe in taking unwarranted presents anymore. I don't do love anymore. I can't take bullshit."

Adonis grabbed her firmly by the shoulders, and the expression on his face was even harder. "Damn it! Stop this. Stop the woe-is-me thing. You can't hold everyone accountable for the actions of a couple of assholes. I won't live in Jasper's shadow."

Daisy held her breath. Claustrophobia snatched her, and the bathroom was becoming too small. She tried to wiggle from Adonis's grasp. "I can't breathe."

Adonis released her. "No, Daisy. *I* can't breathe. You won't let me. You've been trying to make me into someone I'm not. Some*thing* I'm not. You've boxed me into this little world that you've created, and you're wrong."

Daisy regained her composure. "No, I haven't. I haven't treated you like that . . . like you were someone else."

Adonis walked out of the bathroom with Daisy on his heels. "Bullshit!" The bass in his voice deepened with his anger.

She followed him into the bedroom. "What do you mean?"

"Just what I said. You said you can't take the bullshit anymore, but that's a lie. You deal out bullshit. From the day you walked in here, you were full of it. I treated you like a woman—I respected you. But I got unspoken lies in return. You don't respect me as a man. You never told me about you and Calvin, or about having a daughter. And now look at you. I see you sitting at a bar, all dressed up, looking good for someone else."

Daisy stared at the floor, silenced by the truth. She couldn't defend herself. She knew she was wrong; she'd been wrong all along.

She tried to think of what she could say, but knew that dishonest words were empty. "I was afraid," she finally admitted. "I'd held my secret for so long." A tear streamed down her face. "I lied and pretended for so many years that my lies became the truth, even to me. In my mind, my daughter had become my sister's daughter. Until recently. When I saw you again, and I knew that you felt the same way about me as I felt about you, I didn't want to mess it up. I wanted you that badly. It ate at me . . . the guilt. I wanted to tell you about Calvin."

"You could have." Adonis lifted her chin, forcing her eyes to meet his. "I wanted you for who you are. I accept you for you. I wouldn't have judged you."

"Now you're the one who doesn't get it. I had judged myself."

"I believe you. But what about the man you were meeting? I know you had a date—"

"How? Oh, never mind. It was nothing. Just dinner—"

"The truth, Daisy."

"That is the truth."

Adonis shook his head. "And you put this on for him?" He gently slid his hand under her shoulder strap and eased it down. He kissed her collarbone. "Why do you have to be so complex? Just give in." He kissed her again.

Daisy pulled away. Adonis was being sincere, but *she* was still hiding something: her attraction to Jacob. "I can't. I had on these clothes yesterday. I slept in them. I haven't bathed."

"Didn't I just tell you that I want you? That I accept you as you are?"

Daisy nodded.

"Well, let me." He cupped her chin and kissed her, his tongue exploring her mouth—then her body. Before Daisy knew it, he had journeyed to places and depths that only he could.

———————

Daisy awoke in his arms. Feeling his warmth and his muscular form against her back, she scooted closer until there wasn't an inch between them. Adonis tightened his hold as though he never wanted to let go, and a soft moan escaped her. *If I can just stay here forever . . .* She closed her eyes and relished the moment. It felt good to be held, and wanted. Enjoyed. A smile broadened on her face as she thought about the way Adonis had loved her, how good he'd looked while having her. His focused expression, the glimmer in his eyes, had almost made her believe that she was better than anything else he'd ever had. She could still hear him calling her name, and the sexual muskiness still permeated the room. Their juices smelled sweet to her. Delicious. She was almost certain that when they'd kissed, they'd exchanged pieces of their souls.

She reached behind her and rubbed his leg. She wanted him to wake up, to give her more.

The telephone rang, and Adonis stirred.

Daisy sighed in disappointment. She had wanted to be the reason he awoke.

He looked at the clock. "Can you pass me the phone?"

She handed him the cordless, then climbed out of bed and went to check her cell for messages. She input her password, praying that Jacob hadn't called. The last thing she'd expected was to hear Kenneth Burgess's voice greeting her ears, insisting that they needed to meet immediately at his office. It was urgent, he said.

She ran into the bedroom as she dialed his number and picked up her dress from the floor.

"This is Daisy Parker," she said to the receptionist, who immediately put her on hold to transfer the call. *Must be important. She didn't even have time to announce my call.*

Kenneth's voice came on the line in an instant. "Daisy, can you be here within the hour? There's something you need to see."

"Sure," Daisy said as she stepped into her panties. "I'll be right there."

"I'll be waiting." Kenneth hung up.

"I have to go," she said to Adonis, who was now sitting up on the edge of the bed.

"You're going out like that?"

Daisy glanced at herself in the mirror. Her hair was all over her head. Her natural complexion peekabood through her day-old makeup. She needed to shower. "Yes. I have no choice, and I don't have time to fix myself. I have to meet with the attorney. I'm nervous enough as it is. Being late will make me even more anxious. Last thing I want to do is pop a magic pill before I go in."

"I'll go with you. Just jump in the shower for a couple of minutes, while I run the iron over your dress."

Daisy sat before Kenneth's desk, waiting for him to get off the phone. She looked over at Adonis, who was sitting in the chair next to her, and grabbed his hand. She was glad that he'd accompanied her. She'd been waiting a long time for Kenneth to call about Jay's case, but now she was afraid to hear the news. The word *urgent* had scared her to death.

Kenneth hung up and introduced himself to Adonis before turning his attention to Daisy. "I apologize for making you wait." He walked over to a table on the opposite side of the room and grabbed a file. "This is the reason I wanted you to come in. Jasper gave me this a long time ago with specific instructions. I'm sorry I didn't bring it up to you earlier, but I couldn't." He paused, looked at Adonis. "Do you mind stepping out of the room? Attorney/client privilege."

"I want him to stay. I need him to," Daisy said.

Kenneth shook his head. "As I said, Jasper left detailed instructions. You and Jay are the only ones to know what's in this."

Adonis smiled and stood. "I'll be right in the reception area." He kissed Daisy on the cheek and whispered, "It'll be okay."

Once Adonis had closed the door behind him, Kenneth handed the file to Daisy. She hesitated, wondering about its contents, then slowly opened it. Instantly, she recognized Jasper's handwriting: *The next-to-the-last resort.*

"What's the last resort?"

"I'm not at liberty to say. But, if we go to court, you'll find out."

Daisy moved the first paper to the back of the file. She gasped with shock as she read the heading of the second: *DNA Labs of America.* Jay's name was on the report, and so was Jasper's. The report stated that there was a 99.98 percent chance that Jasper was Jay's father.

"I don't understand. I thought Jonathan was Jay's biological father."

"Keep reading, Daisy. This is where it gets interesting."

The second page of the DNA report stated that because Jasper and Jonathan were identical twins, there was no way to conclusively determine who fathered Jay because the men were genetically indistinguishable.

"This can't be. Is it true?"

"Yes, I'm afraid it is."

Daisy swallowed hard. She didn't know whether to believe the documents in her hands. Jasper had been sneaky; how could she trust him? "I understand the DNA part. I'm wondering if Jasper had a valid reason to have the test performed. Was he just trying to legally establish himself as Jay's father?"

"That's a good question. Turn the page."

The next page was a New Jersey address.

"What's this?"

"The address of Jay's relative on his mother's side. The woman you need to speak to is named Peaches. Evidently she has all the information."

"Peaches?"

Kenneth laughed. "Yes, that's her given name. Peaches Marie Pleasant. We didn't know where she lived, so we had to find her. That's why it took me so long to get back to you. Oh, and one other thing. Here." He handed Daisy some money. "Jasper had also left me money to handle the case. I never would've taken yours, but the file was sealed. I didn't know. Call me after you see Peaches. I can't proceed until you do."

Daisy did a final check on the freshly pruned plants, gave them one last misting of food, and headed out into the cold December breeze. She tightened her scarf and hummed an upbeat tune. She'd felt lighter, happier, since Jacob had called her earlier and asked her to come over. "No strings attached," he'd said, then went on to tell her that he'd be moving out in two days.

She smiled wider than she had in a long time. Christmastime had always been one of her favorites, and something within her felt lighter as it approached. The feeling was good, and it gave her hope for her and Jay's future.

With a few hours to kill before it was time to meet Jacob, Daisy turned onto Fifth Avenue and stopped in front of a display window at FAO Schwarz. She had no idea what Jay might want. His interest in toys had always seemed to change weekly, and since he'd been stripped from her life, she'd missed plenty. Lani, she knew, would be satisfied with a Barbie doll or two. Daisy smiled. Lani was just like her in many ways, and being easy to please was just one of them. *Well, I can't go wrong with a video game.* She followed a mass of shoppers inside the store, then bumped into the last person she wanted to collide with. Camille.

Camille, flawlessly made up, wore a full-length mink coat with matching hat and gloves. Daisy wanted to choke her for wearing Jasper's money, for unintentionally rubbing it in that she'd received the whole shebang, but Daisy refused to lower herself.

"Hello, Daisy," Camille greeted her, smiling genuinely.

Daisy paused and stared. She didn't know whether to take Camille's friendliness seriously. The woman had put her and Jay out of their own home. *But I did sleep with her husband and had him taking care of me. Hell, I gave her a run for her money and didn't even know it.*

Feeling somewhat victorious, Daisy returned the smile. "How are you, Camille?"

"Feeling lighter." She patted her stomach.

"Oh, congratulations." Daisy feigned enthusiasm. "I didn't realize that you'd had the baby. What did you have?"

"A girl. Camilla."

That figures. "How nice. Well, it was nice seeing you. I've got some shopping to do—"

Camille suddenly grabbed her by the arm. "I need to talk to you."

Daisy looked at Camille's hand on her sleeve and cleared her throat. Camille let go.

"It's important, Daisy. It's about Jay, and Jasper's mother."

They walked down the street among the Christmas shoppers. Daisy stole a glance at the woman walking beside her, anxiously waiting for Camille to speak first. What could possibly be going through her mind? Why was she being so cordial all of a sudden?

"Do you want to stop in here and grab a cup of coffee?" Camille asked, pointing to a coffee shop.

"Sure." Daisy shrugged. "Why not? It's cold out here, and I've been working all day. I could use something to warm me up."

The two of them waited silently at the counter for the waitress to take their order. The air between them was thick, too foggy for idle chitchat. They stood as though pretending not to be together—not too close, not too far apart.

Camille spoke up first and ordered two medium coffees. Coffee was exactly what Daisy wanted, but she refused to let a woman she didn't like make that decision for her. So, even though it felt juvenile, she declined the coffee and ordered a hot chocolate instead.

"Well, here we are," Camille said, sitting down at a table.

"Yes, I guess so," Daisy said, taking the chair across from her.

The minutes ticked by slowly. Daisy sipped her hot chocolate and waited. *Why the hell did she say she wants to talk to me if she's not talking?*

"I'm sorry, my mind's been somewhere else," Camille said as if reading Daisy's thoughts.

Obviously. "I see. Well, what is it you wanted to discuss?"

"You have to get him away from those people. They're horrible."

"What are you talking about, Camille? Jay's in foster care."

"No, he's not. He's with my mother-in-law."

"Can't be. I spoke to him, and he told me that he was in foster care."

Camille sighed heavily, seemingly as exasperated as Daisy. "I tell you he's not. I saw him over there just last week, when I went to drop off Christmas gifts."

Daisy hoped that Camille was mistaken. If Jay was in the custody of Jasper's parents, her fight would be even harder. They were biologically related and had more money for lawyers. "How did they get him?"

"They're loaded. You'd be surprised how money can fool people. They must've convinced someone that they were good for Jay. But they're not, I'm telling you."

"How come you're so opposed to them having Jay? I know I have my reasons; I'm just wondering about yours."

"They're terrible grandparents—terrible people. Period. You

should've seen how they treated me after Jasper died. You would've thought that I'd turned into the Antichrist or something. They treat Camilla and me as if we have something contagious. When she gets older, I'll be ashamed to tell her that they're her relatives. Lord knows they don't treat her like one."

"Camilla, too?"

Camille nodded. "Yes. When Jasper was alive, and we told them that I was pregnant, you can't imagine how much they loved me—or pretended to. But after he died and the will had been executed, that was it. They shunned me, and my child. Every now and then they call and act nice, as if they care. But it's a facade. Nothing with them is as it seems."

Daisy couldn't understand why Camille would bring them gifts if they were truly as horrible as she painted them to be. "Is it because they don't think you should've gotten all of his money and assets?"

"Are you serious?" Camille laughed. When Daisy didn't join in, Camille stared at her. "You are, aren't you? I didn't get all of anything. I got the house and his car, but that's it."

Unwilling to let Camille see the hurt that was about to surface, Daisy did her best to put on a poker face. "Jay and I didn't get a dime."

Camille's jaw dropped. "Nothing?"

"Nada."

"I'm *so* sorry. All this time I thought that you'd gotten just about everything. I never would've taken the house had I known. There's no way I would've put your son out in the cold! I was jealous. I thought that he loved you more."

Daisy laughed nervously. "No, he didn't love me at all. It's taken a while, but I've figured that out. And I'm pretty sure he didn't love Jay all that much, either. If he had, *he* wouldn't have left him out in the cold. It's not your fault. Any other wife would've done the same."

"Well, I wonder where all his money went."

"If it didn't go to his parents, maybe he had another woman. I know for certain that he was sleeping with someone else. A woman I know."

Camille covered Daisy's hand with hers. "You poor thing. Was it one of the women I met?"

"No, of course not. My friends wouldn't do that to me," Daisy lied. Camille was being nice, but Daisy would never give her the satisfaction of knowing that Jasper had tipped out with someone that close to Daisy. She'd already looked stupid once, when she'd found out that he'd married Camille after being with Daisy for years. *I won't allow myself to look like the same fool twice—even though I was.*

"Back to Jay . . . ," Daisy began.

"Yes, back to Jay. Daisy, please get him out of there. I don't know what it is, but something isn't right. The mother's okay sometimes, although her idea of raising a child is to hire a nanny. But the stepfather was ice-cold toward him. One minute he was smiling, and then, when Jay walked into the room, he frowned like he had a bad taste in his mouth."

Daisy decided to choose her words carefully. What if Camille was setting her up? She said the safest thing she could. "I'm trying to get him back now."

"Please do. And if there's anything I can do, let me know. I'll even go to court, if necessary. Twenty years from now, I don't want to walk into my office and see Jay sitting on the other side of my desk, still trying to overcome the trauma he suffered during childhood. I see cases like that every day, and I don't want him to become one of them." Camille handed Daisy a business card. "Those are the numbers to my office and answering service. If it's after hours, the service will reach me at any time. Feel free."

After Daisy left Camille, she walked toward the ice rink at Rockefeller Center. She blended in with the mass of people on the New York City sidewalks. They were all a blur. Everything was moving too fast. Deep in thought, she didn't feel them bump into her. Didn't hear their muttered curses. Didn't see the Do Not Walk sign at the corner before she blindly stepped off the curb and headed into traffic. Too embarrassed to look up at her rescuer, she thanked whoever had pulled her back onto the curb by her coat collar to keep her from getting hit by a delivery truck.

She leaned against the rail at the ice rink and watched the skaters below, the conversation with Camille haunting her. Jasper's stepfather had to know that Jay was Jonathan's son. From the way Camille described his behavior toward Jay, it seemed obvious. Why else would he treat him so horribly? She had to get Jay out of there. She'd need Ming Li to tell Jonathan's story to the attorney. She wasn't sure if it would work, or if it would be considered hearsay, but it was worth a shot.

"Yuck," she said out loud. Just the thought of having to see Ming Li, let alone ask her a favor, sickened her. She didn't know how she'd be able to face her without strangling her.

The whipping wind stung her eyes. They began to tear, but Daisy didn't wipe them. She needed to cry, and the freezing gust of air was the perfect excuse. But then she remembered Adonis's woe-is-me speech, she held up her head and straightened her shoulders. Checking her watch, Daisy hurried to hail a cab to take her to Jacob's.

———————

Daisy sat on one of the only two seats in the living room. She looked around and smiled at all the boxes. Once, packed boxes had saddened her, but seeing Jacob's made her happy. The sooner he moved out, the sooner she'd be able to move in.

She noticed him in the doorway and realized how much she'd miss seeing him. She didn't even know him, but she loved looking at him. He and Adonis had to be in the top five of the world's most beautiful men.

Jacob smiled as though he was waiting for her to invite him to sit down and join her. Unconsciously she licked her lips seductively and played with her hair. As he watched, the air between them filled with sexual energy. Daisy wondered if Jacob could feel it too. She looked into his warm eyes and was certain that he did.

"Well, aren't you going to sit down?"

He crossed his arms. "No, I like watching you from here. Sometimes, when you're too close, you miss the little things."

Daisy laughed. He was right. "What exactly are you afraid to miss?"

"Nothing in particular. Everything in particular. I like watching you."

Hell, I love watching you with your sexy self.

Daisy stared into Jacob's eyes and suddenly felt the need to look away. He was reeling her in too much. She found herself ready to say yes to questions he hadn't even asked. The game that they were playing was too dangerous, and someone would lose. That someone would be Adonis, and eventually her, if she gave in to Jacob.

"So, do you still want it?" he asked, sitting down across from her.

"The apartment?"

"Of course, the apartment. Was there something else you had in mind?"

Daisy paused a moment too long. "Well, no . . ."

"You mean yes, don't you?"

"No means no."

Jacob went to Daisy and took her hand. "Listen, Daisy. I don't know what it is about you . . . about us—"

Daisy held up her free hand. "Don't. I'm way too complicated for you. I've got too much baggage. Too many problems. I'll run you off without even trying."

Jacob laughed. "I can't be scared off. I run *to* what I'm drawn to, not away. That's always been my problem . . . going after what I want. Sometimes it can be a curse."

Lord, don't I know it. "Well, trust what you know. Consider me a curse. I'm sort of involved with someone."

"Sort of, as in just beginning a relationship, or just ending one?"

"Beginning."

"What if he runs off?"

"I don't think he will. He hasn't yet."

"So, is he the reason you canceled our dinner?"

Daisy looked away. She had known that he'd ask eventually. "Yes, but not intentionally. We'd cut our ties a while back, and then I ran into him at the restaurant. I wouldn't have felt comfortable with both of you in the same place."

Jacob rubbed her hand and studied her intently. For a moment, she wished that she wasn't involved with Adonis. She desperately wanted to kiss Jacob, wondered if his lips were as soft as they appeared. Blinking slowly, she inhaled his breath as he exhaled. It was sweet and inviting. Her mouth watered. *Damn, what have I got myself into?*

Jacob stood and pulled her up by the arm. He was just inches in front of her. She closed her eyes and felt his face in the crevice between her shoulder and head. He buried his nose in her neck.

"You smell delicious."

I bet you are *delicious.*

She opened her eyes and stared directly into his. He was tempting. Too tempting. Before she knew it, she'd reached out and touched his hair. His soft curls spiraled around her finger and seemed to beckon her. Carefully, she pulled away, Ms. Christine's warning playing in the back of her mind: *What looks good to you may not be good for you.*

Jacob pulled her close again, cradling her face in his hands. He kissed her forehead, her nose, then brushed her lips.

Daisy reared back. "I can't do this. I don't even know you. I don't know anything about you. And you don't know me. I can't throw everything away for lust. It seems huge right now, but it's so small compared to life and love. Besides, you're going to be my landlord. And your father's my boss."

Jacob laughed. "But I do know you. You just don't remember me."

Daisy looked at him as if he were crazy.

"I first saw you when you started working for my dad. I'd come and go, hoping to get your attention. We locked eyes one day."

"Are you sure about that? Because I still don't remember you. No offense."

"You may not remember because it was some time ago, but I'll never forget. You looked so beautiful sitting in the front of the flowers. I watched you faithfully. I knew then what I know now."

"What's that?"

"That you're special, delicate. Just like your name. You deserve someone who'll treat you the way you deserve to be treated. You shouldn't be working. You need someone like me to take care of you."

Daisy pulled herself out of his arms again and smiled. She had no idea what kind of energy she exuded that made men think she was helpless. Jacob was as much of a joke as Jasper and Calvin had been. At one point in her life, she'd have believed him. She would have given in and let him manipulate her because she was attracted to power. But Adonis had shown her what real power was. He had loved her without needing to control her.

"I believe that you *would* take care of me. But I'll have to decline. He's—Adonis is too important to me."

Jacob looked surprised. "Adonis, hunh? Well, if his name truly holds meaning, I'd better be careful. I studied Adonis in college. The myth, not the man." Jacob laughed and reached into his pocket. "Here." He handed her a set of keys. "I'll be completely moved out the day after tomorrow. You can move in then, if you'd like."

Daisy kissed him on the cheek. "Thank you, Jacob. Thanks for the apartment, and the very enlightening conversation."

———

Daisy left Jacob's apartment feeling both happy and ashamed. Up to the moment she'd realized he was no good for her, she'd come dangerously close to giving in to him. She'd never been tempted by two men before; she'd never wanted more than one. Although Jacob was breathtaking on the surface, he wasn't Adonis. Jacob would have drained her; Adonis filled her. While she guessed that Jacob could rock her world sexually, Adonis had rocked more than her body. The man had gotten under her skin, and into her mind. He had made her want to utter the three words she'd sworn she would never say again.

"I'll tell him tonight," she promised herself as she stepped onto the porch.

Daisy hurried into the house. She couldn't wait to share her news with Gigi and Ms. Christine. She knew they'd both be happy for her. Her stay with Gigi had been good for both of them. They had been there for each other during their time of need; Daisy had needed a place to rest her head, and Gigi had needed support after her breakup with Marcus. But as close as they were, she realized that they both needed their own space. Too many women in a kitchen would eventually lead to trouble.

As Daisy hung up her coat, she saw Gigi sitting at the dining room table, holding her face in her hands. She was crying.

"What's wrong?"

Gigi shook her head.

"It's something," Daisy persisted.

"Yes, but no one that you're concerned about."

"Why not? Who is it?"

"Ming Li. She's in the hospital. She overdosed."

16

*D*aisy carried the last box into Jay's room and set it on top of the others. She wiped her dusty hands on her jeans and glanced over her shoulder. Adonis's and Ms. Christine's loud laughter floated through the apartment. She hoped the walls were thick. The last thing she wanted was to give her neighbors a reason to complain about her.

She shushed them loudly and sat down on top of Jay's bed. Relishing the sudden silence, she closed her eyes and said a special prayer of thanks. It had been a long time since she and Jay had had a nice place of their own. The room was too small to accommodate all of his belongings, but it would do. She didn't care if his toys were scattered throughout the apartment, as long as they were together. Getting him back was all that mattered.

"You need any help?" Adonis offered from the doorway.

"No, I'm finished for now. I need to paint and buy him some

new linens and curtains, the things he needs to make this room feel like his. But I guess you'll help me with that, right?" She caressed his face softly.

Adonis rolled his eyes in mock disgust. "You sure know how to get what you want. You know I'll help in any way I can, with a little persuasion. Speaking of persuasion, who did you work your magic on to get a place like this?"

Daisy froze. She hadn't yet told Adonis about Jacob, or about renting from him. He'd be upset if she told him the entire truth. She'd tell him only what he needed to know. "My boss's son rented me the apartment. He's a professor, and he's gone on sabbatical for a year. He needed a tenant, and I needed a place. I didn't have to work my magic. You're the only one that I work." She kissed him on the cheek and hurried out of the room before he could ask more questions.

Ms. Christine slid a sofa against the wall. "There," she said with one final shove. "Now, doesn't that look better on this side of the room? It better, 'cause I'm not moving it again. I'm tired, and I have a plane to catch."

Daisy hugged her mother. "Thanks, Ma. For everything. It looks fine right where you put it. I'm going to miss you."

"Sweetie, you don't have to thank me. But on second thought, if you really want to thank me, you can cook me dinner when you come home. I've been cooking ever since I got out here."

"Sure, Ma. Whatever you want, you got it."

"Good. I'll have a list ready for you when you come home to visit. "Come on, Adonis!" Ms. Christine yelled. "It's time to go." She turned to Daisy. "I bet he's lying down. Two days of moving tires anyone out."

"I'll get him, Ma." Daisy headed for Jay's bedroom.

She found him curled up on Jay's bed. She smiled. He looked so peaceful, so tired. She hated to wake him. "Adonis, are you sleeping?" she asked, nudging him gently.

He stretched, looked up at her with sleepy eyes. "Yes. No. I'm up now."

Daisy sat on the bed and rubbed his back. "Ma's waiting for you. You should never have told her you'd take her to the airport."

"I know. You should be taking her."

Daisy knew what he was going to say next, and she didn't want to hear it. She'd been able to avoid that conversation for the last few days. Moving had saved her. "I have a valid reason for not wanting to go. You guys are stopping by the hospital first. Why should I visit Ming Li, after what she did?"

"Women. I love y'all, but I can't take y'all. If it were two men, we'd just talk about it—maybe even fight. But we'd get over it. Besides, you don't know the whole story."

"And neither do you," Daisy said defensively.

Adonis kissed her on the forehead. "Don't put me in this. You know where my loyalty is. I'm just telling you what Gigi tried to tell you . . . what your own mother tried to tell you. There's more to the story."

"I'll think about it," Daisy said drily, and returned to the living room to bid Ms. Christine good-bye.

Her mother hugged her. "Alright, baby girl. I'll call you when I get in to let you know I made it."

Tears welled in Daisy's eyes as she squeezed her mother. She hated to see her leave.

Adonis smiled from the doorway. "Now I see why you don't want to go, baby girl," he teased.

Daisy frowned at him.

Ms. Christine turned and blew Daisy a kiss. "You'll be fine. Pray."

"Yes, pray," Adonis urged her.

"I will, Ma. Adonis, make sure you lock the door behind you. I'm going to lie down."

———

Daisy scrubbed the olive paint from her hands in the kitchen sink. She'd been working alone for two days, fixing up the apartment. She had just finished Jay's room. Her back ached from all the reaching and squatting. She didn't care what the advertisements said, the extendable, automatic-fill paint-brushes weren't any easier to use. She glanced out the tiny kitchen window to see that snow had begun to fall. The first snowfall of the year always made her feel warm inside, and she began humming her own tune as she danced from the sink to the stove. Turning on the flame, she snapped her fingers and did a little dip. She removed the kettle and filled it with water. "Do you remember the twenty-first night of September?" she sang. "Love was changing the mind of pretenders, while chasing the clouds away." She stopped, realizing how silly she must look, but then she remembered that she was by herself. *This is one of the perks of living alone.* Daisy began singing again.

Until the intercom buzzed.

She answered, but didn't receive a response.

"Must've had the wrong apartment." She went back to the kitchen.

The doorbell rang.

What the hell? Who got into the building without me buzzing them in? "Must be Adonis," she said out loud, going back to the door. *Ma must have taught him how to slip in.*

"How'd you get in?" she asked as she opened the door.

Calvin Harris stood before her.

"Damn. How did you find me?"

Calvin smiled halfheartedly. "I'm a detective. It's what I do for a living."

"Well, detect this." She swung the door closed, but Calvin stopped it with his foot.

"That's very juvenile, Daisy."

"And just popping up at someone's house without being invited is . . . what? Being a respectable adult?" She sighed. "Just come in. I don't need my neighbors in my business." She walked into the kitchen to turn off the kettle, which had begun to whistle. Just when she was starting to have fun, the devil showed up. *His horns must be in his pocket.*

She bumped into him as she turned to leave the kitchen. "Damn. I invited you to come in, not get on top of me. Give me three feet."

Daisy had no idea why he was there, but it couldn't be good. Except for the few hot months that they'd shared in college, nothing had ever been pleasant between them. "Have a seat." She gestured to the sofa and waited for Calvin to sit down. "Well?" she asked impatiently when he did.

"I came here to talk to you about Lalani."

"Lani," Daisy corrected. "She prefers to be called Lani."

"Okay, Lani."

The intercom buzzed.

No one calls first anymore? She went to answer it. "Who is it?"

"Mrs. Tompkins, the social worker from the hospital."

Daisy buzzed her in, then hurried over to Calvin, worried. "Sorry, you have to go. Come back in an hour."

"Not until we talk about Lani. I flew three thousand miles to have this conversation, and I'm not leaving until we do."

"Please, Calvin. You don't know what this—" The doorbell rang, interrupting her. "Shit! Okay, Calvin. You win. But please don't say anything. Promise me that, and I'll explain later. We're related. Just go along with that."

Daisy straightened her clothes and smoothed her hair. As much as she hated Mrs. Tompkins, she knew that she had to be on point. With all the energy she could summon, she plastered a fake smile on her face and opened the door.

"Come in, Mrs. Tompkins."

Mrs. Tompkins nodded politely, stepped inside, and slowly looked around the apartment. "Hello, Daisy."

"Ms. Parker," Daisy corrected. If she couldn't address Mrs. Tompkins by her first name, then neither could Mrs. Tompkins call her by hers. "How may I help you?"

"Do you mind if we sit and talk? It's about Jay."

"Follow me," Daisy said, turning toward the living room. She looked at her watch and reminded herself to keep doing so. *If she thinks I have somewhere to go, maybe she'll go back to the hole she crawled out of. Calvin too for that matter. Hell has to have noticed by now that its two biggest demons are missing.*

"Mrs. Tompkins, this is—"

"Detective Harris." Calvin rose from his seat to shake Mrs. Tompkins's hand, then settled himself back down.

Stupid asshole. Now he's going to have this nosy heifer acting even nosier, if that's possible. "He's my cousin, visiting from out of town," Daisy added quickly.

Mrs. Tompkins sat down. "Well, Daisy, I'll get right to the point. That is, if you don't mind me speaking in front of your cousin."

"Oh, no, Daisy doesn't mind. We're a close family," Calvin interjected.

Daisy had to will herself not to roll her eyes and Calvin out of his seat.

"Daisy, I'm no longer handling your case. But I managed to find out quite a bit while I was working on it. And I came here to apologize."

"For what?" Daisy asked, taken aback.

Calvin sat up straighter.

"Well, first off, I know that Jay isn't your son. I also know that he's not your late boyfriend's biological child, either. And for you to fight for him the way you are is wonderful. I've talked to a lot of people about you and Jay: the schools, the basketball coach, the doctors—"

"Mrs. Tompkins, Jay *is* my son. I've raised him almost single-handedly since he was in diapers. That's what everyone fails to realize; I didn't have to give birth to him to love him. If anyone questions who his mother is, they should just ask him."

"I did," Mrs. Tompkins said, nodding, "and he told me everything. How you struggled to take care of him, to keep a roof over his head. How you spent almost all of your money on his sneakers—"

"He wouldn't know all that. I've always protected him from knowing too much. Some problems are only for adults to know."

Mrs. Tompkins laughed. "You know, Daisy, for being such a good mother, you're forgetting something. Kids hear more than we know. I believe they learn more through eavesdropping than they do in the schools."

Daisy decided Mrs. Tompkins wasn't so bad, after all, and

shared the whole pitiful story of her and Jasper with her. Daisy glanced at Calvin, who'd turned into a human sponge. He was sucking up the whole conversation. She had almost forgotten that he was in the room. She didn't have the time to save face, or be too private. Calvin and the whole world could know her business for all she cared, just as long as she got Jay back.

Mrs. Tompkins stood. "May I see Jay's room?"

"Sure. It's right back there." Daisy pointed at the direction. "But let me ask you a question first. I'm sure you've found out information about other cases before. What was it that made you come here to talk to me, other than what you've told me?"

"Off the record"—Mrs. Tompkins laughed sadly—"I grew up in foster care. I was taken away from my mother and never returned. My case was a joke. My foster parents were a nightmare, and I had no real reason to be in the system. My mother's ex-boyfriend called and lied about her, said that she'd abused me. My mother had never laid a hand on me—ever. Long story short, they took me away, and she took her life when she couldn't get me back. I've been in therapy for years. A wonderful, caring psychiatrist we both happen to know asked me about your case, and it turned out to be one that I'd covered. Thank Camille." Mrs. Tompkins walked to Jay's room.

Daisy closed her eyes and tried to regain her composure. She knew how Mrs. Tompkins's mother must have felt. She remembered Camille's words: she didn't want Jay sitting on the other side of a therapist's desk in twenty years.

"One more thing," Mrs. Tompkins said, returning to the living room. "About the stepfather . . . is there anyone you can get to testify?"

Daisy nodded. "My friend . . . someone I know was told the story. Jasper's brother confided in her before he died. He was the one who was abused."

"Good. It'll help us in court."

"Us?"

"Yes. Camille and I will go, if you want us to. The more support you have, the better. I'm sorry I judged you so harshly. If you need me, you have my card. I'll let myself out."

Daisy sank down next to Calvin on the sofa and covered her face. She didn't want him to see her crying anymore. Although Mrs. Tompkins's offer to testify had eased her anxiety, her foster-care story echoed in Daisy's mind. In her gut, she knew Jay was unhappy. She could feel his pain. She knew it must confuse him to be treated badly; he'd never known ill treatment before. Unable to take the anguish, Daisy squeezed her eyes shut and tried to remind herself that everything seemed to be looking up. But her heart had begun to race. *Not another attack.*

"Please," she begged aloud. Calvin reached out and held her. She pressed her face into his chest and sobbed.

"It's okay," he soothed.

"No, it's not. They have my son."

Calvin eased her off his chest and held her at arm's length. Tears were in his eyes, and a crack was in his voice as he spoke. "Why didn't you keep *our* daughter? If you love that little boy as much as you seem to, why would you deny me the opportunity to experience love like that? Why didn't you at least allow me to know Lani? To love her?"

Daisy hung her head. For the first time, she realized how wrong she'd been in keeping Calvin and Lani apart. She'd thought about introducing them before, had even toyed with the idea of telling Calvin. But she'd been too selfish and self-centered to do the right thing. She'd handled Lani's birth all wrong. While it should have been celebrated, it had been condemned, a closeted secret.

"Because I was stupid, so selfish and stupid. I'm sorry, Calvin," she said.

He stood up. "Me too, Daisy. I'm sorry that I got to see the human side of you. My plans would be so much easier to execute if I hadn't seen you cry. I apologize for what I'm about to do, but I have to. I have to be a father to my daughter."

Daisy stared at Calvin. Anything that happened to Lani now would be Daisy's fault. "Please don't," she begged, grabbing his arm. "Don't try to take my baby away. They've already taken one. I can't lose them both."

Calvin yanked himself from her grasp, and his expression turned cold. "What makes you believe that you're entitled to two children, and I'm not good enough for one? You don't deserve Lani. That woman said that you struggled for Jay, but you couldn't even struggle for your own child because you were too weak. Hell, I don't care what that social worker thinks. You're not the good mother she believes you are."

Daisy jumped to her feet. "Fuck you, Calvin! Fuck you, and everyone like you. You don't know me. Never did. And you think I'm weak? Why, because I gave our daughter up? News flash, Calvin: I was never weak. A weak woman wouldn't have been able to do what I did. I did what I thought was best for Lani, and it hurt like hell. I'm so tired of people like you trying to dictate my life, trying to tell me who and what I am. You're nothing but vampires—you suck the life out of people and leave them for dead." Daisy shook her head. "Not anymore. Never again. I did the right thing. I wasn't so sure before, but now I know. I won't allow you or anyone else to make me question myself, or my choices. I'm not a child. I'm a woman who knows right from wrong."

Calvin stood his ground. "Still, you haven't been any more of a parent than I have. But the difference is that you had a choice. You had the option to be her mother, and you didn't choose it." He walked away and slammed the door on his way out.

Daisy's heart pounded against her chest as if it were trying to escape, and her hands trembled. She counted slowly to three and tried to control her breathing. While the argument with Calvin had made her feel stronger, it had also given her reason to worry. Now, there was no question about whether he was going after Lani.

The sudden rise in her heart rate had signaled the need for medication. She didn't want to take it, but knew that she needed it. She couldn't shake the anxiety. Daisy grabbed the phone and dialed the one person who could help her without talking her to death. "Jesus," she whispered when he didn't answer.

The doorbell rang again.

"Please, let it be Adonis," she whispered, her disdain for people who popped up unexpectedly without calling forgotten.

She looked through the peephole, and there he stood. She forced a smile and opened the door.

"I'm so glad to see you." She squeezed him and began to relax.

"What a nice welcome. I thought you'd be upset with me."

"What's a couple of days?" She grabbed his hand, pulled him inside, and led him into her bedroom. "You smell so good." She put her nose to his neck, inhaling his scent just as Jacob had hers.

"What's wrong?" Adonis lifted her chin and searched her face, then put his hand on her chest. "Your heart's beating very fast. Are you having a panic attack?"

"Anxiety."

"Have you taken your medicine?"

"I don't want to. It makes me relax too much."

"Wait here." He sat her down on the bed and left. Daisy listened to his footsteps moving down the hardwood hallway. She knew that he'd do his best to persuade her to take the medicine. She loved that about him, that he cared about her well-being, not just her body. Warmth spread throughout her, and the back of her neck tingled. *Anxiety and goose bumps at the same time. That's a first.*

Adonis returned and held out his hand. "Here. I cut it in fours. Take just a fourth first, and see if that helps." He gave her a glass of water.

"I knew you'd do that." Daisy laughed. "Thank you."

"No problem." He sat down beside her. "What happened to make you so upset?"

Daisy rested her head on his chest and told him the story. She began to cry when she related Mrs. Tompkins's story. Adonis comforted her.

When her tears finally stopped, Adonis looked at his watch. "Come on. Let's go."

"Go where?"

"To Jersey, to see Jay's relatives. It's not too late, and it won't take us long to get there. We should've gone the day that you got the address. It seems to be the only way, and I'm tired of seeing you cry. You don't have to do this alone, you know. I've sat back and watched you try to do it by yourself. But that's what I'm here for . . . to help you."

17

*A*donis put the car in park. Silently, they appraised the neighborhood. Apartment buildings and houses that looked as if they should be condemned stood on one side of the street, housing projects on the other. Unfolding the paper with the address on it, Daisy breathed a sigh of relief when she realized that Jay's relative didn't live in the projects. She didn't want to go there. Was afraid to. Still, she had a bad feeling in her gut. Debris littered the block, along with the loiterers and roughnecks she presumed were drug dealers.

"You ready?" Adonis asked.

"Are you kidding? No, I'm not."

"Don't tell me you're afraid." He laughed.

"Don't tell me you're not at least a little hesitant."

"I'm from South Central L.A. These knuckleheads out here don't intimidate me."

"Billy Badass, hunh?"

"As long as I have Nina with me, I'm straight."

"Nina?"

Adonis opened the glove compartment and pulled out a gun.

"A professional with a gun. I see."

"How do you think I lived long enough to become a professional? You haven't been out of L.A. that long, have you? Besides"—he tucked the gun in his pants—"it's not a *gun*. It's a chrome Desert Eagle, and I'm licensed."

Daisy didn't approve, but she had to admit that there was a good chance they'd need it. She reminded herself that her upbringing had been easier and more predictable than his. Her neighborhood had been safe, and his had been known for gang rivalry. She'd never walked in his shoes, and she didn't have the right to judge him. She stole a glance at him and was thankful that he'd made it. He had beaten the odds. Adonis was definitely not a product of his environment, but had learned a thing or two from it.

Daisy got out of the car and softly closed the door. Although the street was busy, she felt as though she needed to sneak. She didn't want to attract too much attention, as if her closing a car door would be the highlight of somebody's day. She tucked her necklace into her shirt, stretched her hat over her earrings, and slipped off her rings and put them into her pocket. "This is crazy," she mumbled, unable to recall the last time she'd had to be so cautious. She'd felt safer on the New York subways.

Adonis grabbed her hand and squeezed it. "It's okay. I'm here."

Daisy wrapped her arm tightly around his as they crossed the street. Tried to meld with him. Holding hands wasn't enough. She needed to feel as close to him as possible.

Adonis's face had gone blank and hard. She'd seen that look before, the look that made it perfectly clear he was not to be messed with. "I won't let anything happen to you."

She made a conscious effort to walk heel-toe, having once read that the highest percent of mugging victims walk on their toes. No way would she allow herself to look vulnerable. She couldn't look as hard as Adonis, but she tried her best to imitate his confidence. Silently, she counted down the addresses until she came to the one she was searching for.

The building looked exactly the way she'd imagined it—ragged. Several of its windows were broken, and loose pieces of brick jutted out from a wall of lewd graffiti. The cement crumbled underfoot as she stepped onto the stoop. The intercom system was missing, and the front door was barely hanging on its hinges. "Yuck," she said, and pulled her sleeve over her hand to keep from touching the handle.

Daisy opened the door and the overwhelming stench of old piss stung her nostrils. Deep moans and a smacking noise assaulted her ears. She peeked around the banister to the back of the hall. A woman was bent over with her palms pressed against the disgusting wall. She was being screwed doggy style. *Great! First urine and now nasty ass in the air.* She held her breath and blinked quickly, eyes stinging, then headed up the stairwell with Adonis on her heels.

She glanced at the slip of paper again. She was right in front of Peaches' apartment. "We're here," she said nervously to Adonis, and knocked on the door.

"Who the fuck is it?" a voice bellowed from inside.

Daisy didn't answer.

Adonis moved her to one side and pounded his fist on the door.

"Goddamnit! I said, who the fuck is it? Don't be banging on my door like the motherfuckin' po-lice." The door flew open.

The woman was a mess. An ugly mess. Her brown skin was blotchy, with light spots and terrible acne. Her shriveled hair lay flat on her head, and her breasts drooped braless, her nipples peeking out through her shabby robe. She looked directly at Adonis and licked her lips. "*Goddamn,* it must be Christmas, and you must be my gift. Mmm, mmm, mmm. You must be the new delivery boy. 'Bout time Ray Lee got someone that looks good. After all the rock I buy from him. Come on in here with your fine ass and let me unwrap you. I ain't got a tree, but, baby, I got a bed."

Daisy pushed Adonis aside and stepped forward. "Are you Peaches?"

The woman narrowed her eyes. "Who the fuck wants to know?"

"A friend of your nephew's."

"Oh, bitch, you got the wrong place. I ain't got a nephew—"

"So you're not Desiree's sister?"

"You knew Des? Come on in." Peaches stepped to the side, allowing Daisy access. "Ain't you coming?" Peaches asked Adonis.

Adonis shook his head.

"What's the matter, you scared of good pussy? Mine purrs, it don't bite. But you can nibble it. Just don't chew." She laughed.

It took everything Daisy had not to grab the woman by her hair and wrestle her to the floor. "Take it down a notch or two. He's with me."

"Well, if he ain't coming, I ain't talking. That's what you're here for, right? To pick my brain?"

Daisy waved Adonis in. She didn't want him to know Jay's business; it wasn't hers to share. But apparently, she had no choice.

"Y'all come on in and have a seat." Peaches plopped down on the sofa.

Daisy and Adonis remained standing. The apartment was filthy with clutter and old plates covered in mold. Empty forty-ounce beer bottles lined the table and the windowsill. A pint of Wild Irish Rose stood on the floor in front of the broken-down plaid sofa.

"What the fuck you expect, Buckingham Palace? Sit down." Peaches gestured in the direction of a scuffed folding chair and a pleather one sitting opposite it.

Daisy sat on the edge of one chair. Adonis refused.

"Well, I guess you can do what you want. I don't give a damn if you sit, stand, or crawl. I just want to look at you. What are you, 'bout six-two, six-three? 'Bout two forty, two fifty?"

"Are you Peaches or not?" Daisy snapped impatiently.

"Yep, dat be me. And you are?"

"Daisy."

"That figures. A flower, huh? That man right there know how to pluck, or what?" Peaches laughed again. "So, you here 'bout Des? What about her?"

"I need to know about her son."

Peaches nodded slowly and removed a small packet from her pocket. She opened it and poured its white contents on the back of her hand. She held it to her nose and snorted it into one nostril, then the other. She held her head back and closed her eyes in rapture. "I'm sorry, y'all wanted some?" she asked, rubbed the rest on her gums, then sat back with eyes closed, obviously waiting for her hit to hit her.

"No, thanks," Daisy said.

Adonis said nothing.

"Well, whatcha wanna know 'bout Jay?" Peaches was calm now, her whole demeanor changed.

"I want to know about his father."

Peaches giggled. "Shit, I wanna know too. Which one?"

Daisy sat up. "You don't know who his father is?"

Peaches looked at Daisy as if she were crazy. "Oh, so you didn't know Des, hunh? Des was a hot bitch. Couldn't tell that wench nothin'. She thought she was the cutest thing that God gave breath to. Thought she was better than everybody—the whole family. Just 'cause she went to college. Well, if you ask me, the only thing she learned at college was how to fuck. Everybody. They could've gave her a Ph.D. in fuckology. Know what I'm saying?"

"I guess," Daisy said. "But what about Jay's father?"

"Who the fuck you rushin'? Damn, give a bitch a minute to think. You got somewhere to be or somethin'? 'Cause I don't go by the clock, 'less I'm gettin' paid."

Daisy didn't like Peaches' tone and looked at Adonis, who nodded. They both realized that they'd have to put up with Peaches' nasty mouth and matching attitude.

"Well, *Daisy,* all that fuckin' caught up to Des. You know she died from AIDS, right? Anyway, before she caught the monster, she got caught up with them Stevens twins. Them was some fine muthafuckas for your ass too, I'm tellin' you. Des ain't know if she was coming or going. See, one of them had her body, but the other one had her heart. One of them loved the shit outta my sister, because he didn't know that his brother had fucked her. Fucked her good too. That's what Des told me. That Jasper had whipped it on her and dicked her down like never before. She ended up with Jonathan, though. He was the one she loved—the one that believed he was the father of her child. But truth be told, Des didn't know which one she was pregnant by because she fucked 'em both in one week. She met Jasper first and fucked him just 'bout every day that week. Then she met Jonathan, fucked him the same day, and he fell head over heels for her. I guess Jasper saw how much his brother liked Des and didn't tell him that he'd had her. He stepped off." Peaches sat back. "So there you go. Now you know."

Daisy was stunned. "So you don't know."

Peaches laughed. "You a little slow, hunh? That's what I just said. Think about it. Why do you think the boy's named the way he is—Jonathan Jasper Stevens? She gave him both of his daddies' names."

———————

Daisy awoke the next morning to a fresh start. After her conversation with Peaches the night before, she felt a new sense of freedom; liberty from ignorance. She finally knew the truth about Jasper. About the past. More importantly, about Jay. She hoped that Peaches' revelation would give her the sharp edge she needed to cut through the red tape and the Stevenses' suit for custody.

Daisy watched the clock, mentally urging time to pass faster. She needed to talk to Kenneth. Tapping her foot, she dialed his number. As soon as her watch's minute hand struck twelve, she pressed the talk button.

"Kenneth, good news!" she said, excitement pouring from her mouth.

"Peaches Pleasant?"

"Yes. Thank God for Peaches!"

Daisy related the events of the night before, interrupted by an occasional laugh from Kenneth.

"Unbelievable," Kenneth said, sounding as human and friendly as Daisy remembered him being when Jasper was alive. "Well, looks like wa have just about all we need."

Daisy crumpled her brow. "About all? Peaches isn't enough?"

"Oh, Peaches was more than enough, I'm sure. But we still need someone that the court—the state—will take seriously. While Peaches gave us the information that we need regarding paternity, we can't allow her in the courtroom. Not on our behalf. But all the other information that you've gathered will certainly help us. It's a good start—"

Daisy held her smile behind a smirk. "So we need someone upstanding? A good citizen who pays taxes and doesn't have a record?"

"Exactly. That'd be great."

"Kenneth, I know exactly who we need."

———————

Daisy unbuttoned her coat and strutted down the hospital corridor feeling brand-new. The night she'd told Calvin off had brought new meaning to her life and had sparked a fire that hadn't been lit since her teens. She was no longer the weak, needy woman-child she had once been; she was a woman with a mission. She'd get Jay back, and Ming Li was going to help whether she wanted to or not. According to Kenneth, Ming Li was the key to the case, the only living person who could speak for Jonathan.

Daisy paused outside Ming Li's door. *Please, God, don't let me have to snatch this mixed-up bitch out of the bed and beat her.* Then she walked in as if she owned the place.

Ming Li sat up and looked at her, then her eyes dropped. Guilt was written all over her face. Daisy had never wanted to hurt someone so badly.

"I'm glad you came," Ming Li said.

"Uh-huh." Daisy nodded skeptically and sat down. "Look, Ming Li, straight to the point. I need something from you, and after what you've done, I don't see how you can refuse."

"You want me to testify?"

Daisy nodded.

"Sure. I have no problem doing that."

"Good. My lawyer will be in touch." Daisy stood to leave.

"Daisy . . . wait."

Daisy began to walk away.

"Daisy, if you don't listen, then I won't go to court."

Daisy turned, glowering. "I know you're not trying to hold anything over my head. You owe me. I don't owe you."

Ming Li's eyes dropped to the floor again. "You're right . . . in a way." She grabbed a box from the bedside table, opened it, and began shuffling through it. "Here, read this." She handed Daisy a letter.

It was the stationery that Daisy had had designed. "What—you want to rub it in?" She snatched the envelope out of Ming Li's hand.

"Read it, and look at the postmark," Ming Li urged.

Daisy held it to the light. It was postmarked just a month before Jasper died. She shot Ming Li a look, then opened it.

"Can you read it out loud?" Ming Li asked. "I want to be sure that you read it correctly."

Ming Li,

Why do you keep doing this to me? How many years must I chase you? Why won't you take my calls? I'm confused. I offer you the world and you give me nothing. I book trips and dinners and you stand me up. I buy you gifts, and you return them unopened. What more can I do? Tell me what I need to do to get you back because I have to have you. I'll give up everything and everybody for you. I love you, don't you understand that? I've loved you since the first time we slept together. And after the last time we made love, I was sure that you felt the same. It's hard to believe that that was over thirteen years ago. To me, it feels like only yesterday.

Do you realize that you've been avoiding me for almost a decade? It kills me to receive half-hellos and happy good-byes from you. I guess you don't know a good man when you see one.

"So, now you know the real truth," Ming Li said. "I wasn't sleeping with your man. I do my thing, but not with my best friends' men."

Daisy shook her head, confused. "But—"

"There are no buts. I slept with Jasper on a very drunk night a long, long time ago. Back when my body wasn't conditioned to alcohol."

Daisy pointed at the paper. "It says here that you slept with him more than once."

"I did. I slept with him twice. I thought he was cool. I even went out in public with him. You know I don't do that. After I slept with him the second time, he instantly turned into an ass-hole. He wanted me to stay in the house, quit my job—*you* know."

"Why didn't you tell me? We were friends."

"If I'd told you, if you'd known about me and him when you first met me, would you have been my friend?"

"No," Daisy admitted. "I don't mingle with exes."

"Exactly. And I don't mingle with women. But when Jasper brought you back into my shop that day to get your pedicure fixed, despite the fact that I couldn't stand him, I genuinely liked you and Gigi. I'd never had many female friends, and we three hit it off. I didn't want to risk losing you as a friend. That's why I didn't tell you. That's why you conducted all of my business with Jasper."

"If you didn't care about him, why did you keep the letters?"

Ming Li laughed. "Because the bastard threatened to black-mail me a few times. He said if I didn't give him what he wanted, he'd tell you that I went after him. I had to protect myself."

Daisy didn't know what to think. The letter in her hands backed up Ming Li's story, but she was still hurt. "How did you OD?"

Ming Li smiled sadly. "Well, I guess some of us aren't as strong as we pretend to be. I had my secrets, just like anybody else. I've been on Prozac and medication for my hyper disorder for years, and after a while, I guess, they didn't mix too well with alcohol. I overdosed by mistake, but I needed to. If I hadn't, I wouldn't have realized that I'm an alcoholic—among other things."

"What other things?"

"I'll tell you more when they let me out of here."

Daisy took off her coat and sat down. The tension in the air and in her bones withered away. She was glad that she'd decided to confront Ming Li. Otherwise, she would never have believed that she hadn't betrayed her. They chatted for hours, about everything and nothing at all. It didn't matter what they discussed, as long as they were talking.

"So, you're really not going to celebrate Christmas?"

"There is no Christmas without Jay. Maybe New Year's."

Ming Li shook her head. "Count me out. The drinks will be too tempting."

"There'll always be next year. You'll be stronger, and Jay will be back. I know he will."

18

Spring

"Someone's asking for you outside," one of Daisy's helpers informed her.

Daisy turned the sprayer off and laid it down on the marble planter. "Did you get a name?"

"No. He wouldn't give one."

Daisy sighed, took off her gardening gloves, and headed toward the bathroom. Whoever it was would have to wait until she'd washed her hands. She'd been working with pesticides all day and prayed that her unexpected visitor wouldn't prove to be another one. *I work in almost twenty different locations. Whoever it is must've needed to see me pretty badly to track me down. This better be good.* All day, she'd had a positive feeling about Jay and their upcoming court date, and it irritated her that someone was disrupting her mood.

As soon as she walked through the double doors, she ran

into Marcus, who was standing with a blank expression on his face.

"Hey, Marcus." She smiled.

Marcus half-smiled, half-smirked. "I need to talk to you."

"Are you okay?" Daisy genuinely hoped so, even though she had urged Gigi to move on. But his absent look told her that he was still hurting.

"I'm straight."

"Well, I don't know if I can leave just yet." She checked the time. "I've got about forty-five minutes."

"Can't you make an exception for an old friend? You don't have a boss watching over you. I wouldn't be here if it wasn't very important."

"Let me see . . ." She paused as if thinking it over carefully, then finally went on, "They should be able to finish up without me." She called over her assistant, who told her that she'd be happy to finish up.

"I'm ready, Marcus. Where do you want to go?" she asked as they stepped outside.

"Central Park's not far. It's nice out."

"Fine. The park it is. Should we walk or take a cab?"

Marcus walked out into the street and held up his arm. For a second, she thought about declining his invitation to talk. She'd never seen him so standoffish before, and it was beginning to make her nervous. When the cab pulled to the curb, he held the car door open for her, and she got in. She scooted over to make room for him and decided that his behavior was just a symptom of his painful breakup with Gigi.

"Aren't you going to tell me what's bothering you?" she asked as they rode.

He held up his hand to silence her. "When we get to the park. It's private."

As soon as they pulled up to the park, Daisy jumped out. She had started to feel as if she were suffocating in the cab, sitting next to Marcus, who'd consumed the cab's space with labored breathing. An eerie feeling rushed through her. She was beginning to worry. She knew Marcus would never hurt her. Hoped he wouldn't. He had no reason to—unless he knew that she had sup-ported Gigi's decision.

He grabbed her by the arm and led the way to an unoccupied bench. She was thankful that they weren't too far away from other park goers.

"Have a seat," he commanded.

Daisy sat, but not because he had told her to. She was tired. "Marcus, what is it? What's the matter?"

Marcus looked away and began to pace, his steps sounding more like a march than a walk. He finally turned, glaring at her. "You should know what my problem is."

"Gigi?"

"Yep. That bitch of a friend of yours."

Daisy had never heard him speak that way before. "Oh, Marcus. She just needs time, that's all."

"Bullshit, Daisy," he spat. "You know that's bullshit. All three of you bitches are just alike—"

"Whoa!" Daisy stood up, indignant. "Don't disrespect me like that. I didn't do a thing to you. I wasn't the one sleeping with you—I didn't hurt you, or leave you."

"But you *would've* slept with me."

"I would've what? I know you didn't just say that I would've slept with you. You know that's not true. Are you crazy?"

"Maybe so. But I know I could've. Why not? You were so quick to fuck Adonis after Jasper died. Any bitch that moves that fast is in heat."

"I don't like the way this is going, Marcus. I'm leaving."

"No, you're not. Not if you know what's good for you."

"Are you threatening me?"

"No. You're not leaving because we need each other. I need to know something, and I have some information about Adonis that you need to hear. You see? We have a lot of needs."

"Sorry, Marcus. The last time you told me something about Adonis, it wasn't exactly true—"

"Was it exactly false?" he asked sarcastically.

As crazy as it sounded, she had to admit that what he'd told her had had some truth to it. Because of Marcus, she'd found out about Christy. But the game he was playing was dangerous.

"I don't know, and I'm sure I don't know anything that you need to know."

Marcus sat down with a sigh. "What I need is simple. I'm willing to save you a bunch of heartache in exchange for peace of mind. Just tell me who Gigi's been seeing."

As far as Daisy knew, Gigi wasn't involved with anyone. And if she was, Daisy wouldn't tell him. "No one that I know of."

Marcus shook his head. "Try again."

"I'm telling you, no one. She hasn't told me anything about anybody. And if she was seeing someone, she would've told me."

Marcus stood and studied Daisy's eyes. "As much as I don't want to believe you, I have to. Take this for what it's worth. Your so-called man has his other woman from L.A. visiting him."

"No, he doesn't."

"You're incredible." Marcus laughed. "First, you were mad at me for not telling you about Jasper, and now you don't want to believe me about Adonis. Trust me on this one. I know for a fact that Christy is here."

Daisy froze. Marcus had to know what he was talking about. Otherwise, how would he know Christy's name? He hadn't when he'd first told her about Adonis's engagement. She knew for certain that Gigi and Ming Li would never share that information with him. "Are you sure? How do you know?"

"I have my ways. I found you today, didn't I? I also know that Gigi's screwing someone. And I know where you live. Do you want me to tell you your address?"

Daisy shook her head. "That's okay."

"Why don't you take a ride to Fourth Avenue and Twelfth Street tonight, say . . . around eight o'clock? A good game of pool will do you good."

As irrational as Marcus was acting, Daisy had to believe him. Feelings of anger and foolishness rose up within her. "I just may do that, Marcus. Thanks . . . I guess." She turned to walk away.

"One more thing. Tell Gigi that I love her new look, and that

that cranberry-colored thong she was wearing the other night is sexy as hell."

Daisy stared at him. "You haven't been stalking her?"

"Wanna know why I believe that you really don't know anything about Gigi's new man? Because as beautiful and innocent as you are, as smart as you appear, you're a lot dumber than you look. You're blind in one eye and can't see out the other."

"No, Marcus. I beg to differ. Maybe once upon a time you would've been right, but not anymore. I see everything clearly now, including the fact that you don't stand a chance of getting Gigi back. Blind or not," she added with a laugh, "even I can see that she's not in your future." She walked away, hating that she had let herself stoop to his level.

―――――――――

Daisy sat on Ming Li's stoop, waiting for her to arrive. She ran one hand through her disheveled hair and hung up her cell phone with the other. She'd been trying to contact Gigi, but had gotten no answer. She checked her incoming calls and saw that she'd missed two of Adonis's. She had her reasons, she told herself, for deciding not to return them. Although she wasn't sure if she should believe Marcus, she didn't want to talk to Adonis right now. If Christy was in town, she was sure that he'd have some excuse, some made-up business appointment he had to attend. Her words to Marcus echoed in her head. *I see everything clearly now.* "Do I?" she muttered.

"Hey, why are you sitting out here?" Ming Li asked as she walked up. "You could've let yourself in. You know where the key is."

"I just needed to sit outside for a while. I don't feel as alone with my thoughts that way. The traffic helps."

Ming Li unlocked the front door. "Come on in and tell me what's going on."

Daisy followed her inside, then sat down at the bar and put her head in her hands. She needed to talk to Gigi. She and Ming Li had gotten over their misunderstanding, but Daisy still had reservations about opening up to her. Their trust wasn't the same, and neither was their friendship. She hated to be so standoffish with someone she'd once thought of as a sister. But sisters didn't keep secrets like that.

"So, what is it?" Ming Li asked as she pulled up her stool and poured a glass of bottled water.

For the first time, Daisy noticed that all the alcohol had been removed from the once fully stocked bar. All the furniture she'd destroyed was gone as well.

"I . . . I don't know—"

"You don't know what? If you can tell me? If you can trust me?"

Daisy nodded.

"I guess that's understandable. After what I kept to myself, I don't know if I'd be able to, either." Ming Li paused. "Maybe it would help if I told you my truth—the rest of the story."

"Maybe."

"Well, you know how I'm always so hard on men—on everyone? It's been for a reason. I wasn't born this way. In fact, I started therapy to try to cure it."

"Therapy? I always thought you needed it, but I never imagined you'd actually go."

"Ha!" Ming Li laughed. "See, that's just it. I've never been as strong as I appeared to be. It was the cognac—bottled courage." Her eyes misted. She brushed at them, but she couldn't hold back the tears. Before Daisy knew it, Ming Li had broken down sobbing.

Daisy shifted uncomfortably. She'd never seen Ming Li in so much pain, never thought her capable of it.

"I started drinking when I was eight. Bet you didn't know that, hunh? When I was little, my father used to beat my mother. He beat her like she was a child, and she never fought back. She never left him. I couldn't understand it, and I promised myself that it would never happen to me. And I meant it. When they used to fight—no, when he used to pummel her—I'd go into the liquor cabinet and pour a drink. That's what I used to see her do. I guess it was her way of coping. Eventually, it became mine." Ming Li took a sip of water and looked away. "When he was done tormenting her, he used to take her into the bedroom and screw her. It wasn't makeup sex, either. There was nothing intimate about it. There weren't any *I'm sorry*s or *I love you*s—just sex. And I used to hear her beg him not to."

"Ming Li, I'm so sorry," Daisy murmured, rubbing her friend's back.

"Me too. In fact, I was so sorry that I began to pity myself, and I eventually became depressed. I've been on Prozac for as long as I can remember, probably about as long as I fucked nearly every man I found some sort of interest in. I thought sex was the answer, that I could control them with what was in my head and between my legs." Ming Li laughed bitterly. "I honestly thought that was true, because no matter how many times my dad jumped on my mom, right after they had sex he'd hum her a tune. He beat her outside of the bedroom, and she whipped him in it."

"Wow!" was all Daisy could say. As long as they'd been friends, she'd never understood Ming Li the way she did now.

"So," Ming Li went on, wiping her face with a napkin, "enough boohooing. Tell me what's up. Anything I can do?"

Daisy felt at ease now, after hearing Ming Li's story, so she told her about her conversation with Marcus. They both agreed that they needed to find Gigi, but neither one knew where she was. They hadn't heard from her in days. Ming Li suggested that maybe Marcus was right. Maybe Gigi was seeing someone else.

"The panty thing scares me," Daisy said.

"He's been stalking her. Maybe all of us. How else would he know where you lived?"

Daisy shrugged. "I wouldn't put it past him, not after the way he was behaving. It was like he was either on drugs or needed to be."

"Probably so. Well, are we going to shoot a game of pool?"

"Hell, yeah. I'm ready now."

Ming Li shook her head. "No, you're not. Not dressed like that."

Daisy looked down at her work clothes. She was going to bust her man, not put on a fashion show. For all she knew, she might end up tussling, although that wasn't her intention. "I'm fine."

"To whom?" Ming Li laughed. "Seriously, you can't go bust a man like that. Not when he's with his ex and you don't know who your competition is. Not only do you have to walk in and own the place, you have to make her feel smaller than you."

"If she's sneaking around with a man that doesn't belong to her, she's already inferior."

Ming Li grabbed Daisy's hand and pulled her into the bedroom. "Okay, let's see what we have here that you didn't destroy," Ming Li joked. "What size do you wear?"

"None of your business," Daisy smirked. "I'm about two sizes bigger than you."

Ming Li reached into her closet and grabbed something black. "Here, try this on. It has Lycra in it."

Daisy held the short dress up in front of her. "Ming Li, I'm not wearing this little thing, it's too cold. I'll freeze to death."

Ming Li lit a cigar. "Honey, now is not the time to get picky, it's time to get right. Besides, it's not that cold." She held her finger to her lips as if lost in thought. "Now, you're about a size eight shoe, right?"

Daisy nodded. "Yes, you're exactly right. But after all these years, I guess you should know."

Ming Li stepped into her closet and came out with a pair of black, calf-length, high-heeled boots. She handed them to Daisy.

Daisy frowned down at them. "Ming Li, do you see how skinny these heels are? I'm going to kill myself in these. How am I supposed to be cute, if I bust my ass? And they're a size eight and a half. How do you fit into these? You're too tall."

Ming Li pushed Daisy toward the bathroom. "My mother has small feet."

"Oh, that's right, she's Asian."

"No, she's black. My dad's Korean. And enough with the stereotypes. Not all Asian women have small feet, just like not all black women are strong. Stuff the boots with cotton balls. Act like you haven't always had money to buy shoes that fit."

———————

Daisy and Ming Li circled the block several times without seeing Adonis's car. After they checked the surrounding area, they found a parking spot around the corner from Corner Billiards and waited patiently. Daisy drummed on the steering wheel.

"Hyping yourself up, or calming yourself down?" Ming Li asked.

"A little of both, I guess."

"Maybe he's not here. It's almost nine, and we haven't seen his car anywhere."

"That's true. But this is New York. He could've cabbed it or taken the train. Or the Christy chick could've rented a car. We won't know unless we go inside."

Daisy opened her door and carefully stepped out into the cold early spring chill. She shivered. The little black dress was cute, but it wasn't worth a dime when it came to warmth. "Let's do this. I know he's here."

"I thought you said you weren't sure."

"Technically, I'm not. But I feel it in my gut. I used to sit around and guess what Jasper was doing. But this time, with this man, I have to see for myself."

They walked quickly, in silence, their boots clicking in unison against the sidewalk. Daisy wasn't sure if she was going to battle, but she was definitely going to get her man. Her mother had once told her to choose her battles wisely, and this one was worth fighting. Deep in her heart she knew that she loved Adonis; she wasn't fighting for *him,* but for the principle. She'd fight for respect, for the person she'd learned to love the most: herself.

A newfound determination and energy flowed through Daisy's veins as she opened the door and strode into the billiards hall. She was glad that Ming Li had tagged along, but she realized that she didn't really need her. She could handle the situation alone. If Adonis was there with another woman, Daisy wanted to see who she was. She wouldn't embarrass herself. Wouldn't get into a catfight. *My interest isn't in the cat, but the dog.* Then she spotted

Adonis was with a woman at a back pool table and decided that her dog had definitely gotten off his leash. She pumped her fist, nodding to herself. *A choke chain is what he needs. And I've got two hands to choke him with.*

She held her head high and walked toward Adonis's table. Ming Li stopped at the front counter. Adonis glanced up, saw Daisy, and froze. Their eyes locked. Her heart thumped, but this time, she wasn't having an attack. There was no need to panic. *She* wasn't in the hot seat, but she would warm a couple of asses if need be.

"You see this bitch?" Ming Li whispered behind her back. "Now, aren't you glad that I made you dress up?"

Daisy nodded and gave the woman the once-over. She was clearly in need of a meal or two. Christy had to be a size two, if that. Although she was obviously black, she was a living example that black could come in all different shades, sizes, and proportions. She was just above average height, paler than tinged winter snow, and had an ass flatter than a billiards table. Daisy laughed, and her confidence rose.

Ming Li nudged her. "Am I seeing things, or does she have fake titties that are three sizes too big for her bony body?"

Daisy looked at Christy's breasts and winced. Her skin, stretched like elastic, begged for relief. "Ouch. They look like they're going to bust," Daisy said, then turned her attention back to Christy's face. She was pretty in her own way, but the rest of her had to go.

Ming Li grabbed a cue stick and rolled it onto the pool table next to Adonis's. "Straight enough. Rack 'em, Daisy."

"I didn't come in here to play games." She walked over to Adonis and eased between him and the table. She inched her dress down and inhaled his breath. It was minty. *He better not have kissed her.*

"Adonis?" the woman said from behind Daisy.

"Hey, baby," he said to Daisy, ignoring the woman.

"That's all you have to say?" Daisy asked as she poked out her chest.

Adonis smiled seductively and traced her face with his forefinger. "No, I've been trying to tell you this all day." He bent down and kissed her deeply and passionately, as if they were the only two people in the room.

Daisy was still curious, but she succumbed. She wanted to slap sense into him but decided she'd put on a show first and enjoy it. She felt his hands on her back, then under her arms, and then her body rose. He picked her up and sat her on the pool table. They never unlocked lips. Vaguely, Daisy heard the sound of the balls breaking, and then one of them hit her in the butt. She rolled her eyes. *I'd hoped I wouldn't have to toss this heifer.* She hopped off the table and saw Ming Li at the other end, holding a pool stick and smiling.

"Well, why should we pay for a table when they're not using theirs?" Ming Li asked.

"I want you to meet someone," Adonis said.

The woman walked over to Daisy and extended her hand. "You must be Daisy. It's nice to finally meet you."

Daisy studied her face. "Hi. Christy, right?"

Christy nodded.

"I didn't know you knew Christy," Adonis said.

"I don't."

"And neither do I." Ming Li walked over and introduced herself.

"Christy just got into town this morning," Adonis explained. "I was trying to call you earlier to tell you, but you didn't answer."

Daisy didn't care if Christy had only been in town an hour. She didn't want Adonis around her.

"Hey, Chris," someone said from behind them in the deepest voice that Daisy had ever heard.

As Daisy turned, a tall, handsome man two shades darker than Christy walked over to her and kissed her on the lips. Daisy watched them carefully, trying to determine if the kiss was real. She noted with relief that it was almost as passionate as the one she and Adonis had just shared.

"Hey, Rock," Adonis said to the man, "what took you so long?"

Rock held a bag in the air. "Man, I forgot where we parked. If

I didn't need my own stick to shoot with, I would've just given up."

"Oh," Adonis said with a smile. "This is Daisy and Ming Li." Adonis turned to Daisy then. "This is Christy's *husband,* Rock. We played ball together in college." Adonis leaned over and whispered in her ear, "He's been here the whole time. Just forgot his stick in the car."

Daisy smiled graciously and shook Rock's hand. She winked at Adonis and gave Ming Li a knowing look. She knew her instincts had been right, just as she knew she could trust her man.

———————

Daisy awoke in Adonis's arms. She grabbed a peppermint from her bedside table and popped it into her mouth. *No way am I going to ruin the moment with morning breath,* she thought. Then she shivered. Her upper body was warm from his embrace, but the lower part was cold. She looked down and realized that the covers had toppled to the floor sometime during the night. She smiled. *It's no wonder.* She scooted her naked body against his and nibbled on his index finger. Their evening had been eventful, but their night had been magical. She moaned with pleasure, remembering all the things he had done to her, with her, and for her. Adonis had always been attentive in bed, a pleaser. He made her feel as she'd never felt before.

But last night had been different. Although Daisy had never imagined it possible, the sex had been better than ever. His kisses had seemed more delicious, his body more scrumptious. She looked at him while he slept and decided that he was everything she needed in a man.

He stirred and released her. "Morning, baby." He kissed her on the forehead. "I'll be right back." He got out of bed and left the room.

Daisy heard water running in the bathroom and settled in to wait for him. A sweet calm took over her senses as she inhaled his scent on the pillow. She realized how weak she was for him.

Adonis returned and scooped her into his arms.

"What are you doing?" Daisy snuggled close to his warm, naked body. In less than twenty-four hours, she had forgotten how jealous she had been. She closed her eyes and felt herself float higher and higher with each step that he took.

Adonis blew hair out of Daisy's eyes and smiled. "I'm carrying my queen to her bath. What does it look like?"

"Is that right? Your queen, hunh?" she said as he gently set her into the warm, captivating bubbles. She closed her eyes, letting the whole world disappear.

Adonis slid into the tub behind her and wedged his legs on either side of hers. Daisy didn't care that it was almost too snug; Adonis could never be too close.

"Yes, my queen." He laughed.

She rested her head on his chest while he lathered her breasts. "What's so funny?"

Adonis kissed her wet temple. "You were going to fight for yours last night, hunh? You weren't playing. You were just going to walk in there and take your man," he teased.

"Shut up," Daisy said playfully. "It wasn't like that at all," she lied.

"Yes, it was. And I liked it . . . your assertiveness. I didn't think you had it in you. I didn't know you cared that much."

"Are you kidding? You don't know, do you?"

"Know what? Tell me what I don't know."

She stared at him. She hadn't yet told him how she felt, although she had promised herself that she would. She decided to wait until later, until she could set the moment. She didn't want to be in the bathtub when she told him that she loved him.

"Did the sex seem different to you last night . . . better?" she asked, trying to avoid his question.

Adonis smiled and kissed her softly. "It was better. Do you know why?"

Daisy shook her head.

"It was more than just sex." He rose to his knees and turned Daisy around. He laid her down, holding the back of her head with one hand while he parted her legs with the other. Over the next few minutes, she told him that she loved him over and over again.

Daisy studied her face in the mirror and smiled at the after-glow. She couldn't believe that she'd told Adonis she loved him. She'd never thought she'd be capable of loving someone else, of trusting someone else, after Jasper. But Adonis wasn't just someone.

A cool breeze swept through the room, interrupting her thoughts. Adonis walked into the bathroom fully dressed and sat down on the commode to watch as she massaged Palmer's into her skin. He handed her a robe, staring at her legs all the while.

"You like?" she asked, knowing full well that he did.

Adonis shushed her.

"What? You don't want to help?" She lifted her leg and placed her foot high up on his chest.

Adonis stood quickly, grabbed her, and covered her mouth. "Ssh!" A serious look clouded his face. "There's a social worker here to see you," he whispered.

"Here? Now?" Daisy stamped her foot and tugged at her hair. She began to pace, and tears welled up. She looked helplessly at Adonis. "I'm so stupid. I should've know they'd pop up sooner or later. Now how am I supposed to explain us being like . . . like . . . naked? How can I prove I'm a good mom if I'm parading around the house with a man?"

Adonis brushed her hair out of her face. "Don't worry. It's okay."

"But—"

He placed his hand over her mouth. "I straightened up the place before I let her in. She thinks I'm Jay's cousin by marriage, which is true, and that I'd came by to check on you because you don't feel well. So try to look sick. I didn't want to lie, but I figured it wouldn't look good, with your being undressed and all. I'll be in the living room." He closed the door softly behind him.

Daisy practically jumped into her nightgown and robe. She

tousled her hair and rubbed her eyes, trying to make them look red. She'd had no idea that Mrs. Tompkins was coming over. Showing up unannounced was probably part of her job, catching people off guard to see how they really lived. Daisy grabbed a wad of toilet paper from the roll and headed for the living room, praying that Mrs. Tompkins was bearing good news.

As Daisy stepped into the room, she cleared her throat and wiped her nose. But then she froze. It wasn't Mrs. Tompkins standing in her living room, but a woman she'd never met before.

"Hello," Daisy greeted her, trying to summon a smile. All of a sudden, she really didn't feel well. Her heart was pounding, and her skin felt warm and clammy. At least she knew that Mrs. Tompkins was on her side.

The woman in the tan suit smiled. "Hello, Ms. . . . ," she began, looking inside the file in her hand. "Ms. Parker. My name is Edith Stokely. I'm Jay's new social worker."

"Oh, I forgot. Mrs. Tompkins did tell me that she wouldn't be handling our case anymore."

"Yes, she was promoted. I'm really sorry to bother you. Jay's cousin here told me that you're not feeling well. I'll try to make this as quick as I can. May I take a look around your place?"

"Sure." Daisy sat down across from Adonis. She wanted to follow Ms. Stokely, but she didn't want it to look as though she was hiding something.

Shit! She turned to Adonis and whispered, "The bedroom. The sheets—the smell—my panties."

Adonis waved it away. "I took care of all that. Don't worry."

Daisy heard Ms. Stokely in the kitchen next, opening and closing cabinets. *What the hell is she looking for? I know that that's not my refrigerator I hear opening.*

Ms. Stokely appeared in the doorway. She looked in the file again, then began writing. "Okay, Ms. Parker. We'll be in touch."

"Ms. Stokely, when can I see my son?"

"I'm not really sure. I have to take this report back to my supervisor."

"Is Mrs. Tompkins your supervisor?"

"Well, no. She's the head of our division."

Daisy nodded. "Ms. Stokely, maybe you can check with Mrs. Tompkins—"

"I'm afraid it's not that easy. We have rules to follow, standard procedures that must be handled in a certain order."

"Red tape, right? Wait here a second. Adonis, can you entertain Edith? I have to make a call."

Daisy went into her bedroom and searched her wallet for Mrs. Tompkins's card. She dialed her number and prayed that she'd be in the office. Daisy flipped the card over and found her cell phone number on the back.

"Hello, Mrs. Tompkins? This is Daisy Parker calling to take you up on your offer." She explained that she wanted to see Jay. She related what Edith Stokely had told her about going through the required procedures. Mrs. Tompkins listened intently.

"You *are* over the division, right?"

"Yes, I am," Mrs. Tompkins replied with a smile in her voice.

"So you can make it happen? I don't want to get you into trouble with your higher-ups, but you know better than I do how much Jay needs me. And how much I need him."

"Let me speak to Ms. Stokely."

Daisy was grinning as she walked into the living room. She handed Ms. Stokely the phone, then listened gleefully as Ms. Stokely stammered and apologized. Daisy winked at Adonis and held out her hand for the phone after Ms. Stokely hung up.

Ms. Stokely smiled. "Ms. Parker, are you a God-fearing woman? Off the record."

Daisy nodded. She wasn't exactly religious, but she believed. "Yes."

"Good, because you have quite a few angels looking after you—one being Mrs. Tompkins. Anyway, Jay can come visit you for a weekend. I don't know what you've done, but keep doing it."

"Believe me, I will."

19

*D*aisy had shopped until she could shop no more. She shouldn't have spent so much money, but she didn't care. Her son was coming home. It had been almost two weeks since Ms. Stokely had approved her, but apparently they'd had a little situation—namely, Jasper's mother—to deal with first.

Mrs. Tompkins had called and told Daisy that Mrs. Stevens, after hearing about Jay's weekend visit, had gone to court to try to stop it. Mrs. Tompkins assumed that Mrs. Stevens had counted on her money, her status as grandmother, and her social standing to help her. But what she hadn't counted on was the judge asking Jay what *he* wanted.

Daisy hummed as she wrapped Jay's last gift. It was spring, but she was singing Christmas carols, since Jay's visit reminded her of how she usually felt on December 25.

Adonis wiped his hands on his pants. "I've finished hanging the welcome banner. Do you need any help?"

Daisy smiled. "No, this is the last one."

He hugged her from behind. "No, it's not."

Daisy looked around the living room. "I could've sworn this was it."

He massaged her shoulders. "I'll be right back. I have some gifts for him out in the car."

"You didn't have to—"

"Yes, I did. I'm starting to feel like he's as much mine as yours. I want him here just as much as you do."

I am so in love with you, she mouthed behind his back as he left the apartment. Ms. Stokely had been right; someone was definitely watching out for her.

When the buzzer rang, Daisy glanced at her watch. Her heart raced. Jay was scheduled to arrive at any moment. She ran to answer the intercom, pausing to fix herself in the mirror hanging next to the door.

"Who is it?" she sang.

"Girl, it's us," Gigi announced.

Disappointed, Daisy buzzed them in. "It'll be fine," she reassured herself. "He'll be here any second."

While she waited for them to come up, Daisy finished cleaning up the wrapping paper and strategically stacked the gifts around the cake. *It sure is taking Gigi and Ming Li a long time to get up here. They must've run into Adonis.*

The bell rang.

"Just a second," she called out as she maneuvered a box into position.

She opened the door to see Gigi and Ming Li standing there smiling.

"Hey, y'all." Daisy hugged them and stepped aside as they came in, then saw in surprise that Adonis was standing behind them. "Sweetie, why didn't you use the key?" she asked, taking some gifts from the pile in his arms.

He kissed her on the cheek and walked in.

Jay stood behind him, wearing the biggest grin she'd ever seen.

Daisy dropped the presents, and her hand went to her mouth. The whole room disappeared. She held out her arms, and he ran into them. She grabbed him, squeezed him, and kissed him all over his face.

"Hi, Mom." He grinned, brushing the tears off her face before wrapping his arms around her neck.

Daisy pushed him back at arm's length and looked at him. She ran her hands over his wavy hair and began kissing him again. Her tears ran freely when she saw how big he'd gotten, how handsome he was. Her baby had been growing up out of her sight.

"Ah, Mom. Not the waterworks, please," he said, hugging her again.

"I missed you, Jay. I've missed you so much, baby. I'm so sorry they took you."

"He is too."

Daisy looked up to see Ms. Stokely smiling at her. "He told me about it on the way here. He told me everything. Now I see what Mrs. Tompkins was talking about. If it were up to me, we'd skip the whole court process and just let him stay forever."

"That sounds good to me." Daisy wiped her eyes and moved to hug Ms. Stokely. "Thanks for bringing him."

"Happy to. Maybe next time it'll be for good."

"Would you like to stay for his party? I know it's a little strange, but he wasn't here for Christmas."

"I would love to, but I have another case to attend to. Have fun, though. Who said Christmas only comes once a year? I have a feeling that Santa will be visiting you again real soon." Ms. Stokely winked at Daisy and let herself out.

Daisy decided that she must be dreaming. She turned around slowly for fear that she'd wake up and find Jay gone. The past few moments seemed too good to be true. She swallowed hard when she saw Jay's eyes light up as he dug his finger into the icing on his cake. *He's so beautiful. And he's mine, at least for the weekend.*

Daisy tucked Jay into bed after reading him a story. She kissed him on the cheek and stood in his doorway before turning off the light. She just had to study him again. He seemed so grown-up. She hoped that it was simply time that had caused him to grow up so quickly, not his living situation. She wanted to question him, to ask him if his step-grandfather had mistreated him in any way. But she decided not to, not on his first day home. She started to close his bedroom door, but his voice stopped her.

"Mom?"

"Yes, sweetie, what is it?"

"I love you."

"I love you too, Jay. More than life itself." She eased the door closed until she heard it click, then returned to the living room.

"Some party, hunh?" Adonis asked, patting the seat beside him.

"Yes, it was." Daisy smiled, curling up next to him.

"He seemed to really like his gifts."

"Yes, he's easy to please."

She laid her head on Adonis's chest, and neither of them said anything for a moment. They knew the small talk was leading nowhere. While she wanted him to stay and share not only her bed but her happiness, he couldn't. The way he squeezed her hand told her that he didn't want to go, either. But they both knew that he had to. She'd never allow a man, even the one she was madly in love with, to share her bed while Jay was in the house.

————

Daisy sat at the kitchen table and played with her breakfast of turkey sausage and over-easy eggs. The night had flown by, and the reality that Jay had only one more day left was digging into her soul.

"Hey, Mom." He appeared in the doorway.

"Hey, sweetie. Are you hungry?"

"No," he said, shaking his head. "I already ate. I had cereal while you were in the shower."

"Oh, sweetie, are you sure? Wouldn't you like a hot breakfast? It's cool out."

"Nope, I had four bowls of cereal."

"Four? You were that hungry?"

Jay laughed. "Not really. It's just that Grandma Stevens won't allow me to eat cold cereal. She makes me eat oatmeal."

Daisy winced. Jay hated oatmeal. "Well, here at home you can eat whatever you want, as long as it's balanced. You can have cereal for dinner if you want to."

"Thanks." He kissed her on the cheek. "Can you take me to see my dad?"

Daisy winced again and closed her eyes. She didn't want to go to the cemetery, but she had no right to deny him. "Sure, but we'll have to wear jackets. It's colder out than it looks."

———————

Trudging slowly behind Jay on the soggy grass, Daisy surveyed the manicured grounds and fresh flowers adorning the gravesites. If she had thought about it, she would have purchased an arrangement for Jasper's grave. She smiled. Months before, the idea of bringing flowers would have been out of the question. But she'd long been over him. He was dead and couldn't hurt her anymore. She stood back a distance and urged Jay to go on without her. A creepy feeling came to her as she remembered the way she'd pissed on his grave. Guilt tried to creep in, but she quickly dismissed it. He'd deserved a lot worse.

Jay ran over to her. "Mom, someone's already there."

Daisy grabbed him by the hand and led him toward Jasper's oversize headstone. *See, you did this to him, Jasper.*

"Camille?"

Camille turned around. She was holding one of the prettiest baby girls that Daisy had seen in a long time. "Hey, Daisy. I never thought I'd see you here."

Daisy smiled. "And you would've been right," she said, nodding toward Jay, "but he asked me to bring him."

"I'm here for Camilla too. She never knew him, but it's my responsibility to make sure that she knows *about* him . . . the good things, anyway."

"That's what good mothers do. Lucky for her to have a woman like you as her mother," Daisy said sincerely.

Camille walked up to Jay and introduced herself as a friend of his parents.

"Come here," she said, beckoning to Daisy with her free hand. "Let me show you something."

Daisy slowly moved closer.

"Look at the resemblance," Camille went on. "Isn't it scary?" She held Camilla out next to Jay.

Daisy stared in disbelief at their pretty, flawless dark skin, slanted eyes, and deep dimples. "They look just alike, like they have the same parents." She turned to Jay. "Go ahead and visit your father, baby. I'm going to be right over there." She pointed to where she'd been standing earlier. "Let's walk," she said to Camille.

"Just a second, I have to get Camilla out of this air. My mother's waiting in the Jeep. I'll put her in her car seat, and then I'll meet you."

Daisy walked in silence, the vision of Camilla and Jay filling her mind. They looked too much alike, too much like Jasper, or Jonathan. Too much like the Stevenses. *They have some strong genes.* She glanced over her shoulder at Jay, who stood looking like a smaller version of his father.

"Okay." Camille walked up to Daisy, rubbing her hands together. "It's starting to get chilly."

Daisy nodded. She'd asked her to walk because she didn't want Jay to overhear their conversation. "Camille, can I ask you a personal question?"

Camille chuckled nervously. "Daisy, everything between us has been personal. Go ahead."

"Why have you been so nice to me, so good to me and Jay? I mean, I was sleeping with your husband, living with him. I can't say I would've done the same for you."

"Yes, you would've. I can tell that you're a good, caring person. Anyone who fights for someone else's child without having been married to the parent has to have a good heart." Camille paused. "I knew we'd talk about this one day; I just didn't think it'd be so close to *him*."

"Too bad he can't hear us." Daisy laughed. She felt lighter on her feet, just thinking about making Jasper as uncomfortable as he had once made her.

"Maybe he's turning in his grave as we speak." Camille laughed, then turned serious. "I'm nice to you because I have to be. I need to be. No, actually, I have no choice but to be. Don't get me wrong . . . I hated you something fierce. I hated the sound of your name and the very sight of you." She laughed again. "Even though we do look alike. But really, I blamed you for Jasper's infidelity, and just about everything else you can think of."

"The feeling was mutual, believe me."

"I do. But you know what? I realized that you didn't do anything to me intentionally. You didn't even know about me, and I didn't know that you existed. Hell, most of it wasn't our fault. We do have to take some of the blame, though. He did what he wanted to do, but we *both* let him. After I went to counseling—"

"You saw a therapist?"

"I had to. My emotional state was fragile, and there I was, counseling patients. Talk about the blind leading the blind. I think I needed to talk to them more than they needed to talk to me. But actually, most psychiatrists eventually seek therapy. After all the problems we're faced with on a daily basis, we get so wrapped up in helping someone else, that sometimes we forget to handle our own."

"Makes sense."

"Yes, it makes a lot of sense. Therapy helped me tremendously, and it made me realize that instead of trying to hurt you, I should've been trying to help you. We women get so caught up in what another woman is doing with our men that we forget that our men are to blame too. A woman can't make a man do anything he doesn't want to do. It takes two to get down, and if a man says no, then it's a no go."

"Amen."

"And after I saw Jay, after I had Camilla, I realized that I was wrong. Kids aren't supposed to suffer for our mistakes." Camilla paused, lowering her eyes. "I guess you can say that I got over being a woman scorned. I knew he was cheating, just like you did. We just both had our blinders on."

Daisy wanted to hug Camille, but settled for a smile. While she appreciated everything the woman had done for her and Jay, Daisy still didn't consider Camille a friend. "Thank you for helping me—helping us. You and Mrs. Tompkins have been saviors. I don't know what I would've done without you two."

"So, did you get custody yet?"

Daisy shook her head. "Not yet."

"Don't worry, you will. That boy is your son. Jasper gave him to you when he handed over all the responsibility to you. He did it first when Jay was a baby, then again when he died and left you to fend for yourselves. Don't let them take him away."

"I'm not. Whatever it takes—"

"You'll get him." Camille turned to walk away. "Oh, Daisy?"

"Yes?"

"Promise me something."

"What?"

"That as soon as you get Jay back for good, you'll call me. That you'll allow him and Camilla to be siblings."

Daisy smiled and nodded. "What are you doing for the holidays?"

———

Daisy woke up crying. She grabbed her pillow and tried to muffle her pain. The last thing she wanted was for Jay to hear her. Their weekend had been wonderful, but it was coming to an end too quickly. She sat up, slipped on her house shoes, and went to peek into his room. She just wanted to see his face and watch him breathe.

Quietly, she opened his door and peered in. A whimper escaped her. Just the sight of him stirred something inside her. The hurt within her turned to urgency. She needed Jay as much as she needed life. The sooner she got custody, the faster everything would be better. But she knew that for her and Jay to have the life that she wanted for them, she'd have to decide what to do about Lani.

Daisy quickly closed his door and went to call Adonis. She

didn't stop to consider that he was probably still in a deep slumber. He'd been able to soothe her many times before, and she needed him again; not his reassurance, just his support. Instinct told her that she was on the right path, and she'd learned to trust her feelings. She'd get to be a full-time mother again. But in the meantime, letting go was hard.

Adonis answered on the second ring.

"I need you to come over. Please."

"I'll be right there," he said, and hung up.

Daisy went to her closet and turned on the light. She pushed her clothes to the side and shuffled boxes around until she saw the safe. Jay's upcoming departure had brought back her thoughts of Lani, and at that moment, she needed them both more than ever. She carried the small safe from the closet, set it on the bed, and entered the combination. She opened it carefully, and fingered the mustard-colored envelopes that had once frightened her. She opened each of the envelopes and spread the documents facedown on the bed. *One, two, three. Eenie, meenie, minee, moe.* She turned the first one over and looked at it. Lani's birth certificate. *Take a tiger by his toe.* A medical file with her sister's name on it. *My mother told me to pick the best one, and you're not it.* A picture of Calvin.

She arranged the papers neatly in the order that she would handle each problem. *I'll handle Calvin. Then talk to Brea. Then, if all goes well, Lani will be in my life more.* She closed her eyes and remembered her last conversation with Calvin. She was a grown woman who knew right from wrong, and she knew she'd done the best thing for her daughter. Although she wanted her daughter back, Ms. Christine had been right; Daisy didn't deserve Lani, just as the Stevenses didn't deserve Jay. Brea was Lani's mother, and she was Jay's. *If Jay loves me like I birthed him, then Lani must love Brea the same.*

The buzzer interrupted her. She got up carefully, trying to keep the papers from shifting. Adonis knew the whole story anyway, she told herself, so she didn't have to hide them. She padded softly through the apartment. Jay had been sleeping lightly during his visit, and she didn't want to wake him.

"You alright?" Adonis asked as she relaxed into his arms. "I got here as quick as I could."

"I'm better, now that I know what I have to do," she said as she headed back to the bedroom.

"What do you have to do?" he said, following her. "You're not planning on running with Jay, are you?"

"No, of course not. They'd never give him to me if I did something that stupid." She pointed at the papers. "I know what to do about Lani—"

"Are you sure that you want to?" Adonis interrupted. "I mean, have you really thought about it? Have you thought about how Lani would feel being ripped from your sister? Think of Jay, and how he felt being taken away from the only mother *he's* ever known."

Daisy smiled sadly. "You didn't let me finish. I know how Brea and Lani would feel: just as horrible as Jay and I feel being separated. That's why I'm *not* going to try to get custody." Daisy shook her head in disbelief at her past selfishness. "I don't know how I could ever have thought of being so cruel. I was only thinking of myself."

Adonis sat down beside her and held her. "It's understandable. It's only natural to want to be a part of your child's life. But you can. There are other ways, you know."

Daisy smiled. "Yes, there are."

Daisy stayed in her room when Adonis answered the door for Ms. Stokely. Daisy held Jay tightly and promised him that they'd be together soon. She knew that her promise wasn't concrete, but it was something that they both needed to hear, a ray of hope they could both hang on to. She wiped his tears, swallowing her own. Someone had to be the stronger one, and she was the mother, so it had been delegated to her.

"It's going to be okay," she assured him. "Just call me if anything happens, or if anyone bothers you. Or for any reason at all. I don't care what time it is, or where I'm at. You remember the numbers, don't you?"

Jay nodded and sniffled. "I love you, Mom."

"I know, sweetie. I love you too." She took his hand and stood up. "Ms. Stokely is here for you." She swallowed hard. "Be good, okay? It's not her fault. She's just doing her job." Daisy kissed him on his forehead and led him to the living room.

Ms. Stokely smiled at them. Jay turned and grabbed Daisy by the waist and held on as tight as he could. Daisy just nodded at the social worker. She couldn't force a smile when she was crushed.

"I'm sorry, Jay," Ms. Stokely said. "But we have to go now."

Adonis bent down and whispered in Jay's ear.

Jay looked at him and nodded, then let go of Daisy. He stood on his tiptoes and kissed her on the cheek.

Daisy hugged him one last time. "Remember what I told you . . . I'll never leave you."

"We'll never leave each other," Jay said, and walked away. "I love you, Mom," he called out from the hallway.

Daisy turned, ran to the bathroom, and locked the door. She needed time to herself, time to cry as never before. *It's harder when you* see *them take your child away.*

Daisy lay alone in her bed and tried to sleep. Jay's departure had left her not only sad, but uneasy. She looked at the clock and was sure that he too was in bed, and she hoped that he was asleep.

She got up and walked to the window. She opened the curtains and searched for the brightest star. She recalled Ms. Christine's conversation about the star and mouthed the words, replacing names and times as she spoke. "You see that star right there, Jay? That bright one?" She pointed. "That's ours, mine and yours—our connection. For the past minute, I've watched that star, and I knew that you could see it too. I'll never be too far away for you to reach me. Whether I'm home or up there in heaven with Ma Dear, I'm always going to be here for you." She dabbed her eyes and went to brew herself a cup of chamomile tea.

The doorbell rang as she was on her way to the kitchen. How did people keep getting into her building without being buzzed in? *I bet Ma showed them all.*

She opened the door, expecting to see Adonis, but she found Gigi instead.

"Hey," Gigi said softly as she walked in.

"Hey, yourself. What are you doing out so late?" Daisy locked the door behind her.

"Well, I just got off the phone with my mother, and I had to see you."

"Are you going to tell me why, or do I have to guess?"

Gigi walked into the kitchen and sat down at the table. "Well, I have some good news and some bad news. Remember when Ming Li said that Jonathan knew his stepfather had fondled some child? Well, my mother told me how he knew. The woman who caught him lives right here in New York."

"Gigi, that's great! Where is she? Do you think she'll come to court?"

Gigi shook her head. "That's the bad news. She won't talk to anyone about it. Apparently, she was the stepfather's mistress, and it was her son he touched."

"Do you know where she lives?"

"I can find out. My mother said the lady's kept the same telephone number for years, so maybe she still lives in the same place."

"What's her name?"

"Louise Black."

"Call your mother."

Daisy pulled on her shoes and jeans and prepared herself mentally. While she empathized with what the woman had endured, Daisy had her own turmoil to deal with. "Oh, she'll talk. She has to," she muttered as she grabbed a jacket and her purse and headed to the kitchen.

"I got it," Gigi said, then noticed how Daisy was dressed. "Where are you going looking like that?"

"We're going to Louise Black's house. Never mind what I have on. Let's go." Daisy pulled Gigi by her sleeve.

Daisy pulled into the driveway of the quaint brick house in Jamaica Estates. She looked at the illuminated address and sighed. She was in the right place, but with the exception of the porch light, the house was dark. She shrugged. She had no time to think about etiquette.

"You can stay here if you want," she said to Gigi, who looked reluctant. Daisy walked up the sidewalk that led to the front door and rang the bell, then pounded the metal knocker against the door.

Gigi came up slowly behind her. "Are you sure about this?"

"Who is it?" an older woman's voice asked from inside.

"Daisy Parker," Daisy replied firmly, as if her name would be recognized.

She saw a hand pull the curtain back, followed by a face peeking out. "You must have the wrong house. I don't know anyone by that name."

Daisy stood on her tiptoes. "I'm looking for a Ms. Louise Black. I'm Elaine Mitchell's niece," Daisy lied, using Gigi's mother's name. She felt Gigi bump her.

Daisy stepped back when she heard the front door unlock. She held her breath as it eased open to reveal a small, shadowy figure on the other side.

"Elaine Mitchell, you say?"

"Yes, ma'am. Are you Ms. Black?"

The front door opened all the way. "Yes, I am." Louise Black, in rollers and a sheer bed cap, eyed Daisy and Gigi. "Y'all two young ladies alone?"

Daisy nodded.

"Who are you?" Ms. Black asked, turning to Gigi.

"I'm Elaine's daughter, Gigi Mitchell."

A smile spread across the older woman's face. She looked soft and trusting. "Well, I'll say. Elaine Mitchell, hunh? Y'all come on in, then. It's too late for two young women to be out alone." She held the door open, and Daisy and Gigi stepped inside the dark house.

Ms. Black closed and bolted the door, then turned on a lamp. "Have a seat. Is there anything I can get you? Y'all alright? It's pretty late. I was just starting to drift off."

Daisy took a seat on the plastic-covered furniture. "No, I'm not alright, Ms. Black. My son's been taken away."

"Oh, my. That's too bad. But I don't understand why you're here."

"My son is in the home of Elwyn Cane."

Ms. Black gasped and shook her head. She couldn't look Daisy in the eye. "I still don't know—"

"Yes, you do," Daisy said, raising her voice. "I already know what he did to your son. Help me, so he won't do it to mine."

"Please, Ms. Black," Gigi begged.

Vehemently, Ms. Black shook her head. "I can't."

"Why? Why would you allow a little boy to go through what your son went through? My son, Jay, is only nine years old."

"No!" Ms. Black said, rising. "You can leave now. You've over-stayed your welcome."

Daisy jumped up and grabbed Ms. Black by the shoulders. "You're going to help me—"

"What the hell is going on in here?" A man's voice came from behind, and Daisy felt her feet leave the ground.

Before she knew it she was airborne, her body slamming against the wall. She looked up into a large man's angry face. "I'm sorry," she said as Gigi helped her to her feet. "I didn't mean . . . Ms. Black, I'm so sorry. But I need your help." Daisy tried to look around the man.

"Who the hell are you?" he asked.

Gigi jumped in front of Daisy and explained the situation in one breath. "She's only trying to save her son," she explained.

"I need all the help I can get," Daisy said. "And if it takes you throwing me into another wall, then so be it. But I won't leave until—"

"Oh, yes, you will, if I want you to. But I'm not going to throw you out." The man's expression softened. "I'm going to give you what you want. It's not up to Mother to help you. You need me. My name is Thomas . . . I'm the one Elwyn *tried* to molest."

———————

They sat down and talked. Thomas insisted that he be allowed to testify before Daisy even had a chance to ask. Relief coursed through her when he told her to give him the date and time, and he'd be the first to enter the courtroom.

———————

Just as she was about to get into the tub, Daisy's phone rang. The night had been long, and she hadn't slept a wink, thinking about Thomas's agreement to go to court.

"Hello?" she answered irritably.

"Daisy," Kenneth Burgess said, "I got your message about Thomas Black, and I called and spoke to him. He's coming in tomorrow. More good news: we've got to be in court two weeks from Tuesday, at ten A.M. Meet me in my office at nine."

20

*W*earing a black designer suit and an air of confidence, Daisy strutted into the courtroom. She knew she looked good dressed to the nines, and she topped off the look with a huge smile. *If only they knew my whole ensemble came out of Ming Li's closet.* As she strutted alongside Kenneth Burgess to their table at the front of the courtroom, she locked eyes with Mrs. Stevens, who was sitting next to Elwyn Cane.

Daisy sat down, then turned to wave at Ming Li and Gigi. She was glad that they were there to support her. She smiled at Ms. Christine, who had flown in for the big day and was seated next to Adonis. Then she mouthed, *Thank you,* to Thomas Black. After everyone had settled in, Daisy searched the court for Jay. She didn't see him.

"Where's Jay?" she asked Kenneth.

"In the back, in the judge's chambers. There's going to be a lot of things said that he doesn't need to hear. Don't worry." Kenneth patted her hand. "He'll be out to testify."

The judge entered the courtroom and called for order. Daisy sat patiently as the case was introduced, silently praying that whoever had looked out for her before would continue to do so.

She sat back and crossed her legs when Mrs. Stevens's attorney asked the court to grant the Stevenses custody of Jay. He was Jonathan's son. In their eyes, and in the eyes of the law, as they interpreted it, Daisy didn't have a right to a child that was neither hers nor her deceased boyfriend's.

Kenneth patted her hand. "We have this in the bag," he whispered. "Watch what we spring on them." He winked, adding, "I've been saving this for last—you don't know anything about it." She realized he was trying to reassure her, but he'd confused her instead.

"Do you mean 'the last resort'?"

Kenneth nodded and patted his briefcase.

The Stevenses' lawyer closed with how much they'd be able to provide financially for Jay, topping it off with a list of the colleges they could afford. Daisy looked around. There must have been some mistake. They didn't call anyone to testify on their character or suitability as parents. *I guess they do believe that their money talks.*

Kenneth asked permission for counsel to approach the bench. Daisy couldn't hear what was going on, but she could tell from the Stevenses' lawyer's expression that whatever it was, he wasn't too happy about it. She heard him ask the judge not to admit it as evidence. Then the judge said loudly, "This is not criminal court. It's not only my job, but the state's job, to make sure that the child is in the best care."

Daisy sat back and watched Kenneth work. He called Camille to the stand first. She testified that she'd witnessed Jay being mistreated. Camille then gave her credentials as a doctor of psychiatry and urged the court not to let Jay wind up in an office like hers later on in life because the wrong decision had been made. She looked at Daisy and smiled, then pointed to her. "She's his mother, the one he belongs with."

Mrs. Tompkins testified next. She reaffirmed what Camille had said. "And I should know," she added, "because I'm a supervisor for Social Services. I've been a social worker for twenty years."

The Stevenses' lawyer had no questions.

Daisy looked at Mrs. Stevens, who shot her a dirty look. Daisy continued to stare, until she won the stare-down. No way was she going to let some old, stuck-up, no-good grandmother intimidate her. She could show her what to do with her money. She'd raised Jay almost his entire life, and they were the ones who were after *her* son, not the other way around.

Jasper's stepfather sat up and glared at her. Daisy winked at him politely and turned her head. She wouldn't give Chester-Chester the Child Molester a chance to ogle her. It was bad enough that he'd treated Jonathan coldly because he'd heard a rumor of his secret, but he had treated Jay the same way. Daisy admitted that the only reason the man was still breathing was because he hadn't touched Jay. *I'm not your wife,* Daisy thought. *I'd kill you dead first.*

"Any other witnesses?" the judge asked Kenneth.

Ming Li stood.

"Yes, four," Kenneth replied, and accompanied Ming Li to the stand.

Ming Li told her story. Guilt washed over the Stevenses. Their once brown complexions turned gray.

"And Jonathan told you this directly?"

"Yes," Ming Li said as tears ran down her face. "And he cried when he told me."

The court fell silent.

The judge stared at the Stevenses' lawyer as if urging him to speak out in defense of his clients. But he didn't. He sat stiff as a corpse.

Kenneth paused, running his fingers through his hair as if thinking. "Your Honor, I'd like to call someone to the stand that can testify against the Stevens household. Rather, against one Mr. Elwyn Cane, the step-grandfather of the child. Mr. Thomas Black, please come forward."

As Thomas walked toward the front of the courtroom, Daisy watched as uneasiness and guilt unmasked Elwyn. He shifted in his seat and dabbed his forehead with a handkerchief. She smiled when she saw him whisper in his wife's ear and quickly walk out.

Thomas was sworn in. Without hesitation, he told how Elwyn had attempted to fondle him on several occasions, but he'd always managed to escape. Pain and anger rose in his voice when he said that Elwyn had threatened to kill him if he ever uttered a word. Relief filled his voice when he explained how his mother had caught Elwyn red-handed, trying to pull Thomas's pants down.

The court stirred, and the judge called for Elwyn Cane, who was nowhere to be found.

The Stevenses' attorney kept his eyes on the floor and never cross-examined.

Kenneth maintained his professionalism. "Your Honor, I'd like to call Dr. Berkley from DNA Labs of America."

Dr. Berkley approached the stand and was sworn in.

"Dr. Berkley, this is the birth certificate that the state has on file for Jonathan Jasper Stevens, affectionately referred to as Jay. It states here that Jonathan Stevens is his father. However," Kenneth said, holding up the lab report, "this is the DNA lab report from your company, the result of a DNA test performed on Jasper Stevens and Jonathan Jasper Stevens. Could you explain this to the court?" He handed the report to Dr. Berkley.

Dr. Berkley put on her glasses and studied the document in her hand. "Oh, sure. I remember this case, because it was the first of its kind at our facilities. We tested it three times just to be sure."

"Yes, Doctor?"

"Well, there was no way to genetically determine who fathered Jonathan Jasper Stevens, because the potential fathers are identical twins and, therefore, have identical genes."

The judge sat up and stared at the doctor. "Can you repeat that?"

"Sure. There's no way to prove who fathered the child in question. While the birth certificate lists one brother as the father, the DNA test states that the other brother is the father. Even if both men were alive, there'd be no possible way to prove conclusively who fathered the child."

"So," Kenneth said, "let me make sure this is clear. You're saying that either man could be Jay's father—that both men could legally be his father?"

"Well, it's not for me to determine the legal status of the child. But both Jasper and Jonathan are his fathers genetically, because we can't tell them apart by their DNA."

"Thank you, Doctor. That will be all."

A smile appeared on the judge's face. "Well, that's a first for me too. I assume there'll be no cross-examination?" He looked at the Stevenses' lawyer, who declined. "Well, then, let's take a five-minute recess."

Daisy sat at the table feeling victorious, even though the court hadn't yet ruled in her favor. She patted Kenneth's hand in appreciation.

"Here," he said, sliding a blank envelope in front of her. "I forgot to give this to you. It came to my office yesterday sealed in a package addressed to me. That's why it's blank. Open it," he urged.

Daisy opened the envelope. As she carefully unfolded the papers, her mouth dropped. "Oh, no!" she breathed in disbelief as she stared at the insurance policy in her hand. She'd never thought about Jasper's 401(k) and death benefits from work.

Kenneth smiled. "Oh, yes."

Daisy's ears were ringing. Jay was set for life. "I'm so happy that Jasper did this for him." She hugged Kenneth.

Kenneth patted her on the back and whispered, "Look on the next page . . . see what he did for you."

Daisy swallowed and turned the page. "Oh, *shit!*" she said out loud at the sight of all the numbers. She looked around and saw that everyone was staring at her, but she didn't care. Tears ran down her face, and she closed her eyes, smiling. *Thank you, Jesus. Thank you.*

"Sometimes these things take time to clear. That's what took so long," Kenneth chuckled, squeezing her hand. "And 'the last re-sort' that Jasper wrote about is a video tape. While you can't view it—neither can I—Jasper assured me it could save Jay if it ever was needed. Would've told you sooner, but I couldn't."

The bailiff told both Kenneth and the Stevenses' attorney that the judge would like to see them in the viewing room.

Daisy sat as patiently as she could, but it took everything she had in her not to jump up and shout for joy. But she was sad too, thinking of all that she'd had to go through, most of which would have been avoidable had she and Jay received their money sooner. But a person had to suffer to grow, she admitted to herself. She wouldn't be half the woman she was today if she hadn't.

Kenneth hummed on his way back to the table. The other lawyer kept his eyes downcast as he walked.

The judge returned to the bench and banged the gavel, announcing that court was back in session. "Ladies and gentlemen, I want you all on your best behavior. Jay is coming out to testify, and he's nervous. He's a good kid, and I can see why everyone wants him."

Daisy composed herself. She couldn't wait to tell Jay that his father hadn't forgotten him, that even though he was gone, he'd still managed to make sure that Jay was taken care of. She looked over at Mrs. Stevens and held up her papers. *Take that, bitch. He doesn't need your money.*

Jay emerged from the judge's chambers. Daisy smiled at him as their eyes met. *It's going to be okay,* she mouthed.

He nodded and said, "I know."

"What did you say?" the judge asked him.

"My mom told me that it's going to be okay, and I said I know."

The judged smiled. "Your mom's right."

Once Jay was sworn in, he took a seat and kept his eyes on Daisy. Tears were still running down her face, but for a different reason now. She hated that Jay had to sit on the stand and testify. He was too young to go through something like that. But according to the court, he was old enough to express his wants and tell the truth.

Daisy kept her eyes on her lap while he spoke. She didn't want the judge to think that she was influencing his answers. When Kenneth asked Jay how the Stevenses were treating him, Daisy's eyes shot up.

"Okay, I guess." Jay shrugged. "I don't really know them, and they don't really know me. Sometimes I feel like I'm in the way. But my nanny likes me."

Daisy winced.

"What about your mom—Daisy? How does she treat you?"

Jay looked at her and smiled. "Are you kidding? My mom's the best. We do everything together. She knows all about me, and she doesn't make me eat oatmeal. I still have to eat broccoli and stuff like that, but not oatmeal. When I got to visit her, she even took me to see my dad's grave. Grandma Stevens wouldn't."

Kenneth approached the witness stand and leaned casually against it. "Jay, I'm going to ask you an important question, okay? I know you're an honest boy, and I want you to tell me the truth. There is no wrong answer. It's no trick question, and no one's going to get mad at you. Who would you like to live with? Your grandparents, or your—"

"My mom!" Jay interrupted him. "She said she'd never leave me, and I promised her that I'd never leave her. And I don't lie to my mom."

Daisy nodded, blinking back her tears. *Yes, baby.*

"That's all, Your Honor. We rest our case." Kenneth walked away.

"Cross-examination?" the judge called out.

"We rest," the Stevenses' attorney replied.

The judge looked down at his podium and flipped through some papers, then cleared his throat. "Well, based on the testimony heard today and the sealed legal videotape that I've watched, my decision is made. Jasper Stevens spoke from the grave today and asked the court to save his son, Jay. He was thorough with his story, giving just about every detail spoken in this room. And because the court or doctors cannot dispute his paternity I will uphold that he is Jay's father. I will also uphold his request as to where Jay shall be placed. The great thing about this case is that it proves that a person doesn't have to be biologically related to love a child. A lot of the information revealed here was sad and enlightening. The DNA test taught me something I didn't know. However, there was one thing that the DNA test didn't need to reveal: no medical document or court can dispute where this child needs to be. Jonathan Jasper Stevens needs to be with his mother, Daisy Parker. Daisy Parker, I grant you full custody. Jay, you can go to your mother now."

"Come on, baby. Let's go home." Daisy held her arms out and embraced him.

"Forever?"

"Forever. I told you I'd never leave you."

Daisy sat at Ms. Christine's kitchen table and watched through the window as Jay and Lani played outside. She was smiling so hard that her face hurt. Seeing her children playing together was magical, even if she was pretending to be an aunt to one of them.

"They're something else, hunh?" Ms. Christine said as she peeled an orange.

"Yes, they are. They get along so well. Like brother and sister."

Ms. Christine shot Daisy a don't-you-start-that look.

"Don't worry, Ma. I didn't mean it like that."

"Good. Have you talked to Brea? She said she was going to call you."

"I just got here last night, Ma. When did she tell you that?"

"This morning, when she dropped Lani off. Right before she went to work. You know she lost her baby?"

Daisy shook her head. "No. I didn't know. How is she?"

"When you talk to her, ask her. I'm tired of being y'all's go-between."

Daisy bit her lip.

"And straighten your face before I warm your behind."

Daisy laughed. "Do you know how I can reach Calvin? I want to talk to him about dropping his custody suit."

Ms. Christine smiled. "Yes, I have his number around here

somewhere." She got up from the table. "Let me go find it for you."

Daisy got up and walked outside onto the side porch. She leaned against the rail and watched the kids play softball. "You two be careful not to break your grandmother's window. I don't want to hear her mouth."

"Okay, Mom," Jay said as he held the bat and waited for Lani to throw.

"Yes, Aunt Daisy." Lani wound her arm as if she were pitching for the big leagues. "You ready, Jay? 'Cause I'm going to dust you." Her reddish, shoulder-length ponytail bounced with the movement of her head.

"Because, Lani. Not *'cause."*

Lani smiled. "Okay, Aunt Daisy. I'm still going to dust him, though." She giggled.

"You wish," Jay said.

Ms. Christine tapped Daisy on the shoulder and handed her Calvin's number. "Here you go. Use the phone in my room, in case you want to show out again," she teased.

———————

Daisy sat on her parents' king-size bed and propped herself up on the many pillows. *Well, here goes nothing.* She dialed.

A woman, whom Daisy assumed was Calvin's wife, answered on the second ring.

"Hello, this is Daisy Parker. Is Calvin in? I'd like to speak to him about Lalani." Daisy figured she'd give his wife all the information up front. She wouldn't want some woman calling her house and just asking for her husband. She wanted to show her the same respect that she'd want to receive if it were her on the other end of the line.

"Just a second," the woman said cordially, and put Daisy on hold.

"Yeah?" Calvin said.

Daisy cleared her throat. "Calvin, would it be possible for us to meet and talk about Lani? I'll be here until my son's spring break is over."

Calvin was silent for a moment. "Just a second."

Daisy could hear him relating her request to his wife. She smiled when she heard his wife tell him to meet Daisy.

"Where do you want to meet?" he asked when he returned to the line.

"It doesn't matter."

She heard the phone fumble on Calvin's end.

"You can come over here and talk," his wife offered.

"Thanks," Daisy said. "When would be a good time?"

"Now, if it's okay with you. Write the address down. You and Calvin need to come to some sort of agreement."

————————

Daisy rang the bell, stomping her feet to shake off the jitters.

The door opened, and Calvin appeared. "Come on in," he said, holding the screen open.

Daisy stepped inside and looked around, admiring his wife's taste and simplicity. Not a thing was out of place.

Calvin gestured toward the sofa. "Sit down. Would you like something to drink?"

"That's okay," Daisy said, wanting to make her visit as short as possible.

Calvin sat down across from her.

"Where's your wife? She's welcome to sit in. I don't want her to feel as if I'm disrespecting."

"She's in the bedroom. She'll be out to meet you when we finish. Lani's our daughter. She won't take part in any decisions, but she'll support mine."

Daisy shook her head. "Okay. Well, you know I'm here to talk about custody."

"You want custody?"

Daisy shook her head. "You know I'd love to have her. But, no, I'm not going after her. I've done a lot of thinking, and a lot of growing. It wouldn't be fair for me to rip her from the only parents she's ever known."

"You're serious, aren't you?"

"Yes. I just got Jay back, and I realized a lot while I was fighting for him. It hurt both of us when he was taken away. I'm the only mother he's ever known. Call it a revelation—a deciding factor."

Calvin scooted to the edge of his seat. "Daisy, let me ask you a question. How well do you know Lani?"

Daisy swallowed hard. "Not too well. Hardly at all. I'd seen her a couple of times, but then I disappeared for a while. Personal reasons."

"So you understand how much it kills me not to know her."

"Yes, I do. I'm here to ask you to give up on the custody suit, but I'm not suggesting that you give up knowing her. I think I've come up with a solution. If we can convince my sister, then we should all be happy. Satisfied, at least."

"What's the solution?"

"Well, Lani doesn't have godparents. I remember that much. Maybe you and I can be her legal godparents. That way, if anything should ever happen . . ."

"I gotcha." He paused. "As much as I'd like to say no, it may be a good idea. It wouldn't be fair for us to disrupt her life. If we were her godparents, we wouldn't be yanking her away from Brea, we'd just be adding to her circle."

"Exactly."

"Well, if it's done legally, I don't see why not."

———————

Daisy sat on the swing next to her sister as Jay and Lani played on the park's playground. She looked over at Brea and thought she was still just as beautiful as she'd been when they were teenagers. Her thick, sandy-brown hair still hung down her back, and her deep brown eyes were still as wise as if she'd lived a few times before.

Daisy smiled and prepared herself for the talk that she hoped wouldn't end up as an argument. They hadn't had a friendly conversation in a while, and Daisy realized how much she had missed her sister. *Maybe we can be friends.*

Brea turned to her as if on cue. "So, what are we here to talk about?"

Daisy nodded toward Lani.

Brea stopped swinging. "Daisy, I don't know why you want to take that child away from me. You don't even know her—"

"Let me stop you right there before this gets ugly. I didn't bring you here to fight."

"Then what did you bring me here for?"

"Well, me and Calvin—"

"You and *who?* I know you and Calvin aren't trying to cook something up to take Lani away from me. I should've known—"

"Wait, Brea. Hear me out."

Brea stood. "No, you hear me out. You're not getting her."

"We don't want custody. Calvin and I have decided against it."

"You and Calvin don't want custody? Yeah, right."

"I'm serious, Brea. I went to his house yesterday and talked to him. But we would like to be in her life."

Brea crossed her arms. "See, I knew it was a trick."

Daisy flung up her hands in surrender. "No tricks. She'll be yours legally. She'll still be your daughter. We won't ever try to take her away from you. All we want is to be her godparents. Nothing more."

Brea grabbed Daisy by the chin as she had when they were little. "Say it again. I want to see your eyes when you say it. I can tell if you're lying. You know I can."

"I said no tricks, Brea. She'll be legally yours. All we want is to be her godparents. We just want to do godparent things with her."

"I don't know. You, I can deal with, but Calvin . . . I don't trust him."

"He said he'd sign away his rights if necessary, if he has any."

Brea looked thoughtful. "Let me think about it. I have to talk to Phillip before I make any decisions. He *is* her father, don't forget."

———————

Daisy sat on the sofa pummeling the control with her fingers and yelled as she made her first touchdown. Jay looked at her as if she were crazy, but she didn't care. He'd been beating her for hours, at every video game he owned. He'd mastered all of them. She looked at her control and wondered whatever happened to Atari. *Now, that was a game.*

"Come on, Mom. Press the button. You're holding up progress."

"What difference does it make? You're winning anyway."

Jay huffed, and she tapped the back of his head playfully.

Jay laughed. "See, you're a sore loser."

The telephone rang.

Thank God. She set the control down. "Play the computer. I'm tired."

"Tired of losing," she heard Jay giggle as she went to answer. "Hello?"

"Daisy?" It was Mr. Wiles.

"Hey, Mr. Wiles. How are you?"

"Good. Good. Listen, the reason I'm calling is that I nominated you for that apprenticeship-training program I told you about, and I wondered if you'd be interested."

"I don't know. You never said what kind of program it was, where it's located, or when it starts," she said, laughing.

Mr. Wiles laughed too. "Guess I didn't tell you much. It says here that it starts in July. It lasts for a year or so, depending on which program you sign up for. There are three in total. Two you already know about: horticultural things and landscaping. I know they sound the same, but as you know, they're not."

"Yes, no need to preach to the choir," Daisy joked.

"Amen. The other is designing golf courses. Oh . . . and you can take it in Florida or California."

"I don't know, Mr. Wiles . . ."

"It'll pay you more than I do. Think about it. It's a great opportunity, and I'd hate to see you miss out on it."

"Okay, I'll let you know."

"By Friday. They want an answer by Friday."

Daisy hung up the phone, went back into the living room, and asked Jay to turn off the game. The more she thought about the opportunity, the more it appealed to her.

"Jay, how would you like to live near Grandma, Grandpa, and Lani?"

Jay turned to her and smiled. "That'd be great. Why? Are we moving to L.A.?"

Daisy shrugged. "Maybe, maybe not. We'll see. I'll let you know." She patted him on the back, kissed his cheek, and went into her bedroom. She lay down to think and closed her eyes. *What should I do?*

The next thing she knew, Jay was shaking her by the shoulder. "Hey, Mom. Adonis is here."

Daisy sat up. "What? What time is it?" She looked at her clock on the nightstand.

"It's almost seven. You've been asleep for over two hours."

"Tell him I'll be out in a second."

"Okay," Jay said. "He brought pizza. You want me to fix your plate?"

Daisy smiled. *This boy is too polite. He's going to make some woman very happy one day.* "No, thank you, sweetie." She followed him out of the room, but detoured into the bathroom to brush her teeth and wash her face.

Someone knocked on the door.

"You hungry?" Adonis asked.

"No. Jay already asked me."

"Can I come in?"

She heard the doorknob turn.

"If I say no, are you planning on coming in anyway?" She yanked the door open.

Adonis tumbled inside. "What did you do that for?" He kissed her on the cheek.

"Because you turned the knob like you were so sure I'd say yes."

He closed the door behind him, gently lifted her chin, and kissed her deeply. "You say yes to everything else."

"You do too."

"How can I say no to you? Last time I checked, I loved you." *Now is as good of a time as any.* "Well, since you can't say no, I guess you'll be moving back to California with me and Jay."

Adonis's hands dropped. "What?"

"What's the matter?"

"When did you decide to move back home?"

Daisy shrugged. "Just now, I guess."

"Why?"

"Well, Mr. Wiles offered me a great opportunity to get into this training program to learn how to design golf courses. It'll pay me more than my current salary."

Adonis laughed. "Are you serious?"

Daisy frowned. "Yes. And do you know how much people get paid to design golf courses?"

Adonis shook his head, a sober expression on his face. "No," he said, and then his tone became emphatic. "I thought we had something, that we were together."

"Adonis, I don't see what the big deal is. Your job has you moving from place to place. You were going to have to go back to L.A. soon anyway."

"But why are you concerned with the training program? You don't need the money. You don't ever have to work again if you invest it right."

Daisy held up a finger. "See, that's where you're wrong. I may be set financially, but I do have to work. Besides, I have to set an example for Jay. I don't want him to grow up thinking he doesn't need to work because his dad left him a lot of money. That's not how the real world works. Furthermore, I don't want him to wind up with some lazy woman because he saw me sitting home all day."

Adonis looked crestfallen. "You're right. You have a point. I'll have to think about it, though. When does the training program start?"

"July."

"Give me some time."

"Take all the time you need, Adonis. I love you, and I would love nothing more than for us to be together. But you must understand something: I once sacrificed my identity and what I wanted in life for love, and I lost myself in the process. It cost me too much, and I won't do it again. I was dead, and I resurrected myself. If I stay here because you want me to, I'll have done all that for nothing. If I throw all my hard work out the window, I might as well be pushing up daisies."

Epilogue

*D*aisy lay back on the beach lounger and adjusted her visor. She closed her eyes and relished the warmth of the California sunshine. She smiled and nodded her head to the music blaring from the radio.

"Hey, Mom, look!" Jay hollered.

Daisy sat up and pushed her sunglasses down on her nose. She smiled and waved at Jay to let him know that she was watching.

"All right, baby!" she cheered as he putted successfully.

"Look at me too, Momma Daisy!" Lani called as she planted her feet firmly apart on the course and took up her stance.

Daisy giggled. She loved the name that Lani had been calling her ever since she'd been christened as her godmother. "I'm watching you too, baby." Then, when Lani's attempt to hit the golf ball was unsuccessful, Daisy added, "Good try."

237

"Looks like we have us two future PGA competitors," Adonis said as he watched the kids.

"Maybe so." Daisy rubbed his leg. "Did Gigi call the house?"

"Yes. She left a message and said she'd be here in a couple of weeks. I guess she had no trouble transferring her job."

"That's good. She and Ming Li will be moving here around the same time."

"So, Ming Li's salon out here is doing pretty well, then?"

Daisy nodded. "You know she's always had a head for business. She knows what she's doing. Plus, she has a fiancé to help her out. I still can't believe it."

Adonis laughed. "Lucian Anto-something, right?"

"Antonopoulos."

"Looks like the single life is overrated."

"Yeah, Gigi's getting married in the fall. Can you believe that she and Thomas hit it off so quickly? And poor, deranged Marcus. He thought she had a man all along. She had Marcus out there acting like a fool. I heard that he's okay now. Camille's his therapist."

Adonis chuckled. "Gigi and Ming Li will probably need to see a therapist next. For a while, I thought you needed to consult one. Remember how stressed you were?" Adonis paused and gazed into her eyes. "Would you do it all over again?"

"Yes," she answered honestly, admiring her wedding band. "Planning a wedding is stressful, but it's worth it. Everyone thinks that marriage changes things, and they're right. It makes everything better."

Adonis tackled her playfully and kissed her. "I make everything better."

"We make everything better."

"I agree," he whispered in her ear. "How do you think Jay'll feel about me adopting him?"

Daisy's eyes misted. "I guess we'll have to ask him and see."

A golf ball flew past their heads, followed by a chunk of grass.

"They're going to tear up your course."

"Well, someone has to break it in. Might as well be the loves of my life, after all the hard work I've put into it."

Adonis propped himself up on his elbow and handed her a bottled water. "So do I get to break in something too? I *am* one of the loves of your life."

"It depends."

"On?"

"Whether or not you win the bet on the fight tonight."